Enterpris...

Three ladies taking...
and the men wh...

The Champagne Magnate

When Emma finds herself at the head of the family's struggling wine business, she must partner with neighboring vineyard owner Julien Archambeau, the brooding, reclusive Comte de Rocroi.

The Retailer

To honor her late husband's legacy, Antonia is on a mission to turn the ramshackle London property she inherited into the ultimate shopping experience! But she must rely on the guidance of her handsome rival, Lord Cullen Allardyce!

The Publisher

Saddled with extreme debt and an ailing publishing house, Fleur needs an investor to revitalize the business. But sparks soon fly when that investor comes in the form of Jasper Bexley...

Find out what happens to the Enterprising Widows in

Liaison with the Champagne Count
Alliance with the Notorious Lord

Available now!

And look out for the final book, coming soon!

Author Note

Each story in the Enterprising Widows series is about different ways people process loss. In Antonia's case, she wants to finish her husband's store as a way of completing his legacy. When this does not fill her with the sense of purpose she thought it would, she comes to realize that the most important legacies are not necessarily those of the brick-and-mortar variety, but ones of the heart. Her husband's legacy of helping others endures in the lives he's transformed, starting with hers and ending with that of his business partner, Cullen Allardyce, a man shunned by his own family. Together, Antonia and Cullen navigate the shoals of the past in order to plot a course into a future that honors their hearts and their memories, even though living their new dreams will come at a cost for them both.

I enjoyed the backdrops for this story. It was fun to research the London of the early 1850s. It was indeed true that women could eat out (a huge improvement), but there were only six restaurants where they could eat out at (there were other smaller venues and confectionaries they could go to, but in terms of a "real" restaurant, there were only the six). It was also fun to pick a hotel for Cullen to stay at. Mivart's has an interesting zoning history as to why it was allowed on Brook Street. Its founding was surrounded by much controversy, which was resolved by not having food services on the premises. But most fun of all was using Tahiti as Cullen's point of origin. This offered a little chance to look at Britain's presence in the South Seas in the mid-nineteenth century. There's a huge bit of nineteenth-century history unexplored there. Hmm. Ideas are brewing already...

Life is precious, my friends, and time is short—love deeply.

Bronwyn

Alliance with the
Notorious Lord

———

BRONWYN SCOTT

Recycling programs
for this product may
not exist in your area.

ISBN-13: 978-1-335-59606-2

Alliance with the Notorious Lord

Copyright © 2024 by Nikki Poppen

For questions and comments about the quality of this book,
please contact us at CustomerService@Harlequin.com.

TM and ® are trademarks of Harlequin Enterprises ULC.

Harlequin Enterprises ULC
22 Adelaide St. West, 41st Floor
Toronto, Ontario M5H 4E3, Canada
www.Harlequin.com

Printed in U.S.A.

Bronwyn Scott is a communications instructor at Pierce College and the proud mother of three wonderful children—one boy and two girls. When she's not teaching or writing, she enjoys playing the piano, traveling—especially to Florence, Italy—and studying history and foreign languages. Readers can stay in touch via Facebook at Facebook.com/bronwynwrites or on her blog, bronwynswriting.blogspot.com. She loves to hear from readers.

For B who always has the best ideas and who can recite disk seven of *How to Ruin a Reputation* by heart. Good luck at college. I am going to miss you.

Prologue

February 5th, 1852

There were some among society—mainly jealous old biddies with unmarried daughters—who would say Antonia Lytton-Popplewell was simply born lucky. Antonia would disagree. She'd been born with something much better than luck—optimism. Luck was haphazard at best and held one at its mercy without any indicator of when or where it would strike. But optimism was constant and that constancy made many things possible—like allowing oneself the pleasure of trusting others and believing that life would work itself out, which it invariably did.

Just like this current hand of whist. It had started out as an ordinary hand, but was working itself into a grand slam one trick at a time, thanks to her partner's extreme skill. If anyone could turn a mediocre hand into something spectacular, it was her friend, Emma.

To Antonia's left at the table, her other friend, Fleur Griffiths, gave a pre-emptive sigh of defeat. 'Four tricks to go. You're going to make it, Em. I can't stop you.' She tossed the seven of hearts on the pile.

Their hostess, Mrs Parnaby, matched her with a grimace and played a powerless card. 'Me neither.'

Fleur played her last heart and cast a wry smile in Antonia's direction. 'Once again, you have all the luck. Emma did all the work, but you'll win the night.' They'd played a round robin, rotating partners so that everyone had a chance to play with each other. As a result, Antonia had accumulated the most individual points for the evening, which had started hours ago after dinner. They'd sent their husbands home at nine. It was now after midnight.

Antonia laughed at Fleur's begrudging congratulations. 'I had complete faith Emma would see the potential in my little hand and maximise it.' Optimism always saw potential. Just as Antonia had seen the potential in the trio's friendship eight years ago when they'd been three new brides married to three powerful, older men who adored their young wives. Antonia had turned the wives of her husband's two best friends into her own best friends. Now, the three of them were as inseparable as their husbands, their bonds just as strong. The only bonds stronger were the bonds of their marriages.

'Well done.' Antonia applauded as Emma took another trick. She was genuinely enjoying herself. This evening was exactly what she'd needed. No matter how much she loved her husband, Keir, it was good to have some time with her friends, sans husbands. The last few months, she and Keir had been immersed in his latest business venture, an abandoned building in London he wanted to turn into a first-rate department store to rival the *grands magasins* of Paris. They hadn't had a moment to themselves since the project had got underway and it had taken a toll on them.

When Emma's husband had asked Keir to accompany him to check on the soundness of a mill in Holmfirth as a potential investment, Antonia had jumped at the chance to mix a little business with pleasure and turn the trip into a partial holiday. She hoped to rekindle a little romance between her and Keir. Between overworking on the new project and the looming disappointment of eight years of marriage in which he'd amassed a fortune but no family, Keir had begun to struggle in the bedroom of late. As a consequence, she'd felt the stress, too.

They'd begun to wonder if time had run out for them when they hadn't been looking. Where had the years gone? Keir had been forty-nine when they'd wed, a man who'd been determined to have a financial empire *before* he committed to marriage and a family so that his wife and children wouldn't struggle as he'd struggled growing up. She'd not been bothered by the age of her husband. Instead, she'd been optimistic that children would come eventually. But now, she wasn't so sure. The business and pleasure trip was going well in restoring her hope, though.

Antonia's cheeks heated at memories of last night. Perhaps she'd wake Keir up when she got back to their rented home on Water Street, crawl under the covers, slip her hand beneath his nightshirt and…

Someone banged on the front door, shouting, 'The river's in Water Street!' Emma's last trick went unplayed, their hands forgotten as the women exchanged a look of consternation and ran for Mrs Parnaby's lace-curtained windows. There was nothing to see, only to hear. To Antonia, it sounded like the whoosh and whirl of a roiling wind. But that made no sense...

'The dam!' Emma gasped, grasping the situation, wild panic lighting her grey eyes. 'It must have burst and the river's flooded.'

'The men!' Antonia cried, Emma's panic contagious. Their husbands had gone back to their Water Street quarters after dinner at the Parnabys', determined to make it an early night before the business meeting about the mill in the morning. Emma's gaze clashed with hers for a horrified moment.

'Garrett,' Emma whispered and then she was off, racing for the door.

'No! You mustn't,' their hostess cried. 'If you go out now, you'll be washed away, too.'

Washed away, too.

The terror of those words galvanised Antonia into action. She and Fleur grabbed for Emma, dragging her bodily from the door, Mrs Parnaby assuring them they would all go out in the morning for news. There was nothing more they could do at present.

Except to wait.

Except to think about the horror of Mrs Parnaby's words. Mrs Parnaby thought it was hopeless. She'd already consigned their husbands to death along with the other residents of Water Street, aptly named because of its location to the River Holme where Hinchliffe Mill preceded the town of Holmfirth.

The four women sank into the stuffed chintz chairs of Mrs Parnaby's parlour. A frightening silence claimed the room. No one wanted to speak the truth. No, it wasn't truth. Not yet. Antonia stopped her thoughts. She would not let herself go down that path—a path that led to the conclusion that Keir, Garrett and Adam were dead, drowned in a river that had flooded its banks when the dam above it burst. Antonia reached for Emma's hand. 'They're strong men. They can take care of themselves.' The idea that perhaps they could not was unthinkable.

Antonia let those words sustain her throughout the long hours ahead. She called on images of Keir in her mind as he'd been tonight. Happy. Laughing. Content. The way he'd looked at her from across the table had assured her that no matter what they faced in life, they faced it together and his love for her had not, and would not, diminish. Nothing could mar their happiness. Nothing could intrude into their private world.

But the world, like water, had finally found a way to seep in. When morning came, Mrs Parnaby led them through waterlogged streets choked with mud and debris. Animal carcasses, iron machinery wrested free of its anchorage, household odds and ends—nothing had been spared the river's wrath. Antonia had never seen anything as thorough as this destruction, all of it proof of how violent the flood had been and how dangerous. Waters strong enough to break down a building, to wrench iron equipment from its restraints and dismantle it, would have been unnavigable for even the most capable of swimmers. Her heart sank as they reached the Rose and Crown Inn where the displaced were gathering. If tons of steel had not survived, how could mere flesh and bone? And yet some had.

James Mettrick, one of the men they'd come to do business with, who was also a Water Street resident where they were renting, had survived. He was battered and bruised, but alive. He'd found his way to shore. If he had, perhaps Keir had as well. Perhaps Garrett and Adam, too. Antonia exchanged a glance with Emma and knew she was thinking the same thing. There was still hope.

Antonia clung to that hope as she threw herself into helping the bedraggled. She served hot drinks and food, wrapped warm blankets about shaking shoulders, toted lost children on her hip who'd come looking for parents, and held strangers' hands as they struggled to process the magnitude of the flood. Jobs, lives and homes had been washed away. Many were just starting to realise there was nothing and no one to go back to.

She stayed busy, but each time the door opened, her gaze strayed towards it, her heart hoping Keir would walk through it. Each time she was disappointed. She consoled herself in knowing that *when* he did come, it would be late. He would be out helping others, putting others first. He would not come until all who needed him had been helped. Then they would go home to London, to their town house, and this nightmare would be over.

At ten o'clock in the morning, it was not Keir who walked through the inn door, but George Dyson, the town's coroner. He was grey and obviously fatigued. Antonia's heart went out to him. What must the poor man have endured in these past hours! He'd spent the time since the flood bearing the worst news to friends and neighbours. She froze as she watched him approach Emma, a polite hand at her elbow as he said something to her in low tones. Colour drained from Emma as she gestured for Antonia and Fleur to join Mr Dyson in the inn's private parlour. For the first time Antonia could recall, her optimism faltered.

In the parlour, she gripped Emma's hand, the news falling like a blow despite Dyson's attempt to soften it. 'Lady Luce, Mrs Popplewell, Mrs Griffiths, I wish I was not the bearer of bad tidings. I will be blunt. Water Street never stood a chance. The river hit it from the front and the side, absolutely obliterating the buildings.' The man paused; his Adam's apple worked as he swallowed hard. She wondered how many times today had he already made the same speech? Antonia gripped Emma's hand tighter as if that grip could hold back the inevitable. Perhaps he only meant to tell them hopes were slim because of that damage? She did not care how slim the hope was as long as that hope still existed.

Dyson recovered himself and continued. 'James Mettrick's family and the Earnshaws, both acquaintances of yours, I believe, are gone. Their homes were entirely destroyed.' Antonia bit back a cry, her sliver of hope all but extirpated.

'James Mettrick survived. He was brought in this morning,' Emma argued, the jut of her stubborn chin saying plainly, *Don't tell me there are* no *survivors when there were*. Antonia had never loved Emma more than she did in that moment. Emma, who was willing to stand between them all and the Grim Reaper with her arguments and quick mind. But Emma could not out-argue, could not out-reason this. At the realisation, something turned cold in Antonia. She felt as if the very life of her was seeping away as she waited for the *coup de grâce*.

Dyson gave a shake of his head, his tone gentle with Emma despite her scolding. 'The bodies of your husband and his friends have been recovered, Lady Luce. Your husband was found in the Victoria Mill race. I *am* sorry.'

'No!' Antonia let a wail. Not Keir. No, this wasn't real. The world became a series of fragmented moments. She was on the floor, sobbing. Beyond her, Fleur yelled her rage and smashed a plate against the parlour wall. Then Emma was beside her and they were in each other's arms, each of them trying to support the other against the unthinkable. Fleur came to them and they clung together, crying, consoling, rocking, reeling, until they found the strength to rise and do what needed doing: identifying the bodies.

One of Dyson's assistants stood with Antonia in a tent acting as a makeshift morgue behind the inn. He drew back the sheet and Antonia gave a sharp cry at the mottled, cut face of her husband. She'd thought she was prepared. She'd seen death before. She'd been at her grandmother's bedside, her grandmother's passing peaceful, her hand in her daughter's, a serene smile on her face as she left the world. But *this* was nothing like that. Keir didn't look peaceful. He looked…angry, like a warrior who knew the forces arrayed against him were too many, that his best fight wouldn't be enough, but he'd fight anyway.

Out of reflex, Antonia reached to smooth back the dark mat of his hair and gasped at the gash revealed on his forehead. If she needed further proof, there it was. This had been a violent death. Something had struck him. She thought of the heavy machinery she'd seen in the street this morning. Had one of those pieces hit him? Had he been knocked unconscious? She reached for his hand. No, his hands were cut and scratched. He'd clawed at something, gripped something. He'd fought. Perhaps he'd clutched at a piece of furniture as he'd been swept into the current. Perhaps he'd clung to a branch at the riverbank, trying to hoist himself ashore.

She wanted to push the images away. She didn't want to think about Keir's last moments and yet she must. She would not be a coward, not when he'd been so brave. Had he been afraid? Keir had never been afraid of anything. No risk, no enterprise was too daunting for him. Her thoughts went to the inevitable. Had he thought of her at the last? Had there been time to whisper a silent goodbye as he'd gone under? Had she been with him at the end at least in his mind?

'Ma'am? Are you all right?' the assistant enquired nervously. He was young and no doubt the day had been overwhelming for him, too.

She nodded the lie. How would she ever be all right again? All the light, all the love in her life, had just gone out. 'I'd like a few moments alone, please.' She'd always be alone now. It was a sobering thought.

The tent flap closed behind the assistant and Antonia

sank to her knees, Keir's limp hand still in hers. This would be the last time she saw him, held him. She willed the memories to come with their bittersweet comfort. 'I remember the first time I saw you,' she murmured. 'It was at the Gladstone Ball and you were my knight in shining armour.' She felt a soft smile cross her lips at the remembrance. 'We surprised everyone,' she whispered.

She'd come to London that Season armed only with a wardrobe that flattered and the Lytton optimism that her looks would be enough to save her from genteel poverty and spinsterhood. She'd done more than save herself. She'd married Keir Popplewell and lifted not only herself up financially, but her family as well. Keir had paid her father's debts, relieved the country estate of its burdensome mortgage, and purchased an officer's commission for her brother. More than that, though, she'd married a man she loved and who loved her in return.

As for Keir, he'd gained a foothold in society with his marriage to a baronet's daughter, something many had thought impossible. Who would tolerate the rough-mannered, blunt-spoken businessman despite his fortune? He didn't *act* like a rich man. He was notorious for talking to servants—his *and* the servants of others. That was just the tip of the *faux-pas* iceberg. He paid attention to the poor. Keir Popplewell had a heart for the outcast.

Antonia had fallen in love with that kindness. It was a rare man who knew when to be ruthless in business and kind in life. Now, that rare man was dead. Tears smarted in her eyes. He was gone and there was no heir left behind, no piece of himself, no legacy. There was no one left but her. She and Keir had indeed run out of time.

'I think it's time to go.' Emma's words pulled Antonia out of her own reveries by Mrs Parnaby's front window four days later. Most of those days had been spent in front of that window, thinking, remembering, crying, railing at a fate that had left her a widow before she was thirty, before she could be a mother. Keir was supposed to have died of old age; they were supposed to have had more time.

Antonia looked between Fleur and Emma in the silence that ensued. Emma's words were not far from her own thoughts. Somewhere in the sleepless darkness last night, Antonia had come to the twin conclusions that she had to pick up the pieces of this tragedy and, secondly, she had to carry on. She couldn't do either of those here in Holmfirth surrounded by strangers. She needed to be home, in London. Keir's business and his employees would be counting on her to continue the work.

Perhaps Keir himself was counting on her, too, from the Great Beyond: to go home and finish their dream. She nodded when Emma finished speaking. 'I need to return to London and see how things stand. Keir was in the midst of restoring an old building. He had plans to turn it into a department store.' Antonia drew a shaky breath, debating her next words. If she said them aloud the dream would become real.

'I think I'll finish for him. I think it's what I must do, although I'm not sure how. I'll figure it out as I go.' She looked to Fleur. 'Shall we all travel together as far as

London? It's a long train ride from west Yorkshire when one is on their own.'

Fleur didn't meet her eyes. 'No, I think I'll stay and finish the investigation Adam began on the dam for Garrett. There are people to help and justice to serve. People deserve to know if this tragedy was a natural disaster or a man-made one.' Eighty-one people had died that fateful night. It wasn't only their husbands that had been lost. So many families had been affected by the loss of loved ones and livelihoods.

Across the room, Emma spoke sharply. 'Do you think that's wise, Fleur? If it is man-made, there will be people who won't appreciate prying, particularly if it's a woman doing it. You should think twice before putting yourself in danger.'

'I don't care,' Fleur snapped and Antonia's head swivelled between her two friends. Something more was going on here. What had she missed? Fleur's tone was strident. 'If Adam died because of carelessness, someone *will* pay for that. I will see to it and I will see to it that such recklessness isn't allowed to happen again.' Antonia wished she had half of Fleur's courage.

'And Adam's child?' Emma shot back, the remark catching Antonia by surprise. She'd been so wrapped up in her own grief, she'd thought nothing of Fleur's hand finding its way to the flat of her stomach, a gesture she'd made several times over the past days. The thought of a child struck a chord of sad longing within Antonia. How wondrous it would have been for her to have one last piece of Keir, but there was no chance of that. Her courses had arrived that morning, not that she'd been expecting it to be otherwise.

Fleur shook her head, her voice softer when she spoke to Emma, her earlier anger absent. 'I do not know if there is a child. It is too soon.' But not too soon to hope, Antonia thought privately. Fleur suspected there was a chance.

'Just be careful, dear friend. I do not want anything to happen to you.' Emma rose and went to her. Antonia joined her and they encircled each other with their arms, their heads bent together.

'We're widows now,' Emma said softly.

There would be enormous change for each of them over the next few months—the death of their husbands was just the beginning. Widows lost more than a man when husbands died. Society did not make life pleasant for women who hadn't a man beside them even in this new, brave world where women were demanding their due. But amid the chaos of change, Antonia knew she could depend on two things: the friendship of the women who stood with her now and the realisation that, from here on out, nothing in her life would ever be the same again.

Chapter One

Late August, six months later

Eggs. Again. Antonia scooped a serving on to her plate and made her slow progress down the sideboard, adding the usual two sausage links and two slices of toast with a resigned sigh. Everything was the same. In the past six months since the flood had claimed Keir, *nothing* had changed. Not even her breakfast. The loose ends of the will were still, unfortunately, loose, and Keir was still dead, except when she lingered in the blissful state of half-wakefulness each morning when she wasn't quite conscious yet, when the day hadn't quite started and anything was possible. In those precious moments she forgot he was gone. She'd reach for him and then she'd… remember and the day would begin in full.

Antonia took her seat at the head of her lonely table and resolutely tucked into her eggs, her tongue hardly noting their creamy fluffiness. Her tastebuds had gone numb months ago along with the rest of her. Where once she'd enjoyed long meals with Keir filled with conversation and courses, she now ate quickly for fuel alone when she remembered to eat at all.

There was no pleasure in the meal. Meals, like everything she did these days, were for purpose only. In February, she'd returned from Holmfirth and got straight to work. She'd buried herself in that work, in fact, just as assuredly as she'd buried Keir in the ground at Kensal Green.

Her strategy had helped up to a point. She'd kept herself too busy working, too busy attending meetings with solicitors and city officials in charge of construction permits, negotiating with builders and buyers, to feel or to think about all she'd lost. She feared if she *did* allow herself permission to do either of those things— think or feel—the precarious house of cards she'd taken shelter in would come crashing down.

The illusion would be destroyed that she was all right, that 'things' were all right, that it was business as usual at Popplewell and Allardyce Enterprises, that the store was progressing as it should, that her life was 'getting back to normal', whatever *that* meant these days. In reality, neither was true.

The store was *not* progressing as it should be. Things *had* come to a screeching halt last week over a paperwork legality she could no longer overlook. As for her being all right and life getting back to normal, right and normal were not words that resonated with her these days. Her hands clenched about her coffee cup. The anger she kept close began to smoulder. Without Keir, her world would never be 'right' or 'normal' again.

The pain she could tolerate. In fact, she welcomed it. The pain kept her company. She wore it like a blanket, a second skin. What she could not tolerate was the ridic-

ulous snag with the store. It was why she was meeting
Mr Bowdrie, her solicitor, this morning. Since Keir's
property had transferred to her in the will, the agreements between her and Keir's silent partner needed to be
re-signed in order for the partnership to be legally official.

It was a mere technicality. Keir's partner had spent
the last several years content to leave the running of the
businesses to Keir. All she needed was his signature and
she could carry on with renovations. The problem was
that Keir's partner was nowhere to be found. Until he
was, she'd done as much as she could on the store. Without his signature, everything had ground to a halt. Which
had spawned another problem. If the store stalled, she
was in danger of having too much time on her hands,
time to do the two things she wanted to do least: think
and feel. If she didn't find another way to stay busy soon,
she wouldn't be able to avoid the twin devils.

You could have gone to France for Emma's wedding,
the voice in her head prodded gently.

The wedding had been earlier this week. Emma was
on her brief honeymoon now with her new husband the
Comte du Rocroi, Julien Archambeau. Emma was a
French countess now. In her letter, Emma had sounded
deliriously in love after having just lost Garrett months
earlier.

Antonia wasn't sure how she felt about that. She
wanted to be happy for her friend. But in all honesty,
she wasn't sure how she could be. On the one hand, Antonia was willing to admit to some jealousy. Emma had
done the one thing Antonia was desperate to do—move

forward. On the other hand, Antonia was in large measure appalled at the speed of Emma's new marriage. How was it even *possible* to love another so soon after losing the man Emma had proclaimed her soulmate?

It called into question the idea of having a soulmate at all. In doing so, it stole the romance right out of marriage and commuted it to something more pragmatic—that people could have successful relationships with multiple others as long as they had enough in common to start with. The optimist in Antonia counselled that she ought to find hope in that new revelation. She needn't be alone. Might she too also find a new husband? A new partner? A new love that could fill the void left by Keir?

Yet she wasn't ready to believe that. She could not imagine loving someone the way she'd loved Keir, of sharing the emotional and physical intimacy she'd experienced with him. It seemed…wrong, unfaithful. But *not* contemplating it meant she'd remain alone. Loneliness was not optimistic of her.

She had to stop such maudlin thoughts. This type of thinking was *exactly* why she stayed busy. Antonia pushed back her chair, scolding herself. One lapsed moment of not focusing on the store and her thoughts were already wandering in dangerous directions designed to drag her down into the morass of grief. She would *not* let the abyss claim her so easily. She called for the butler. Action was an effective buffer against the blue devils. 'Beldon, have my carriage brought around. I have an appointment with Bowdrie. He hates it when I'm late. Tell Randal I need my gloves and hat.'

She strode to the office she'd claimed as her own after Keir's death and gathered the papers required for the meeting, a sense of purpose resettling itself on her shoulders along with her resolve. *Today* she'd find a way around needing Keir's absent partner's signature. She had one last good argument to make to circumvent that need. Today, things *would* be different. She would not allow herself to think about it being otherwise.

Optimism was more difficult to maintain when faced with the inconvenient logic of the law. Twenty minutes into the meeting it was clear to Antonia that if the well-meaning but unimaginative Mr Bowdrie continued the conversation in this direction, today was *not* going to be different unless she found new answers, new solutions, to present to him. She suppressed a sigh as Keir's long-time solicitor explained yet again why nothing further could be done until they'd acquired Cullen Allardyce's signature on the paperwork.

'Simply put, Mrs Popplewell, the partnership between Mr Allardyce and yourself needs to be established since the partnership between Mr Allardyce and Mr Popplewell has terminated with Mr Popplewell's death. You are a *new* partner and that requires a new contractual agreement between you and Allardyce.' He gave a kind smile, tired resignation in his eyes that communicated he knew this was not the news she wanted to hear, but it was all he had to give.

Antonia felt his weariness. She was tired, too. This issue of a legitimate partnership had set the two of them at odds since the will had been read and not by choice.

Keir had trusted Bowdrie with the legal paperwork of Popplewell–Allardyce Enterprises for two decades, had hired him straight out of university. Antonia knew Bowdrie to be a good man. Keir had trusted him and she wanted to give him her trust, too. But trusting him meant delaying progress on the store. In her frustration, she had to remind herself that Bowdrie was not the problem, merely the messenger. Still, she had to try.

'I do not doubt your interpretation of the letter of the law. However, I am suggesting we approach this from a perspective of the spirit of the law.' She'd spent hours, days, poring over legal texts in the months since the will had been read. The letter of the law wasn't going to save her. 'I am not a *new* partner. There is nothing to re-establish. I've inherited Keir's shares in the company. I was married to him. By extension, I have become *him*. Marriage, in fact, makes that true. I am subsumed legally into my husband.'

It was not a law she liked, but it was useful at the moment. 'I am legally not a separate entity. I am a continuation of what Keir and Allardyce have already settled between them,' Antonia argued patiently from the edge of the red Moroccan leather chair set on the guest side of the wide, polished desk. She was careful to keep her words even and pleasant so as not to give vent to her own exasperation. 'The name of the company won't even change.' Perhaps she could help him see how pointless this exercise was in requiring a signature.

He shook a head just starting to show the first signs of grey at the temples. 'Mrs Popplewell, it is not me who needs convincing. It does not matter what I think about the situation.'

She leaned forward in earnest, warming to the argument. 'I disagree. *You* need to believe it more than anyone because you and my husband's legal team are the ones who need to defend it if my decision is challenged.' She had shocked him and she regretted that. She didn't want him shocked. She wanted him supportive, even if it was in support of upending centuries of English law.

'Ma'am, you can make all the logical arguments you wish, but that does not change the fact that the partnership needs to be re-established. That was made clear in February and it is still the case. The law has not changed.'

'Nor is the law going to. But our understanding of it can,' Antonia pressed on confidently. 'If questioned, we need to say that after further reading and research, we now believe that there is no need to re-establish the partnership because it is not terminated.' She'd known this moment was coming. She'd spent the last six months doing all that could be done at the building site without the required signature, hoping Allardyce would surface in time. Now, she'd run out of those things and Allardyce was nowhere to be found.

Bowdrie remained sceptical. 'That argument has never been made. There is no precedent.'

Antonia flashed a smile meant to charm. 'Then let's make one.'

'You intend to forge ahead without Allardyce's signature?' Bowdrie asked, his agile mind leaping forward to the consequences of such an action.

'Yes.' Antonia opted for directness. 'It's either that or do nothing. I cannot accept the latter.' Antonia flashed a stubborn stare in Bowdrie's direction to see what he made of the admittedly rash declaration. Sometimes rashness was the only way to break through an impasse.

'Allardyce won't like the idea you've decided to out-flank him in his absence,' Bowdrie warned.

'Then he can dissolve the partnership. In any case, I won't need his signature,' Antonia said staunchly. The more she talked, the more solid her grounds felt. If Allardyce returned and wanted to remain in partnership, he could sign the contract and all would be well. If he wanted to stay in the partnership he wasn't likely to complain over her decision to move forward. If he didn't want to remain in partnership, she would buy him out and all would still be well.

Bowdrie arched a brow. '*That* is desperation talking, ma'am. I would not recommend it.' He returned her stare with a look of long consideration. 'Do you know much about your husband's partner?'

'I know he's not here,' she replied smartly, truthfully. She knew, too, that her husband had admired him, found him brilliant. But she'd never known him. Cullen Allardyce hadn't been in England for at least eight years. He'd not attended her wedding to Keir and he had not attended the funeral. That last was a definite strike against him. What sort of friend was absent for a decade of another's life?

'You might have more use for him than merely his signature. I'm not sure I'd be quick to terminate the partnership,' Bowdrie cautioned. 'His pockets are deep as is his need for privacy, but that should not be a strike against him. Your husband trusted him and I think his presence may be reassuring to those investors who might prefer a more veteran presence at the helm.' Bowdrie pushed his glasses up to the bridge of his nose, a sure tell that he was uncomfortable with the conversation.

'You mean those who would prefer a man,' Antonia said plainly, reading between the lines of Bowdrie's well-intentioned delicacy.

Bowdrie cleared his throat and shifted in his seat. 'Well, yes. But there's more to it than that. To lose Mr Allardyce's support could send a message of uncertainty to the company's usual investors. They might question why he didn't stay on. If he leaves for whatever reason, it may encourage others to do the same. Especially since I do not believe it was Mr Popplewell's intention that the partnership be severed. His leaving would be viewed as a "shocking development".'

'You are inferring my husband's intentions on that front, are you not?' Bowdrie had given her an opening. 'Where does it say in any of Keir's papers that he means Mr Allardyce to be a permanent partner?'

Bowdrie shook his head. 'It doesn't, but I think it can be safely assumed.' He shut his mouth, but it was too late. He'd already walked into her trap.

Antonia smiled in victory, her point made. 'Spirit of the law, then? That *is* what you're talking about?'

'You are taking a risk, ma'am, with your argument.' Only because a woman was making it. In that regard it was the same risk she was taking heading up Keir's company.

'I have every faith my husband's legal team can defend my position.' She'd rather not have to test it, though. 'Have we had no luck yet? Do we even know if our letters have reached Allardyce?' The search for Keir's partner was the living embodiment of looking for a needle in the haystack. If Allardyce wasn't in England, that left the whole rest of the world. He could be anywhere, and the clock was running.

She'd prefer to act on plans for the store *with* his permission since she was cognisant that his funds were invested in the enterprise, too. But if she waited on him, it would mean she had to admit that without his signature she couldn't access the business accounts, she couldn't pay workers, she couldn't move forward on the department store. In addition, there was the possibility that they might never find him. If that happened, she didn't want to be in the position of having already admitted she needed his signature in order to operate legally. She would be stone-walled indeterminately.

It would be one thing if he was dead and that death could be proven. Then the company would revert to her, but if he wasn't conclusively dead, merely missing, it would take years for her to be given control and that was intolerable. No, she would not cede that ground easily. She had to push on as if she had every right to.

'We have sent letters to the usual places,' Bowdrie assured her. 'As you know, those letters went out the first of March.' Five months ago. She knew what that meant. The longer the letters went unanswered, the further away he was likely to be. At this rate, they could eliminate the Continent. He wasn't in Europe. If he were he could have been in England within a month of receiving word.

'If he's not in Europe, then where he is?' If she knew, it would give her a schedule of sorts. Africa? India? Those were far-off places. To reach them took more time than she had.

'Tahiti, Singapore. Burma, Ceylon. The last letter he sent to your husband came from Tahiti, but in it he mentioned his plans to travel between the islands on business.'

Antonia sighed. Such exotic locales. Usually just saying the names conjured up a yearning to see those places, but today, the words conjured worried. These places were outposts at the furthest reaches of the empire. No wonder they hadn't heard. She did the timetables in her head. If the letters had gone on the Steam Route through the mid-east and across the strip of land in Suez and on to a steam packet from Suez to Bombay, they would have reached India within two months, barring any delays.

It would take six months if the letters had gone around the Cape, but mail was unlikely to travel that route these days. Still, even on the Steam Route, one needed to add in another month at least for letters to arrive at the more remote outposts in the South Pacific that Bowdrie had named. That assumed a letter had found him directly. If it did not, it might take a ship several stops as it island-hopped to locate him. That would add months. Then there was the return trip to account for. If Allardyce left immediately, it would take him three months minimum to make the journey home, longer if he felt compelled to take ship around the Cape.

Her hopes sank. That meant she'd be lucky to hear from him by Christmas. More likely, she would not see him until after the new year, which seemed ages away from now. It strengthened her resolve, her belief in her position. 'Then it's a good thing we are not waiting for him. It could be another half-year before there's any word or chance of his arrival.' Another half-year before her decision would be contested. By then, who knew what might happen? What successes she might have to show him to prove her actions worthy of her decision? 'We will forge ahead.' She smiled broadly, but Bowdrie fixed her with a sad stare.

'Mrs Popplewell, waiting might not be a bad idea. Perhaps you ought to view this as a holiday interval? Might I suggest taking some time for yourself?' Bowdrie said, not unkindly. 'You've done admirably for your husband's holdings. As they say, you "hit the ground running".' His eyes were gentle and soft. They made her uncomfortable. She did not want his pity. It would tempt her to weakness, to give in to the grief buried beneath the surface of her life. 'But perhaps such efforts have come at an expense to yourself. Maybe now it is time for you to rest, to stop and draw a deep breath.'

Antonia blew out a short breath. She knew what he meant: she ought to take time to grieve, time to mourn. But if she stopped for even a moment, to consider all she'd lost, she would shatter. She'd never be able to put herself back together again.

'I appreciate the concern, Mr Bowdrie, but I do not think it necessary.' Forward was the only motion she knew. When the family had teetered on bankruptcy and everything depended on her ability to marry well, she'd not stopped to think about what would happen if she failed and she would not stop now. The key to optimism was much like the key to tightrope-walking: never looking back, never looking down, only looking ahead. There was only moving forward.

She rose to pre-empt any more of Mr Bowdrie's well-meant enquiries about her personal well-being. She had what she came for: the ability to move forward. 'Thank you for your time, Mr Bowdrie. Please let me know when you have word from Mr Allardyce.' In the meantime, the department store would move forward and so would she. Time and tide waited for no man and neither did Antonia Popplewell.

Chapter Two

Tahiti—October 1852

*O*ne, two, three. One, two, three. Reach, catch, pull. Repeat.

The tide was with them, the current at its quickest and the outrigger took full advantage, the six-man crew straining together as one, a fast, watery waltz. Cullen Allardyce's oar dug into the waves, his shoulders and arms burning from exertion even as the exhilaration of slicing through the water urged him and his crew to greater speeds.

'*Ka hi!*' The call came up from the steer man, his best friend, Rahiti, and Cullen executed a sideways stroke on his left, making a strong turn, using the speed of the waves to best effect , making sure not to break the team's rhythm and tempo. Big Puaiti in the power seat mid-canoe gave the call to change and Cullen shifted his oar to the other side. They were nearly there. The beach came into view, lined with people excitedly awaiting the outcome of the race. Despite his aching muscles, Cullen increased the crew's tempo as another outrigger pulled close, his nemesis, Manu, in the stroker's seat.

Cullen flashed a competitive grin at Manu across the water. They would not lose, not today! These races were in honour of Rahiti's marriage and Rahiti had selected his crew with an eye towards victory. Cullen was not only his best friend, he was also the best stroker in the village, although it galled Manu to no end that an outsider had taken the accolade away from him.

Cullen leaned forward and reached for the waves, digging his paddle in deep, catching turquoise water and pulling hard. Manu resented more than losing his oar position. Manu resented that Rahiti's sister, the lovely Vaihere, preferred Cullen's company to his own. The chief, Rahiti and Vaihere's father, had preferred his company, too. So much so, he'd made Cullen an adoptive son and given him a new name. Kanoa. The Seeker.

That had been years ago. He was one of them now. There was nowhere on earth he'd rather be and no other people he'd rather be with. Here in Maravati Bay, he was home, surrounded by family and friends and freedom. Freedom to do as he pleased, to *be* as he pleased. Which was all Cullen Allardyce had ever wanted.

The shore neared, turquoise waters meeting with a taupe line of sand. Cullen could see Vaihere on the shore standing beside Rahiti's bride, cheering for him. From the power seat in the canoe, Big Puiti called the change, his voice strong despite the gruelling length of the race. Their outrigger surged faster with each catch and pull. The soreness of Cullen's body was nothing compared to the sensation of this, of skimming across the waves, chasing victory.

With a final effort, they crossed the finish line half a

boat-length ahead of Manu's team. A joyous cry went up from the beach. Villagers splashed into the water to celebrate the victory. Vaihere was there and Cullen jumped out of the canoe, sweeping her into an embrace as she settled a hibiscus lei about his neck. 'You were magnificent, Kanoa.' She laughed up at him, the ocean-wet length of him dampening her *pareo.* 'I thought Manu was going to catch up,' she confessed with a mischievous glint in her dark eyes.

'His boat was too slow at the turn,' Cullen confided. 'Their steer man didn't read the waves as well as he should have at the halfway point. They spent themselves trying to catch up and had nothing left for a final sprint.' Rahiti had taken a great chance asking him to take the canoe out as fast as he had, but the crew was strong and had the endurance to hold the pace.

Rahiti, his new bride on his arm, waded through the surf and embraced him. '*Me tuâne*, you have brought me victory today.'

'Not me alone,' Cullen corrected. 'You made the choice to go out fast and Puaiti gave us encouragement with the strength of his calls. Truly, it was a team effort.'

Rahiti clapped his shoulder good-naturedly, his eyes dancing with happiness, not all of it attributed to his victory. 'But you were my stroker, you set the pace and you kept the team to it. Manu did not.' He grinned. 'Come and eat with me. We have a whole day of feasting before us.'

The *ahima*, the underground ovens, had been busy cooking suckling pig and the rich aroma of meat filled the air as they reached the village. Cullen and Viahere settled on a woven mat to eat, taking turns feeding each other from the collection of food and laughing. She listened intently as he recounted key moments of the race, but her gaze strayed often to where her brother and his new wife sat, eyes only for each other.

'You are happy for them,' Cullen said, letting his own gaze follow hers.

'They love one another. That is a rare thing.' She sighed and gave her hair a toss behind her shoulder. 'How wondrous for them that the person they're meant to spend their lives with was on the same small island as they.'

Cullen gave her a soft smile instead of disabusing her of the fairy-tale notion that people had soulmates. He didn't believe in soulmates any more than he believed in love—romantic love anyway. He had brotherly love for Rahiti and familial love for Rahiti's mother and father. But romantic love was merely lust. Quickly satiated. He'd slaked it often enough with different women to know it was not eternal, nor was it particular about whom he satisfied it with. But today was not the day to make that argument.

He shifted on the mat and fed Vaihere a bite of *umara* in an attempt to distract her. He was not entirely comfortable with the conversation. He was well aware that if he should offer for Vaihere, the offer would be welcomed by both Vaihere and her father. He was also aware that he would not make that offer. He wasn't a marrying man for philosophical and practical reasons. Philosophically, marriage was in direct opposition with his ideas of freedom. He liked women—plural. He loved their bodies, he loved exploring pleasure with them.

He could not imagine having only one lover the rest of his life.

Practically, there was much about his life, his past, that he would not willingly subject Vaihere to. This was her home and it was his, but his permanence here was not the same as hers. Some day in the far-off unknown future, if he should ever leave here, he would not willingly take her from this place, from her family, from the life she knew, and put her in danger. He knew what England did to unsuspecting foreigners from untouched corners of the world. He'd been six when the Hawaiian King and Queen had visited England and died there from measles.

He did not wish such a fate for Viahere. Nor did he wish other fates for her such as being tied to him. He did not think a woman like her who valued love, a sense of place and family would be happy with him for the long term. He was a man without a country, a man whose politics and scandal had alienated him from England. Family was important to Viahere and some would say he'd betrayed his.

He felt differently, of course. He thought it was the other way around: his family had betrayed *him*. Still, his own experience suggested that while he might crave the concept of a family of his own in theory, the practice of acquiring one was far less likely. Knowing that he would not offer her the things she wanted only deepened his guilt. She was waiting on him. He could not prolong her wait much longer. He needed to marry her or set her free. He could not see his way to doing the former, so it must be the latter.

Vaihere reached up a soft hand and caressed his cheek.

'I did not mean to upset you, Kanoa. Today is for happiness.' She took his hand and whispered, 'I understand more than you think.' Then her eyes changed, dancing with playful lights. She tugged his hand. 'Come with me to the lagoon. No one will miss us today.'

The lagoon was exactly what he had required, Cullen concluded hours later as he lay exhausted beside Vaihere. Despite the exertion of the race, his body had needed exercise. They'd swum in the aquamarine lagoon, dived beneath its waters with the sea turtles and lounged on the clean white sands of its hidden beach until the sun began to sink towards the horizon, a hot orange ball lowering into cool blue waters.

'We should go back,' Vaihere murmured against his shoulder. 'There will be dancing and food. I confess, I'm getting hungry.' She sighed reluctantly.

'One more swim.' Cullen pushed himself up with a grunt and brushed the sand from his legs. He waded into the water and executed a shallow dive. Of all the things he loved about Tahiti, it was the water he loved most. There was no water like this anywhere in England. A man could swim year-round here. Even if there were no politics, no scandal keeping him from England, he'd still choose to stay here for the water and weather alone.

He let the water cleanse him, letting it push back the long tawny tangle of his hair and wash the sand from his skin until he was ready to go back to the village, to join the wedding festivities and celebrate the perfection of this day: the tides, the weather, the racing, the victory, the pleasure of a full belly and a beautiful woman beside him. Life did not get more perfect than that.

He waded towards shore, his *malo* soaking and slung low on his hips, water sluicing from his hair as it hung down his back, his arm about Vaihere. He had his face turned to the sky, his gaze intent on the early stars peeping through now that the sun had settled, when Vaihere gave his arm an unmistakable warning tug. *'Aito,'* she whispered. Soldier.

He was instantly alert. Soldiers were a less welcome sight after the French-Tahitian war six years ago that had resulted in France establishing a protectorate that recognised Tahiti's sovereignty while reducing the Tahitian Queen, Pomare's, powers. The French Commissaire, Moerenhout, ruled alongside the Queen these days. Cullen was not fooled as to what it meant: Tahiti would shortly lose its autonomy. This was the way of empire building. The usual disgust he felt over the politics of colonisation unfurled in his belly at the thought. He'd seen such strategies before from the English in India.

Cullen squinted in the evening light and studied the man on the beach standing at rigid attention, taking in the navy-blue cut-away coat with its officer's gold braid. The man's bearing and uniform was that of someone who held significant rank. Cullen drew three immediate conclusions. First, that man must be incredibly uncomfortable in all those clothes. Secondly, he was military but a sailor, not a soldier. Third, he was not French, but British. Which meant the man was here for *him.* Cullen stepped in front of Vaihere, gently steering her behind him for protection although the man on the beach would think it for modesty.

'Lord Cullen Allardyce?' the man called, his stare unflinching as he gave Cullen the same intense perusal. Let him look. Cullen was not ashamed, although he could guess the direction of the man's thoughts. He knew how he must look to that proper European gaze, his long, sun-streaked hair hanging to his waist, his body tanned, half-naked, and tattooed. Well, the man couldn't see his tattoo *yet*, since it was on the back of his shoulder, but the man would see it soon enough.

Cullen strode from the water, ready to dispatch the man. Men had come to look for him before and he'd sent them away, but no one had come for years now. There were days when he almost allowed himself to believe he'd finally succeeded in breaking the chains that bound him to his old life. Here in Tahiti, neither his scandal nor his *outrageous* politics—that was his father's word for them—mattered.

'If you've come from my father, I have no wish for correspondence. Go back to your ship.' Cullen planted his feet shoulder width apart and crossed his arms over his chest. Let the man look. Let the man carry back heathen reports about his appearance and the news that the Marquess of Standon's son had gone native. Cullen was sure he wouldn't be the first to report on it. But he knew his assumption was wrong as soon as he spoke. His father had not sought him out for years now. There was no reason for him to do so. His father was as pleased as he, apparently, to have that tie severed.

'I've not come from your father,' the officer said

evenly. 'I'm Admiral Connant and I have a letter for you. It's come through many circuitous routes to reach you as no one was sure exactly where you'd be and I've been charged to put it in your hands whenever I found you. You're a hard man to find, my lord. We had the address in Papeete, but we were told there was no guarantee you'd be there since your business takes you all over the South Seas.'

Cullen shrugged unapologetically. He kept the small office in Papeete with its room overhead for the purpose of giving the rare letter a place to go and for himself on days when he had to see to the paperwork of the business, which was about twice a year—once when Keir's ship left and once when the ship came in. 'I am not often in Papeete, not since the war.' When the French had emerged the victors in the Franco-Tahitian war, Cullen had preferred the village in Ha'apape to the colonial centre.

The man offered a wry smile. 'I know. I gave you a week to show up while we resupplied.' The man was tenacious and intrepid, Cullen would give him that. Not everyone would travel the island, looking for a man who didn't want to be found. That piqued Cullen's interest and his concern. Who would mail him if not his father? He had few friends left in England who knew where to find him or, even if they did, who would need to go to the effort of doing so. It was too early for Keir's annual report. 'Who sent you?'

'Mr Bowdrie. A solicitor. He insisted it was urgent that you be found.'

He recognised the name. Bowdrie was Keir's solicitor.

Technically, *their* solicitor. For a moment the wariness eased. Keir must have money issues to discuss. Perhaps informing him money was being sent to an account, or informing him about an expenditure, likely a large one if Keir felt he needed permission. Perhaps there were papers needing his signature. If so, Cullen hoped Admiral Connant had had the foresight to bring them with him and not leave them in Papeete. He didn't relish the idea of going into the town just to sign papers that could just as easily be signed here and the Admiral sent on his way.

'Mr Popplewell has died, my lord.' The words snapped Cullen back to attention, the wariness returning.

'What did you say?' Cullen ground out. He'd heard the man clear enough, but what those words meant was too unbelievable to accept. Surely it wasn't possible. Keir was healthy, a big, strong man. He'd make a great power seat in the outrigger. But it had been ten years since he'd seen Keir.

There'd been the occasional letter and the annual reports from Keir regarding their investments, but all had seemed well. Very well. The man was besotted with his wife. Business was exceedingly good. Keir was always expanding, always looking for the next big thing, always depositing more money into accounts for Cullen that Cullen never looked at. Money didn't mean much out here.

Connant cleared his throat. 'Mr Popplewell has passed. The solicitor has written on behalf of Mr Popplewell's widow. I have the letter—if there is some place where we might talk?'

The question drew Cullen from his stunned stupor.

'Here, we can talk here. There are wedding celebrations in the village. I would not take this news into their midst.' He turned to Vaihere. 'Go to the village and quietly tell your father. I do not want anyone to worry.' To the Admiral he said, 'Allow me a few minutes.' He took those minutes to gather what wood there was and start a small fire. The swim and the news had left him chilled. Keir. Dead. The man who'd mentored him when his father had despaired of him. The man who'd respected his ideas, who had taught him about business and investing, who had encouraged him to see the world.

When the fire was going, Admiral Connant passed him the letter, the seal unbroken. He rose. 'I'll give you a moment of privacy to read it.'

Cullen slipped his finger beneath the wax seal. For a letter that had come thousands of miles, over sea and across desert, it was quite…short. It might as well have been a missive sent across town, one solicitor to another. There was the usual salutation for bad news.

I regret to inform you that Keir Popplewell has passed away.

No mention of the circumstances leading to his death.

All his personal and business affairs have been left to his wife…

Also not surprising. Keir had no children.

There are matters that require your immediate attention and physical presence in London in order

*for business to move forward since the partner-
ship between Keir Popplewell and yourself needs
to be renegotiated.*

That part made him wince. He was being recalled to
the last place on earth he wanted to be. Surely he'd find
a way around that. He and Mr Bowdrie could exchange
letters for years perhaps before an appearance was necessary. But it was the following lines that grabbed his
attention and caused his heart and hopes to sink.

*Failure to appear in person to resolve these
issues will result in the eventual collapse of Popplewell and Allardyce Enterprises since the company will cease to be able to access bank accounts
and conduct business as usual. Be advised such a
situation would negatively affect Mr Popplewell's
widow and those dependent on the company for
their livelihoods.*

That struck at the core of him. If it had just been about
his money, he'd have let the company dry up. He had
enough and he'd simply start over, build something from
scratch if need be. One did not need money in Ha'apape.
He might be a rogue, but he was not irresponsible. The
operation here was for the benefit of others more than
it was for him and Keir. They had set up the South Seas
import branch of the company in order to find a way to
assist those who struggled in the Empire, indigenous
peoples whose ways of life were being squashed beneath
the heal of colonisation.

Keir had been part of the Prometheus Club, headed by the Duke of Cowden, and the club had encouraged them to invest in people by buying regional arts and crafts from cloth to pottery to sell back in England. It was Cullen's job to traverse the South Pacific looking for things to send back to England and setting up relationships with clans and tribes in order to establish a regular pipeline.

Should the company dissolve, it wasn't just Keir's widow who would suffer, but hundreds of people who depended on the company for income—an income that wasn't always paid in coin but in goats and pigs, that allowed for trade and prosperity, that allowed people to feed their families.

Cullen sat beside the fire and stared out over the dark waters for endless minutes. There was no choice, not one that he could live with, anyway. He looked at the date on the letter. March. It had been sent a little over six months ago, almost double the time a letter should take to reach him. The urgency Bowdrie alluded to had grown old while Connant had searched for him.

He was cognisant, too, that, as a naval officer, delivering the letter wasn't Connant's only responsibility. Official military duties had likely added to the timeline. No doubt Connant had been charged with delivering the letter in India when he'd received orders. Nevertheless, Keir's widow would already be in the throes of worry, unable to do anything without his signature. There were workers counting on wages, ships unable to sail with their cargoes without payment. 'How long do I have?'

'My ship will dock in the bay come morning,' Connant offered quietly as if he could understand the magnitude of what leaving meant.

Cullen nodded. He'd have tonight to say his goodbyes. There was nothing in Papeete he needed. Material items had become less important to him. Everyone he cared for was here in the village. Vaihere would be strong. She would wait to weep until after he left. Her mother would pack an enormous basket of food and hand it to him with sad eyes. Rahiti and his father would argue with him, counselling him to find another way, to take time and think it through. He could not allow himself to be swayed by that very desirable, persuasive position. Too much time had already passed. People were counting on him.

He felt weighed down by the finality of the decision. How quickly everything had changed. The pleasantness of his life was upended, the distance he'd craved destroyed. Just hours ago, there'd been no thought of returning to England, a place that held only bad memories for him.

He'd gone to the ends of the earth and he'd still failed to outrun the arm of England. But England could not hold him. He would not stay. This was just a temporary inconvenience. He would sign those papers and see that all was taken care of. Then he would leave on the first available ship. There, beside the fire on the shore of the lagoon, he promised himself he would be back here, home again, this time next year.

Chapter Three

London—February 1st, 1853

He'd never thought to be here again. Lord Cullen Allardyce looked out the window of the train as it slowed, pulling into Charing Cross station, the South Eastern Railway locomotive completing its journey from the Channel terminus in Folkestone. A porter knocked on the door of his private compartment to let him know arrival was imminent. *Imminent.*

After three months of travel with its inevitable setbacks and myriad transportation experiences that included everything from steamers to camels and a night journey overland to the Port of Cairo, another ship to Marseilles, trains through France, the ferry to Folkestone out of Boulogne, and one last train from Folkestone to London, he'd finally arrived in more ways than the geographic.

Cullen tugged at his waistcoat, still accustoming himself to its tight fit. The journey had been one of transformation as well as transportation. He wouldn't do himself any favours walking around London sporting long hair and a *malo*. Besides, it was damned cold in this part of the world.

That last night in Ha'apape, he'd packed away his *malo* and said farewell to his hair. Vaihere performed a private version of the *pakoti rouru* ceremony and lovingly cut his hair to a more English length. Now his tawny waves skimmed his shoulders instead of his waist. He'd also said farewell to Vaihere. She need not wait for him. It wouldn't be fair and she'd understood that, when or whether he returned, their relationship, as it had been, was completed.

The farewells continued. At the Port of Cairo, he'd said goodbye to Admiral Connant and the culottes he'd worn aboard the ship. He used the delay at Shepheard's in Cairo to purchase two ready-made European suits of clothing and had worn them ever since. Cullen ran a finger between his neck and collar, missing the freedom of his *malo*. He'd not worn this many layers of clothing for years.

The train came to a halt and Cullen reached into his waistcoat pocket to check the address one last time. He'd visit Bowdrie straight away. Then he'd have to find accommodations. Thankfully, it was February and not the middle of the Season. A hotel room shouldn't be difficult to come by and a modicum of privacy. How long the privacy lasted would depend on discretion.

He'd need to visit Coutts and draw on his accounts, find a fast tailor and set up a meeting with the Duke of Cowden. It was inevitable word would leak out that he was in town, so he could only hope for a slow leak. He sighed and leaned back against the cushions of the seat. He'd not had to think of such things for ages, nor had he been this busy. The moment he stepped off the train, he would be absorbed into the hustle that was London, a place that was about as far from Ha'apape as one could get in ways that went far beyond geography. He rose and shrugged into his greatcoat—layer four—and exited his compartment.

He disembarked, fighting a wave of homesickness for the village, for slow days, for swimming in the lagoon, for blue skies and turquoise waters. But he could not regret his decision. He owed Keir. When his own family had despaired of him, Keir had not. He had once needed Keir, now Keir and the dream they'd built needed him. One month was all he'd need to see to business. He'd give himself until March and then he'd be back on board a ship heading home. Cullen drew a deep breath, and plunged into the melee.

'Welcome back, my lord.' Robert Bowdrie bustled out of his neat-as-a-pin Gray's Inn office within seconds of Cullen being announced. The speed was dizzying. The clerk had barely gone into the inner office when Bowdrie had come bounding out. Cullen speculated the usually reserved solicitor had likely leaped over his desk to reach him that quickly. Bowdrie pumped his hand energetically. 'What a relief it is to see you looking so well, my lord. Won't you come in?'

Cullen winced at the address. 'Mr Allardyce is fine, as it always has been.' It was one more thing he had to get used to all over again and one more reminder how far from Tahiti he was.

'Mr Allardyce then, will you come this way.' Bowdrie ushered him towards the inner office and shut the door behind them.

Cullen looked around the familiar space. He'd visited often with Keir. It was odd to think so much time had passed, time in which he'd lived an entirely new life, but this office had changed so little, hardly at all. Some folks said there was comfort in constancy, in knowing that things never changed. But Cullen found only sadness in such a premise. Change meant growth, learning, new places, new people, new thoughts. It meant testing the validity of tradition, something his father had been rankly against. His father would approve of Bowdrie's office.

With the exception of a few more grey hairs, Bowdrie looked the same. The office looked the same. The big desk still dominated the space, the red Moroccan leather chairs, a gift from the Duke of Cowden for long years of service, were still there for visitors. The sideboard still held the same four decanters—whisky, American bourbon, brandy and high-end gin from James Greyville, another of Bowdrie's clients.

Perhaps there were a few more books than there had been. Cullen tugged discreetly at his collar, feeling hemmed in. For such a small space, there were so many *things*. Shelves stuffed with tomes and masculine accoutrements, a compass, a globe, scales, paperweights. The English did like their objets d'art.

Bowdrie was at the sideboard, holding up a decanter. 'Would you like a drink? It's only eleven, but you've had quite a journey. A strong drink is in order as is a bit of celebration. I think no one would condemn our indulgence.'

Cullen shook his head. 'No, thank you.' Other than an occasional rum or a rare French brandy to keep up appearances in Papeete, he seldom drank alcohol any more. He'd discovered he had better things to do: swim, fish, train in the outriggers, and, of course, carry out company business between the islands for Keir. His days were full. He'd had to re-accustom himself to the prevalence of alcohol on his journey given that fresh water had been at a premium most of the trip. But his refusal had left Bowdrie feeling awkward and unsure how to continue the conversation. Cullen offered him a lifeline. 'Why don't we just jump straight into it? Tell me what's happened.'

Tell me what's happened since my friend died, since the one man in England who believed in me is no longer alive.

He'd had the whole journey to accustom himself to that, too, and he'd been as unsuccessful with it as he'd been getting used to the clothes and the alcohol. How was it possible he'd ever felt at home here? Or perhaps he never had?

Bowdrie returned to his chair behind the massive desk. 'I can update you, of course. The short of it is that Keir's death requires the partnership to be re-established, as I explained in the letter. But it is more than that. Banks also need reassurances that the company continues to be viable,' Bowdrie added meaningfully. 'I would never say this directly to Mrs Popplewell—she's had a difficult enough year as it is—but she is a woman in a man's world. Stepping into Keir's position as if she is Keir himself, the head of Popplewell-Allardyce Enterprises, does not help the business. The banks are concerned about a woman at the helm.

'It has not been an issue so far, but if there comes a time when loans are needed or short-term credit is required for purchases, or deals need to be brokered, it will be an issue. They will not do business with a woman. Any misstep on her part will be magnified ten times over because of her gender. Having you here will go a long way in offering reassurances.'

Cullen crossed a leg over one knee. Bowdrie was talking as if he would be here indefinitely. That would not be the case, but now was not the time to talk about leaving. 'How is the company faring now? Keir sent annual reports and from all accounts it looks to be thriving.' He hoped that was the case. The less of a mess there was to clean up, the faster he could be back on a ship. Keir had always been a fastidious bookkeeper so there was hope in that direction.

'The company is doing well at present. So far, we've minimised any financial backlash from Keir's death.' Bowdrie splayed his hands on the polished desktop, slightly hesitant. 'There are plans for growth. Mrs Popplewell has ideas, but I think it would be best if you heard them from her. She's the one at the helm these days and the one you'll need to work with to sort everything out. She is anxious to meet with you.' That was a warning sign if ever there was one. Very well, he'd been warned and he'd be on alert.

'I imagine she is. Without me, her hands have been tied. I am sorry for it. I am sure it's been an added difficulty,' Cullen offered. 'I hope not too much has come to a standstill. I will, of course, help her get things started again.' He meant it as a prompt, an invitation for Bowdrie to fill him in. Hopefully the whole supply chain had not been damaged yet. He and Keir had invested considerable effort in building it, one relationship at a time. But Bowdrie offered nothing. Cullen had the distinct impression Bowdrie was a little bit intimidated by Mrs Popplewell, if not more than a little. It did pique his curiosity about the woman Keir had fallen in love with.

Bowdrie shifted in his seat. 'Yes, well, she can explain all of that to you. I can have her meet you for lunch if that's not too soon. Where are you staying?'

'I don't know yet.'

'Mivart's on Brook Street would be my recommendation. It's not far from Mrs Popplewell's town house and Mivart's prefer long-term guests who stay for a month or more. It will be perfect for you, although there's no coffee room or club room on the premises. You'll have to eat out, but there are several restaurants nearby. I'll have my clerk make the arrangements and a reservation for lunch at two at Verrey's. Women can dine there,' he offered as an aside. 'That will give you time to settle in and unpack.'

He called for his clerk and gave instructions. 'Now that's taken care of, tell me what you've been up to. We have an hour or so before your room will be ready.'

Cullen gave a dry chuckle at the thought of condensing ten years into an hour. How very efficiently English. But perhaps it was possible when so few things changed.

Bowdrie raised his glass in a quick toast. 'Cheers.'

'Yes, cheers,' Cullen replied, offering a silent toast of his own. *Here's to being back.*

Chapter Four

Cullen Allardyce was back. Antonia stepped down from the town carriage at number two hundred and thirty-three Regent Street in front of Verrey's Café Restaurant and took a moment to gather herself. The news had put her emotions into a flurry since it had arrived three hours ago. There was the elation of relief—he was back, loose ends could be wrapped up, things could be finalised. The limbo she'd been navigating could be resolved at last.

But that relief was tempered against the anxiety of knowing such resolution would now require full disclosure on her part about what she'd done with *his* money *without* his technical permission. She was within her rights. *She* wasn't the one who'd ignored the business for years. If he disapproved of the current state of their affairs, he had to acknowledge his part in how they'd got there. He'd also have to acknowledge that she'd done quite well on his behalf in his absence. She'd spent his money, not lost it. There was a difference.

Antonia gave the skirts of her plum ensemble a final smoothing and stepped inside the restaurant. She approached the maître d' in his crisp black and white at the podium. 'I have a reservation at two o'clock for two.

It should be under Popplewell.' It was ten minutes to the hour. She was counting on being the first to arrive. She could stake out her ground.

'Yes, Madame. Right this way, your guest is already here.' Drat. She'd hoped to be early, to be able to study anyone who came through the door. It would have given her a little extra time to form a first impression. The maître d' wound his way through round bistro tables where a few groups of ladies gathered for a late lunch after shopping. Other than that, the heavy lunch crowd that gathered at Verrey's for its *dejeuner à fourchettes* had departed. He led her towards a table near the back wall with its mirrored panels that ran two-thirds its length, the effect making the restaurant look larger.

A man rose as they approached. The first thing she noticed about him was his height. He was a tall man and, up close, a large man. There was breadth to his shoulders and a muscled thickness through his arms that denoted developed biceps lay beneath the fabric of his clothes. And those trousers. They fit rather *well*, too well, something that the cut of his charcoal frock coat emphasised instead of hid.

Although it was shame on her for noticing. Antonia quickly brought her eyes back up, past the blue and white floral pattern on the grey waistcoat, to the sharp features of his face: the razor cut of his jaw, the precision-carved length of his nose and the tawny wildness of his eyes. Those eyes were mesmerising. It would be best not to look at them too long.

On first impression, he was a striking man, a man who possessed both physical and charismatic power to a point that he was almost overwhelming—but just almost. She'd never admit to being overwhelmed by anyone.

In truth, it was hard to know what to make of him. She'd never seen such a man who dressed as a gentleman, but looked more like a gentleman's ancient predecessors. The word feral came to mind, a term oft applied to an animal that had contrived to avoid domestication. The description suited him all too well, this man who had been gone from civilised London for over a decade.

'Mrs Popplewell.' He gave an inclination of his head. 'I'm Cullen Allardyce. I don't believe we've had the chance to meet.' He moved to the empty chair at the table and pulled it out for her. 'I took the liberty of ordering a tea tray so it would be ready when you arrived. But if you'd prefer something else?'

Antonia sat, her senses on full alert. Those manners could not hide the ways in which he was trying to control the interaction; the early arrival to claim the ground, the invitation to sit at the table as if *he* owned it, the ordering of the tea tray—although he'd been careful to balance that with an option. Still, she saw through the efforts.

These were subtle ways in which a man exerted dominance. The politeness of consideration easily created dependence in the recipient. Once people did things for you, you came to expect people would always do things for you and, before you knew it, you could do nothing for yourself. She knew. They were tactics she'd used often enough herself to know their effectiveness.

She leaned forward, a polite smile on her lips as her gloved hand brushed a feathering touch on his arm. It was time to establish some ground of her own. 'I *do*, in fact, prefer something else.' She turned to the maître d' with that same smile, never mind that she usually skipped lunch. This was about the principle of the matter. 'I'll have the *potage au vermicel et le petit pain du beurre* and a pistachio ice for dessert.' The maître d' left them and Antonia wasted no time grabbing the reins of the conversation. 'It is a pleasure to meet you at last, Mr Allardyce. I'm sure the journey was arduous, so your arrival is doubly appreciated.' Given that it had taken almost an entire year to effect.

He nodded. If he'd heard the nuanced critique of his tardiness, he made no sign of it. He merely offered, 'We were delayed longer that I would have liked in Cairo and the winter weather once we reached Europe was not in our favour.' His tawny eyes held hers, his voice sincere and private in its low tones as he changed the conversation. 'I am so sorry to hear about Keir, Madame. He was a true friend to me and he wrote glowingly of you. Your marriage made him happy.'

Antonia felt her throat tighten, the familiar lump form. How was it that after a year, after having officially left mourning behind, such words could still bring her to the brink of tears? There ought to be a moratorium on such reactions. It was hardly fair.

The trays of food arrived and their conversation halted until the dishes had been laid out. The respite was long enough to dislodge the tightness. 'He was a good man, the very best,' Antonia managed to say.

'I do not doubt it,' Allardyce averred. 'How are you getting on? I trust things have not been too difficult despite your need for my signature? If Bowdrie had sent the papers, I would have signed them and sent them back.'

And not come back in person. Antonia didn't miss the rebuke there. He'd not liked being summoned. He no more wanted to be in England than he wanted to be in that suit of clothing. 'If it could have been done, I would have done it. The documents need to be notarised, which requires you being here in person. You are not the only one who has been inconvenienced by these events.'

She would not have him thinking she'd asked for his return on the grounds of an uneducated, selfish whim. 'Bowdrie believes that we have to re-establish the partnership since it is no longer between you and Keir, but between you and a new entity. Myself.' She watched as he polished off his fifth triangle of a ham sandwich. Perhaps it was good after all that she'd ordered on her own. He'd already made quite a dent all by himself in the enormous, tiered tea tray. It would take loaves of finger sandwiches to fill a man his size.

He chewed thoughtfully, his gaze intent on her. 'Do you not agree with Bowdrie?'

Antonia braced herself. They were at the heart of the conversation now, the part that would decide how their relationship together might proceed amicably or otherwise, or not proceed at all. 'I feel there are more options. There was always a chance that we might not find you or that you were dead. In that case, I felt it best we have a contingency. To cede to the idea that we could not move forward without you would be to put ourselves in an untenable position, a ruinous position even, if the worst had happened to you.'

'You mean yourself,' he corrected. 'When you say "we could not move forward", you really mean *you*, singly, could not move forward.' He speared her with a stare, perhaps daring her to respond. She chose to stay quiet, letting her silence press him to continue. He clearly had more to say and she was not disappointed. 'Bowdrie is not a partner; he is an employee even if he was also Keir's friend. He serves at your pleasure. He offers opinions when asked, but he does not decide. There was no "we", Mrs Popplewell. There was only you and now there is me. So, when you use the term "we" from here on out, it means you and me. I think it's important we're precise about our terms. Don't you agree?'

Whatever was feral about his appearance, it did not extend to his mind, which was agile and well trained. Of course, she should have expected that. Keir had thought him a brilliant investor, a man with an eye for all the angles of a market. 'You're as sharp as Keir said you were,' she complimented. It couldn't hurt to sweeten the pot a bit before they went much further.

He sat back in his chair, the delicate teacup looking ridiculous but comfortable in his big hand with its surprisingly long, elegantly slender fingers. 'Sharp enough to notice that only Mr Bowdrie believed you needed to wait for me to move forward. Did you wait?' Those tawny eyes speared her again. 'You don't strike me as a waiting kind of woman, Mrs Popplewell.'

Part of her bristled at that—how dare he make such assumptions when he'd known her for less than an hour?—and the other part of her took fair warning. He was right. His instincts were unerringly accurate on this particular issue.

He set his teacup down and leaned forward, his tawny eyes intent on her. 'So, tell me, Mrs Popplewell, what have you spent my money on? After all, that is what "forging ahead" means in this discussion.'

She hid her surprise at the extreme bluntness of his question and at how quickly he'd decoded the carefully worded conversation. But she would not shirk from offering an equally direct answer. 'Wages, salaries, warehouse rents, cargoes. In short, the usual. I would welcome the opportunity to discuss the cargoes particularly with you so that I understand what the company is doing there. We could cut our overhead by manufacturing goods here at home—' she began to say, only to be almost vehemently cut off.

'No, that's not part of how it works.'

'Then you'll have to explain it to me.' She answered his heated response with her own coolness. 'Perhaps tomorrow we can start going over the accounts in case I've overlooked any nuances. Income from the property holdings continues to come in, as does money from investment dividends, and of course money continues to go out. Now that mourning is behind me, I intend to continue Keir's association with the Prometheus Club. I'd like to be up to speed on that by May when the Season begins and everyone is in town. I will appreciate any introductions you can make and, of course, I will appreciate your presence.'

Although at the moment she wasn't sure that was the

truth. Now that Cullen Allardyce was here she definitely had mixed feelings the longer she thought about what his presence might mean. She'd spent a year doing things on her own and while there was an element of the unknown when one learned as they went, she was now used to being independent, answering only to herself and occasionally Bowdrie. She would have to share now. Would he share? Yet running Keir's businesses was a lot of work. Sharing it with someone who already knew how the business worked would bring its own type of relief.

He frowned. 'The Prometheus Club is ambitious. I'll do what I can.' The non-committal nature of his response worried her. Was it non-committal because, like her, he was still assessing this new territory, still assessing her as she was assessing him? Or was it more? Had he thought of assuming Keir's position in the club? Would that be a first step in putting himself forward as the new face of the company? A first step in forcing her into an invisible role? She took a bite of her newly arrived pistachio ice to cover her worry.

'Is that all you've been doing? Paying wages? Maintaining the status quo?' he queried. 'That doesn't sound like moving forward.'

She wouldn't lie. If they went over the books, he'd discover it anyway and there was no way to hide a building. Antonia met the question squarely. 'There is one more thing. A few months before Keir's death, he'd purchased a building he meant to turn into a department store. I've decided to finish it, as a legacy to him. I can show you tomorrow.'

'A department store?' His brows went up, incredulity evident.

She couldn't decide if his incredulity was out of agreement, disagreement or merely surprise. 'Yes, one to rival the stores in Paris. Keir felt department stores were the way of the future, that eventually they'd come to replace individual shops. They certainly make shopping more efficient by having everything in one place.' *Keir felt.* It was still hard to talk about him in the past tense. She took a final spoonful of her pistachio ice to hide the emotion.

'That's another very *ambitious* undertaking, Mrs Popplewell.' He gave a sardonic lift of a sandy brow. 'Is there anything else you've done with my money in the last eleven months?'

'No, I think that covers it. As I said, we can tour the property tomorrow. I have a meeting scheduled with the site manager.' That seemed a good note to end on. The meal was finished, as was all they could accomplish for today which had essentially boiled down to taking one another's measure. She beckoned for a waiter. 'The bill, please.'

Allardyce leaned towards her and said quietly but sternly, 'Mrs Popplewell, I'll handle lunch,'

'Nonsense, this is a business meeting and you are my guest,' Antonia argued politely, determined not to be beholden or to give up one iota of the control she'd spent the lunch wresting back.

'I am your partner,' he corrected in undertones as the bill was brought to the table.

'Then you may pay your portion,' Antonia countered, 'if you feel that strongly about it.'

'I do.' Allardyce placed some money on the table. 'As apparently do you.'

'It's nice to see we agree on something. Hopefully this is the first of many agreements.' Antonia smiled and rose from the table. He rose with her and she was reminded again of his height, the largeness of him. She allowed him to see her out and wait with her while her carriage was brought around.

He looked out of place here with his longish hair and his busy eyes that constantly darted about the street. The bustling atmosphere made him edgy, she realised. He was having a bit of culture shock perhaps after being away so long. A thousand questions swirled in her mind about that time away. Why *had* he stayed away? Was there family who'd missed him? Keir had never mentioned any. She'd always had the impression Cullen was alone.

Her carriage arrived and she turned to him one last time. 'Mr Bowdrie's note mentioned you were staying at Mivart's. I will call for you there tomorrow at ten. Thank you for meeting me, especially when you've only been home for a few hours.'

He handed her into the carriage, his big hand engulfing her smaller one. 'I am "back", Mrs Popplewell. I am *not* "home".' There was a story there, perhaps answers to her questions, but not today. Or perhaps ever. He was her business partner now. Despite Keir's friendship with him, she needed time to form her own impressions before she decided to mix business with friendship.

Today had been a start, nothing more. As much as she liked to argue with Mr Bowdrie that this partnership was a continuation of something already in existence, it was a beginning, too. Cullen Allardyce was unlike any man she'd yet encountered. Dealing with him would require his very own rule book. One lunch was enough to know that working with him would not be business as usual. Well, she reasoned as the carriage pulled away from the kerb, she'd learned on the fly to manage Keir's holdings. She would learn how to manage Keir's silent partner, as well.

Chapter Five

Keir's wife would need some managing. Marvels usually did and Antonia Popplewell was definitely a marvel, a golden-haired whirlwind dressed in a deep green ensemble the shade of Tahiti's lush teak forests and, Cullen noted, a shade that also matched her eyes—eyes that sparked with energy. She was all brisk efficiency as she toured him through the establishment that took up numbers twelve and thirteen in Hanover Street. But that didn't stop the man in him from appreciating the sway of skirts up the steps. It was no wonder Keir had been enchanted by her. She was a twin wonder of brains and beauty. Not all men appreciated brains of course, but Keir had.

Inside, Popplewell's Department Store was well underway, though it was still something of a construction zone. They stepped around ladders and tools and cabinets waiting to be installed, but much of the hard work had been done. Individual departments were delineated with crisp wallpapers and protective sheets covered polished hardwoods.

'Let me take you upstairs to the third floor.' The heels of her half-boots clicked confidently on the polished oak stairs with its curved banister and elegantly turned spindles. It was no wonder mild-mannered Robert Bowdrie was intimidated by her. She was one part charming, with those golden English good looks and sparkling green eyes, and two parts unnerving with her shrewd intelligence.

He followed her up the steps, only half listening to her narrative. He was too busy processing the larger message of today's tour. She was absolutely on her game and he knew exactly what her game was: she wanted to show him she'd invested wisely in this project even if there was an emotional attachment behind it. She also wanted to show him that she was entirely capable of managing Popplewell and Allardyce Enterprises.

She understood that both the store and herself were on a trial of sorts. She knew he didn't have to renew the contract. He could walk away, which would create difficulties for her going forward, as Bowdrie had alluded to yesterday. What she didn't know, though, was that he'd not walk away. There was too much at stake, too many people's livelihoods.

This tour had shown him what she wanted. She wanted him to invest in the store and to invest in her, which meant signing the papers and leaving. Interestingly enough, that was what he wanted, too. Sign the papers, leave and let life go back to what it had been when Keir was alive. After Bowdrie's allusions yesterday, though, he wasn't sure those goals were mutually attainable. Without Keir there would be no going back to business as usual.

It *was* possible for *him* to go back, however. It would

require walking away and letting her find her own level until the banks pulled the rug out from under her or until they accepted her. She and the business that he and Keir had built would be the sacrifice required for his freedom, for finally cutting all ties to England. But that did not get her what she wanted—to keep Keir's business alive along with his store. In order for her to have that, he had a sneaking suspicion it would require sacrifice on his part. As if travelling halfway around the world wasn't sacrifice enough already.

'This will be the women's department,' she announced, turning to face him, her arms spread wide to embrace the entire floor. 'Ladies will be able to buy all the accessories necessary to complete an ensemble right here without having to traipse from one store for gloves and to another for shawls or...' she paused slightly, the first slight hesitation he'd heard her make all morning '...undergarments.'

Cullen decided to have a bit of fun with her. Could she be teased? He suspected she could. She was brisk, but not dry. All that charm had to have some humour with it, although she'd not had much to laugh about in the last year. Perhaps she needed to remember. 'You mean corsetry? Chemises? Pantalettes? Stockings? Nightgowns? That sort of thing?' He dropped each word into the conversation as if they were shockingly hot coals.

A hint of rose stained her cheeks, but she was up to the tease. 'Yes, exactly that sort of thing, Mr Allardyce. It's why we've devoted an entire floor to ladies only, so that they might have the freedom and *privacy* in which to shop,' she replied archly, giving him a smug smile that said she'd guessed his intention.

'*Touché*, Madame.' He flashed her a disarming smile and for a moment her eyes danced with a bit of laughter before she turned back to her tour, walking in that fast, brisk clip that matched her tone as she pointed out different areas.

'This will be where women can purchase ready-made gowns, some of which have been imported from Paris. We'll have alterations available on site. Here is where women can be fitted for their gowns just as if they were visiting a modiste on Bond Street.' Men were at work as they passed to install cabinets and shelves done in a soft, feminine ivory.

'This space has a woman's touch imprinted all over it. I can see your hand in all of this.' A good hand it was, too. She had an eye for colour, for creating an environment that would visually appeal and invite. But there was one thing that worried him. 'Women like to shop, Madame. This is all so efficient. It will shorten their pleasurable experience. Perhaps they would prefer to traipse from shop to shop, as you put it.'

She laughed and tossed him a smile full of womanly knowledge. 'Have you ever asked yourself why women like to shop? It's an excuse to get out of the house without needing a formalised reason, like attending an event or going to someone else's house. You do realise how few places there are for a woman to go in London while men have their pick of clubs and restaurants? For women, shopping is an *escape*.' The subject brought a different shade of pink to her cheeks, a passionate pink. This was a subject near to her heart. His friend had married a firebrand.

She wasn't done yet. 'We ate at Verrey's yesterday because it was one of six restaurants a woman can lunch at. One of six in a city this size,' she repeated for emphasis. 'Which brings me to the pièce de résistance of the ladies department.' She stopped before a space currently curtained off and drew back the draperies to reveal little tables and chairs and bakery cases still in need of installing. A bank of tall arched windows overlooking the street was hung with floor-long portières trimmed in elegant gold braid, letting in plenty of daylight.

'Popplewell's café,' she announced proudly. 'Ladies can lunch here or take tea. This way they can shop as long as they like, stop for tea, then shop some more without ever leaving the store. I want to make this one of the finest restaurants in the city, a place for women to come to when they want to escape their homes.'

'I like it.' Cullen nodded. He'd not thought of shopping as an escape before, although he could certainly appreciate the notion of wanting to be somewhere outside of the house. Growing up, school had at least been a chance to leave the archaic strictures of his father's domain. He looked about the space, seeing what it could be, what it was very close to being. 'It's a sound business decision. We want customers to keep their attentions on all things Popplewell. We don't want them leaving the premises to satisfy a need. We want to anticipate and satisfy those needs here.'

Passionate, intelligent, insightful—Antonia Popplewell knew how to make an impression. If he could see why Bowdrie was intimidated by her, he could also see why Keir had been captivated. Unfortunately, there were more Bowdries in the world than Keirs. Now, he also saw why Bowdrie was worried. Intimidated people often tried to squash out that which they feared. His father was like that. The man had spent his life trying to dampen his younger son's democratic zeal and sense of fair play.

She motioned that they should sit at one of the tables. 'You've seen the store, now tell me what you think.'

Cullen stretched out his legs. 'I am impressed that so much has been done under the circumstances. You have had a very difficult year and yet all this has moved forward. That is commendable.' He was not Bowdrie. He was not intimidated by a forthright woman with vision. He would give credit where it was due. 'All that remains is to hire staff, stock shelves and finish acquiring product. You should be able to open in July.'

That earned him a sharply arched brow. 'I mean to open at the end of April in order to take full advantage of the Season.'

He did not want an argument with her, so he said, 'What does your site manager say about that?' In fact, where *was* her site manager? She was supposed to have a meeting with him. Cullen had expected him to have been here when they'd arrived, but they'd completed the tour and there was no sign of him.

Her own response was equally evasive. 'I've got warehouses of cargo just waiting to go on to shelves and an agency that has already begun to hire staff for me. All that remains is getting the fixtures up so the store can be filled. Surely, if we started stocking shelves the first of March, we'd be ready by April.' It was a subtle argument to counter his timeline. Her timeline suited his plans much better. It ensured he could make a spring sailing. But his conscience pricked over his motives for agreeing to it. He felt compelled to offer a word of realism.

'*If* the final details can be completed. There's a lot left to do,' Cullen cautioned. Especially if her site manager made a habit of not showing up for work until noon. He asked the second question that had been prodding at him. 'Do you have a store manager in mind?' With a store this size, she'd need someone with experience. Department stores didn't run themselves. She didn't just need staff, she needed a manager and that manager would need his own department managers. There was a whole hierarchy that needed to be in place for each department.

He noted the subtle squaring of her shoulders and braced himself for her answer. 'I will manage the store.'

'Surely Keir didn't intend to run the store himself?' It was a terrible idea. 'Have you ever managed a store of any size before?' This was precisely the kind of thing Bowdrie had feared. 'Stores are time-consuming jobs that don't keep regular hours. A good store may *look* like it runs like clockwork, but that is an illusion only, a play if you will, for the customers' benefit. It takes considerable effort behind the scenes to make it appear "easy".'

'Have *you* run a store, Mr Allardyce?' she countered smoothly.

'Not one of this size. But Keir had me running his

fabric warehouses down on the docks for several years. Drapers would come to do the shopping for their stores. I know a little something about the concept of "retail".'

She gave a tight, polite smile. 'I appreciate the concern. I assure you, I have nothing but time.'

It was a poignant reminder that for all her charm, she had no husband, no children, to give that time to. It was a reminder also that although she'd approached the execution of the project with level-headed thoroughness, this was above all for her a passion project, a memorial for her beloved husband. To be at the store was akin to being with him, a way to hold on to what she'd lost. Beneath the honour and bravery of taking on such a memorial, Cullen wondered when such bravery became an obsession, when honouring a loved one became an unhealthy pastime of walking with ghosts?

There was rustling at the draperies that cordoned off the restaurant. A worker appeared, knit cap in hand. 'Mr Mackelson is here, ma'am. You wanted me to let you know when he arrived. He is downstairs.'

'Thank you, I'll be there at once.' She rose, but Cullen reached out a hand to stall her. She would think him out of line, but he'd risk it.

'On second thoughts, send Mr Mackleson up here,' he instructed with a stern look that sent the worker hurrying. Once the worker had left, he explained, 'Mackleson answers to you, not the other way around. When you go to him, you give him power. If he shows up for work at noon or whenever he feels like it, you've already given him too much of that.'

'Like showing up for lunch early enough to claim the table first?' she shot back.

He shrugged a shoulder. 'Something like that, indeed.' Then he smiled. 'You were early, too, as I recall, so perhaps you're familiar with the strategy?' That won him a little smile from her just as Mackleson came huffing up the stairs. Cullen took in the beads of sweat on his brow with distaste. A heavy man was a man with no self-discipline. No self-respecting warrior in Ha'apape would ever allow himself to look so slovenly.

Antonia Popplewell stood. 'Mr Mackleson, I wanted a report on the cabinetry for the men's department. When we last spoke, we'd determined they were supposed to be installed this week, but I see they haven't even arrived.'

Mackleson gave a long-suffering sigh. 'They'll get here when they get here. It's difficult to find enough delivery drays to haul a large order like that. I can't do anything about it.'

'We're supposed to open in two months,' she reminded him. 'Every delay creates more pressure the closer the deadline approaches.'

'I'll send an errand boy over again,' Mackleson grumbled. Cullen was not impressed. Something didn't ring true.

'That's not good enough,' Cullen interjected. 'They won't listen to an errand boy. You go yourself. You're the manager on this project. You should take responsibility. Who are the cabinet makers you're using?'

'Weitz and Sons,' Mackleson supplied with a sneer. Cullen knew them. They were very good, high quality. Unless that had changed in the last ten years. They'd done work on his father's town house when his mother had redecorated the library.

Cullen turned to Mrs Popplewell, whose eyes had narrowed to green cat-like slits. 'Did you pay full price?'

'Yes, absolutely. My husband always used them. They're a little more than other companies, but definitely worth it.'

Mackleson looked him up and down with another sneer. 'Who might you be, butting your nose into other people's business?'

'I'm Cullen Allardyce, Keir Popplewell's partner.' Cullen offered a cool smile, enjoying the looks of unpleasant surprise, then worry cross the man's bloated face. 'I'll expect a report by the end of the day and I'll expect that you'll return the money you've skimmed tomorrow morning, or you'll be removed from the job.' Cullen would like to remove the man altogether, but he had no one at present to replace him with. The moment he did, however…

'Now listen here, I haven't taken any money,' Mackleson blustered. 'You can't come in here making accusations like that, I don't care who you are.'

Cullen patiently cut him off. 'Then perhaps you can explain the delay to me. Weitz and Sons deliver their cabinets. It's included in their price. They have their own fleet of drays. Delivery is never a reason for delay with them. The only exception to that is for those who choose to pick up their own orders. Those folks get a fifteen per cent discount,' Cullen countered.

'The reason the cabinets are delayed is that *you* cannot find enough drays to pick them up without eating into the fifteen per cent you pocketed. Mrs Popplewell believes she paid them full price, but I would wager that when we look at the final invoice, it will show that you placed an order that specifies you will pick them up yourself.' Cullen paused long enough to let that sink in, his stare never wavering. 'If I were you, I wouldn't stand around. I'd hustle over to the cabinet makers and change my order and make sure those cabinets are here tomorrow morning.'

At least the man knew good advice when he heard it. Silence stretched long after Mackleson departed, but Cullen could practically *hear* Antonia Popplewell thinking. He didn't expect her to say thank you, but if she was angry, she had only herself to blame.

A thousand thoughts raged through her head, most of them inappropriate for voicing out loud, many of them beginning with *how dare he*. How dare he upstage her in front of an employee, how dare he thrust himself into the middle of her conversation, how dare he take things over. She wanted to rant at him, wanted to yell. But that was Fleur's way, not hers. She'd always prided herself on expressing her anger through more diplomatic means. She'd worked too hard today to show herself in the best possible light as a capable businesswoman. She wasn't going to ruin it with a rant.

Finally, Antonia found a collection of words she *could* say out loud and still maintain a modicum of professionalism. 'Do not ever do that again,' she ground out, pleased she'd kept her voice even when what she really wanted to do was scream. Keir never upstaged her. He'd always been conscious of boundaries.

Cullen gave her one of his sardonic brow lifts. 'Don't do what? Call out a man for stealing from us?' He rose from the bistro chair and began to pace. 'When a man steals from *me*, I have a tendency to want justice. When a man lies to me, I want justice. When a man is late to work and takes liberties with his position, I want justice. He was taking advantage of you and you were either too blind to notice, or you *did* notice and were unable to bring him to heel.'

The 'how dares' started up in her head again. She tamped them down. 'You have no right to speak to me that way. *You* have been absent for the entirety of this year. I have managed quite well on my own.'

'With *my* money,' he reminded her. 'With acting in my name as if you already had my signature *and* approval, two very large assumptions I would not tolerate from you if you'd not been Keir's widow.' If she was used to men backing down in the wake of her simmering fury, she would find that strategy didn't work with him. There was more than mere chivalry at stake. 'You have done well, all things considered, but you will need to do much better. You were not managing him.'

'And to be clear, Mr Allardyce, you are not managing me.' Antonia strode towards the exit and tossed him a look over her shoulder. 'Are you coming? We have books to go over. That's next on our agenda.' She set off down the staircase at a brisk clip, her self-sustaining mantra playing over in her head for strength. She was *not* going to let him get to her.

She was Antonia Popplewell, she'd come this far, she'd survived near-genteel poverty, the cats of the London Season, the tragic loss of a beloved husband, the first year of picking up her life without him. She would certainly survive the intrusion of Cullen Allardyce despite his commanding ways, piercing gaze and broad shoulders.

She *would* get through this. She *would* see the store opened. She would because she knew she would not give up. But she also knew Cullen Allardyce was right. If the store was to succeed, she had to do better. The truth hurt. She'd made some mistakes out of sheer naivety.

Keir had had a lifetime of business experience behind him when he made decisions—she had mere months of self-taught insights to fall back on. He had networks of people to consult. She had no one except Bowdrie, yet she was trying to run a business empire that required that lifetime of knowledge with the meagre experience she had. It was like trying to pull a coach with only one horse when one really needed four.

She'd not realised Mackleson had pocketed part of the cabinet money. She'd not picked up on the reason the delivery hadn't been made. She should have. Such things came with experience and time, neither of which she had at this point. Mackleson had been a thorn in her side almost from day one.

In truth, it was something of a relief to have Cullen deal with him since her methods had failed to obtain the desired results and she was running out of options. It was just one more way in which she secretly felt her inadequacies on this project, despite her efforts to learn quickly.

Her carriage waited at the kerb. She climbed in and a

moment later Allardyce joined her, his big body filling the space completely. 'Were you going to leave without me?' he asked as the carriage lumbered into motion before he was barely seated.

'No.' She wasn't ready for a full-blown conversation just yet. Apparently, Allardyce couldn't take a hint.

'How did you know I'd follow you?' He stretched his legs, his calf bumping against her skirts, making her aware of him on a less business-orientated level.

'Because I asked you to, Mr Allardyce.' She looked out the window, trying to make it plain she didn't want to talk.

'Cullen, please, Antonia,' he insisted. 'Since we are to be partners, perhaps it would be best if we dispensed with the formalities.'

'Fine.'

'But how could you be sure I *was* following? You never looked back to see if I was coming,' he persisted.

She turned her gaze, pinning him with a strong stare. 'I never look back, *Cullen*.' And she certainly wasn't going to start now.

Chapter Six

The woman never stopped. A week spent in her company was more than enough time to confirm it. Antonia Popplewell was a tireless whirlwind of activity, somehow managing to be everywhere all at once, whether it was meeting the new employees sent over by the agency, discussing accounts with him, or taking delivery of the disputed cabinetry, which, Cullen was pleased to note, arrived bright and early the morning following his scolding of Mackleson.

Cullen wondered if she ever slept. Sleepless or not, she called for him with the carriage each morning at nine o'clock sharp at Mivart's, hair in a shiny, perfect, golden twist, her appearance immaculate, her clothing fashionable and above reproach. She favoured fine wools in darker colours—greens, blues, subtle purples—and ensembles with a military cut to the jacket, all designed to project an image of competent confidence—something that either impressed or intimidated, Cullen noted on repeated occasions. The latter continued to worry him. Many men didn't know how to respond to a competent woman in business, as Mackelson's situation proved. It further proved that Bowdrie was right to be concerned.

Did this morning's previously unscheduled meeting have anything to do with those concerns? Cullen stretched his long legs across the carriage and studied her. She'd broken with her usual attire this morning and worn a red and taupe plaid gown cut in the apparently timeless redingote style—a variation of a style he recalled from before he'd left. Taupe-coloured boots dyed to match peeped beneath the beige underskirt where the redingote fell away to allow one to appreciate the full skirt. Her tiny gold earrings were still in place as was her perfect twist.

The earrings and perfect twist wouldn't save her from his curiosity or his conclusion that the meeting with Bowdrie had her concerned. Everything about her signalled unease. She *was* worried. The red plaid was out of character for her, perhaps a hurried choice in order to accommodate Bowdrie's urgent summons. They weren't supposed to meet with Bowdrie until next week, but the solicitor had sent a note this morning that had them re-organising their day. It also had them setting out earlier than their usual nine o'clock.

'Did you eat breakfast?' he asked. Whirlwind that she was, she often forgot to eat. He had to remind her on several occasions to eat lunch and it made him wonder if she regularly ate dinner after she dropped him at Mi-vart's in the evening. She was pale today and her usual charm was absent. Her thoughts were clearly elsewhere. She'd not said anything beyond 'hello' to him since he'd got in the carriage and her gaze had remained fixedly straight ahead on the empty seat across from her.

'Coffee. That's all there was time for.' Ah, yes, her

coffee. She drank it religiously in the mornings instead of tea and she took it strong and black without any embellishment.

'That's not breakfast. We'll have Bowdrie's clerk go out for something. You need substance.' So did he. He was starving. When she said nothing more, he tried another prompt. 'Is there anything I should know before we get to Gray's Inn? I'd like to be prepared instead of surprised.'

She shook her head and he let it go, knowing it for a lie. He'd know soon. It was enough for now to recognise that any worry on her part meant there should be worry on his. That was how partnerships worked, whether those bonds were ready to be tested or not.

He was right. Bowdrie wasted no time ushering them into his office and shutting the door even though the clerk had been dispatched for breakfast and there was no one to overhear them. Bowdrie took his seat behind the desk and began without preamble. 'It's the bank. They are foreclosing on the loan Keir took out to buy the building. They're asking for payment in full.' He handed Antonia a letter, but he flashed Cullen a look that said, *This is what I've been fearing.*

This was what she'd been fearing—the other shoe to drop. Things had been going too well for the most part. Her emotions roiled, forming a pit in her stomach, her mind raced with consequences and conjecture regarding all she stood to lose if she lost the building at this point. No. She was not going to panic. Antonia took a deep breath to steady herself. 'That is a twenty-year mortgage. Payments have been made on time. Keir has done business with them before. They know he's reliable. Did they say why the sudden change of heart?'

She didn't miss Bowdrie's swift downward glance as he gathered himself for what was likely to be an unfavourable response. She had her guesses, but she wanted to hear it from him. 'Because Keir is not at the helm any longer. Their loan was with him.'

Antonia scanned the letter. 'Why now? Why have they waited this long to make a fuss?'

Bowdrie fidgeted with a paperweight. 'They wanted to be fair, to extend you the courtesy of a mourning period and a chance to get affairs in order.'

Antonia sat up a little straighter and curbed her temper. 'Fair? What about fair warning? That would have been fair. What is not is this letter the moment I came out of mourning.' She leaned forward. 'It is as if they had a calendar in front of them and were counting down, which suggests this was premeditated. They didn't just wake up today and say, "Let's foreclose on the Popplewell building today." They've been planning this from the start, ever since they'd learned of Keir's death.' That property, situated as it was so near the Bond Street shops, was highly lucrative.

Condemnation surfaced amid her emotions. She should have seen this coming. Keir would have. But Keir would never have been put in this position simply because he was a man. But she was female and that made her fair game. 'We can pay them, or we can fight them.

We can take them to court for breach of contract and negotiating in bad faith.'

'Or perhaps there is a third option.' Cullen spoke, splitting his gaze between her and Bowdrie. 'Please don't forget I am in the room. I believe I was summoned from the other side of the world for exactly this situation. They need reassurance that the company is in good hands. Let them know that I am here, that there is no cause for alarm.'

'Are you certain? It takes you rather into the public eye.' Bowdrie looked almost apologetic, concerned in a way that had nothing to do with the situation at hand. A glance passed between he and Cullen that Antonia could not decipher, some secret she was not part of. It only served to fuel her anger. She was tired of men and their secret, male-only lives she was not privy to.

This was too much. She was the aggrieved party here. Antonia turned her anger toward Cullen. 'The company is in "good hands" because a man is here? Is that what you mean by giving them reassurances? A man who has been absent from the business for ten years is somehow *more* reassuring to the bank than a woman who has overseen everything personally for a year. Do you hear the ridiculousness in that?' She was spoiling for a fight. After a year, her efforts had earned her none of the respect she deserved.

But Cullen wouldn't bite. 'What I *hear* in my suggestion is *reality*,' he offered coolly.

Antonia wrestled her temper into submission. 'This is how it begins. This is how you take the company from me. I won't have it.' This was what she'd feared that first day at Verrey's: he'd come to install himself in Keir's place and slowly relegate her to the background. She would lose the last piece of Keir she had left. She felt herself begin to shake, dangerous emotion overcoming her. She could not lose him, she could not. She'd fought so hard, so long, and she was almost there. The store was perched on opening in sixty days. Her mind grasped for her mantra.

I am Antonia Popplewell, I've survived the threat of genteel poverty, the cats of London…

She laced her hands together to keep them from shaking. If she could stop trembling, she could stop this wave, this *tsunami* of emotion that threatened the shores of her control.

'Antonia, are you all right?' Cullen's voice was somewhere in the fog.

'I am done here.' She heard her voice as if it came from someone else. She struggled to her feet.

Just put one foot in front of the other, through the outer office, down the stairs, to the carriage.

Her mind knew what to do, but her body was not willing. She made it to the outer office, bumping into the clerk who was valiantly juggling coffees and pastry before she collapsed. Only she didn't fall, not all the way. Arms engulfed her, caught her, lifted her with their strength, their wondrous, warm strength…

Strong, hot coffee. Was there any better smell in the world? Antonia struggled towards consciousness, lured by the aroma. But consciousness was confusing. She was in the carriage. How had she got there? She'd been in

Bowdrie's office… Ah, the bank, the foreclosure, Cullen asserting his blasted authority again as he had with Mackleson. She groaned. She'd let her temper get the better of her in there and the dam of her restraint had broken in front of Cullen Allardyce, whom she was desperate to impress.

She gave another moan of regret. Instead of impressing, she'd collapsed in his arms. Such hysterics would only give him grounds to challenge her authority. Someone shifted on the seat opposite and she knew when she opened her eyes, she'd see Cullen sitting there. She had to face him. She hated weakness, in herself more than anyone else. Optimists couldn't afford weakness or cowardice.

She forced her gaze open and there he was, in that damnably well-tailored new suit of his that showed off those broad shoulders, a reminder that she now knew first-hand what those shoulders were capable of. Genuine concern *for her* was etched on his face.

'Sip this, it's hot.' He passed her a tin cup full of steaming coffee. She wrapped her hands about the cup, the warmth seeping into her.

'Thank you.' Hopefully that would cover it without having to itemise what she was thanking him for.

'Here, there are rolls, too. You need to eat something. Did you have dinner last night after I left?'

'Yes.' But she knew she'd hesitated too long.

'What was it?' Cullen insisted.

'I don't remember.' Maybe she hadn't eaten. Some nights she didn't. There was so much to do and mealtimes were the hardest without Keir, that time of day when everything in their busy world receded and it had been only the two of them.

'Just as I thought.' Cullen gave her one of his raised-brow gazes.

She cleared her throat and took a begrudging bite of the still-warm roll. She tried for normalcy, something to restore equilibrium between them. 'That's a new jacket.'

He gave a self-conscious tug at the lapels of his dark jacket. 'My clothes order is starting to arrive. I can now expand my wardrobe beyond the two suits I came with.' He gave a low chuckle. 'I bought them in Cairo while we were delayed. They served their purpose.'

She hadn't known that. 'You came to London with only two changes of clothes?' She'd assumed he'd arrived with trunks, multiple trunks.

'One doesn't need a great many clothes in the South Pacific, although we've yet to convince the Europeans there of that. They insist on wearing all of this folde-rol.' He gave another tug of his lapels for emphasis this time. 'In the heat, it's downright absurd.'

It was on the tip of her tongue to ask what he did wear, but she thought better of it. Her mind had been surprisingly captivated by the words *'one doesn't need a great many clothes in the South Pacific'* and her stom-ach had given a queer, not unpleasant flip, at the images of Cullen Allardyce sans shirt and waistcoat. Was his chest as tanned as his face? Were golden hairs sprin-kled along a tanned, muscled expanse of forearm? What about the rest of him? Did not needing a 'great many clothes' involve wearing something less than trousers?

She rapidly took another bite of the roll. She desperately needed to eat if that was where her thoughts were headed. No doubt those thoughts were brought on by multiple factors: stress, the lack of food, the growing list of questions she had about him and the amount of time they'd spent together.

She'd not spent so much extended time with another outside her family since Keir had died. The closest connection she had was her weekly meetings with Bowdrie. But Bowdrie never said anything interesting like not needing clothes. She knew without doubt in all the time she'd known him she'd *never* been tempted to imagine Robert Bowdrie without even a single article of clothing missing. But such imaginings were definitely a temptation when Cullen was around.

'I have an idea.' Cullen reached for a roll of his own, apparently satisfied she'd keep eating without his vigilant prompts. 'Let's take today off.'

She stopped in mid-chew and stared at him. Was he insane? 'The bank wants to foreclose on the store, didn't you hear Mr Bowdrie?' They had appointments to make, they had bankers to meet with, plead with, and if that failed, they had to go over the accounts and assess what it would mean to pay the loan in full. 'This is not a day to take off.'

'On the contrary, I think it's the perfect day to take off.' As usual, Cullen was infuriatingly unbothered by her hard words. Just once she'd like to get a rise out of him. He didn't strike her as a passionless man or a dry man, but he was definitely the master of his emotions. He gave nothing away. 'We've worked literally since the day I arrived.' He paused, his expression stern. 'When was the last day *you* had off?'

She didn't answer and Cullen gave her a smug *told-you-so* smile. But he misunderstood. It wasn't that she didn't remember. She *did* and it was simply too painful to say it out loud. She knew the answer. February the fourth, 1852. And she'd spent the evening playing whist with Fleur and Emma instead of being with Keir, thinking just how much she'd needed a girls' night. Instead, it turned out she'd wasted the last four hours of Keir's life being away from him.

'We've taken care of work, Antonia, but we've not taken care of ourselves,' Cullen was saying. 'It didn't occur to me until the bank's letter today that we should mark the anniversary of Keir's passing. I know I arrived after the official date, but I haven't been out to pay my respects. I would like to. He was more than a mentor to me, he was a friend—the best friend I'd ever had. A father figure to me, too, at times. I feel badly that I didn't think to go earlier.'

He reached for her hand and she was acutely conscious of his grip, warm and strong like the arms that had held her and the chest that had cradled her. 'Will you come with me? I would like your company. I would like to do this together.'

It occurred to her that she'd like his company as well. She nodded and drew a deep breath. She'd had flowers sent to the grave on the anniversary, but it was her secret shame that she'd not gone last week on her own. She had buried herself in work instead, telling herself that the work at the store was time-sensitive and she couldn't afford the day away. She'd been afraid if she went, she'd fall apart and not be able to put herself back together. But if Cullen was there, she'd have a reason to keep a rein on her grief. She could not afford another breakdown. This morning had been a close call.

He smiled and released her hand. 'To Kensal Green, then.'

Chapter Seven

Kensal Green made death look beautiful with its tree-lined avenues and elegant tombstones, a place of serenity located in the Chelsea–Kensington borough off the Harrow Road, at least three-quarters of an hour by carriage from Gray's Inn. There was plenty of time to prepare herself and yet her trepidation grew as they passed through the triumphal arch made of Portland stone that guarded the entrance. The carriage could go no further out of respect for the dead.

Cullen handed her down and she drew her mantle close against the chill wind. It had been grey and gloomy the day she'd buried Keir, too, a day not unlike this one. Cullen offered his arm and she took it, grateful for the chance to hold on to something, to someone.

The day of the funeral it had been her father's steady arm. Her brother was posted in Canada and had been unable to come. She had not cried at Keir's committal, understanding that any sign of weakness would be held against her by those in attendance. The funeral party had been made up of her father and mother and some of Keir's chief business partners, primarily the Duke of Cowden and members of the Prometheus Club. They would be watching her, judging her, and she'd need their approval.

'It's a beautiful place, very peaceful,' Cullen commented in hushed tones as they strolled the centre pathway, either side lined by Gothic-styled monuments of the wealthier citizens interred there. 'It's rare to see so many trees and so much *green* in town.' He was trying to put her at ease. It was kind of him. The optimist in her wanted to lean into that kindness, but her usual optimism had been tempered a bit this year. She'd been forced to ask questions about people's motives and forced to admit that not everyone had the best interest of others in mind.

She had to ask that question now in regard to Cullen Allardyce. What did *he* want? She was acutely aware that they'd not yet signed the partnership papers. After today's setback with the bank, perhaps he might not sign at all, perhaps he might rethink his words in Bowdrie's office. He'd seemed, at the time, quite willing to advocate against paying the foreclosure. Perhaps after further thought he'd change his mind and decide it was too much trouble. That worried her. She would be hard-pressed to buy him out and pay off the loan in full simultaneously.

'Keir is just over here.' She steered them off the main path towards a grassy space beneath a spreading oak. Her wreath of flowers was draped over the stone cross that topped his grave marker. The roses were already dried and withered, a reminder of how futile her gesture was.

Cullen studied the grave marker. She watched his eyes move over the big, etched letters.

Keir Catton Popplewell
Beloved Husband

Would he think she'd chosen rightly? Should she have chosen 'businessman' or 'friend of the Empire'? Goodness knew he'd made England enough money alongside his own. Cullen gave her a small smile. 'Beloved husband. He would have liked that. He had no family when I met him, except for the family he'd made with Luce and Griffiths, and then perhaps with me if I am not too bold to suggest it.'

'You are not. You were dear to him.' Her throat gave a tell-tale tightening. How odd to be offering comfort, assurances, to this man beside her, who was perhaps seven years her senior, who exuded strength and confidence as if he were untouchable. But in this moment, he was the vulnerable party relying on her for a change. It was the least she could do after what he'd done for her this morning.

'Thank you for that, Antonia.' Cullen bowed his head and she gave him a moment of privacy with his thoughts. For a fleeting second, she was jealous of those thoughts, of those memories that he had of Keir that she didn't. What did he know of her husband that she did not? Shouldn't a wife know a husband better than anyone? After a while, he raised his head. 'Did Luce and Griffiths come to the funeral?'

She pressed a gloved hand to her mouth as the terrible realisation hit her. 'You don't know, do you? No one told you.' Because that someone should have been her. She was his only point of contact to Keir, outside of Bowdrie. This was what they should have talked of that first day at Verrey's. But she'd done what she'd been doing for the last year—burying herself in work, moving forward, never looking back, trying to ignore what was behind her.

'What don't I know?' He looked seriously alarmed. As well he should be. Today had been full of alarming surprises for him: the foreclosure, the loan, and now this.

Antonia gathered her strength. She never talked about *it*, but she must talk about it now. There was no one else. 'They were all killed in the same accident.'

He had her arm again, leading her to the stone bench between the oak and the grave, his voice quiet and coaxing. 'Can you tell me about the accident?'

'It was more of a disaster than an accident. We had all gone to Holmfirth in the west Yorkshire dales, to look at a mill Luce wanted to buy. He wanted Keir's opinion, and Adam Griffiths came along to look into the environmental situation. There'd been concerns before about the safety of the dam upriver,' Antonia said slowly, but the more she talked, the more her words became like the River Holme, surging against the confines of that dam until the walls of her restraint could no longer hold them.

They flowed in torrents as she recounted how the flood had destroyed Water Street, how eighty-one people had been killed, how whole mills had been washed away, the mangled machinery she'd seen left in the streets the next morning, haphazardly deposited by the river, how the river had raged—she'd never heard water make such sounds.

'They took me to see his body after it was recovered.' Her voice softened now, her own rage receding and with it her strength. There was a tremble in her voice when she spoke next. 'He'd fought hard. He'd struggled against the river. His hands were torn, there was a gash in his forehead.'

Cullen's hand wrapped around her own at the first sign of trembling. Perhaps he was trying to stave off a recurring episode of this morning's tears. 'You don't have to say any more,' he offered quietly.

But she did. Now that she'd started, there was so much more to say. 'I should have been with him,' she whispered her shame. 'We had gone to Holmfirth because I'd encouraged it. Yes, Luce had invited him, but Keir had been reluctant to go. We'd just acquired the store and we'd been working non-stop on renovating the interior. He wanted to stay in London and keep working. But I pushed for it.' It was the first time she'd admitted it out loud. 'I was selfish. I was tired of sharing him with the store.'

She shot a glance at Cullen, watching his face for a reaction. 'We were trying for a child. It had been…difficult.' She would not say more in that regard out of respect for Keir's memory. She would not tell Cullen her husband had been semi-impotent at the end.

'We were trying for that family Keir had so desperately wanted and I thought some time away from London would help. Instead, it killed him. *I* killed him. If I'd let him do as he wanted, he'd have stayed in London. He would be alive right now.' She cleared her throat against the rising emotion. She needed to stop talking, but she couldn't and it was going to be her undoing. 'But he did as *I* wanted and he died for it.

'All I have left of him now are his dreams—his businesses, his store, his project in the South Seas with you—and if I lose those things I will have failed him in both life and death. I will have failed him entirely.' She choked on the last word. It was too late to save herself. Emotion rose fast and hard, an irresistible siege. Oh, God, she was going to lose the fight this time. But she was not alone. Cullen Allardyce's arm was around her, drawing her close, letting her head bury itself in his shoulder, her fists clinging to the lapels of his jacket as the sobs racked her.

She had not cried like this since those early days in Holmfirth, sitting by Mrs Parnaby's lace-curtained windows, staring into nothing. The cry left her exhausted, purged. She drew a long, cleansing breath. 'I've soaked your coat.' She straightened, finding herself reluctant to leave the shelter of his arms. He'd been patient. He'd not offered platitudes or tried to argue with her feelings.

'It will dry.' He smiled and withdrew a white handkerchief. 'And so will you. Feel better?'

'I'm not sure.' She took the handkerchief and dabbed at her eyes. It smelled of him, all vanilla and spice and warmth. 'I must apologise that I've gone to pieces on you twice today, but I fear I might do it again.' She offered a watery smile and a half-laugh. 'I've been afraid that if I let myself feel too much, I'll just go on feeling, hurting, and I'd never pull myself together. Seems like maybe I was right.'

'Perhaps crying it out is the best way to hold yourself

together. You can't *not* feel, Antonia. I think no less of you for it,' he assured her. The optimist in her wanted to believe him.

She drew a deep breath, trying to find her centre, still feeling the remnants of her tears. 'There is no crying in business, though,' Antonia reminded him. 'Everyone always says women are too emotional. It is the chain they bind us with.' And now she'd proven it.

'This isn't business, though, is it? This is life and I think grief is a way of savouring life, of commemorating it, as long as it doesn't drag us down.' He gave a nod towards the wreath. 'You were here last week?'

She shook her head. 'No, I sent the flowers, but I couldn't bring myself to come. It was cowardly, I know.'

'But then I made you come; I am sorry,' Cullen said quietly.

'I needed to come. I just didn't need to come alone.' She knew it was true the moment she spoke the words. 'How are you doing? I must apologise for not having told you sooner. It didn't occur to me that you didn't know. I feel horrible about it. I didn't stop to consider *your* feelings, what it must have been like for you to get the news.' She apologised, but he was quick to absolve her. She wasn't sure she deserved that.

'I had the whole journey in which to come to terms with it. I didn't have details, true. But dead is dead. I had months to process that. Although, I do admit, being here today makes it more final, more real.'

It was her turn to offer comfort. She reached for his hand. 'He was your friend.'

'He was also my family, just as you said.' He offered

her a smile and something akin to peace began to unfurl within her.

He'd been generous today, this man who was a stranger to her, known to her in name only and little else beyond her husband's affections, until last week. She wanted to reciprocate as a show of her gratitude. What could she offer him in return? She'd needed to talk—perhaps he needed the same? 'Tell me a story about you and Keir. How did you meet?'

'Did he never tell you?' Cullen laughed. 'I suppose not. It's maybe not a tale for a wife's ears.' It felt good to reminisce like this, with someone who'd known Keir. Admiral Connant had been a polite companion on the voyage and certainly had done his best to commiserate over his loss, but Connant had not known Keir.

He'd talked *to* Connant about Keir, but there'd been no one to talk about him *with*, no one who knew what he'd looked like, who knew how he laughed—a big expansive sound that started from deep within him and warmed anyone who heard it—who knew all the ways in which he had championed the underdog because he'd been an underdog, too, before he'd climbed his own way up the ladder to a fortune. Of course, Keir had already been in possession of a goodly amount of that fortune when Cullen had met him.

'Now you have to tell me. With a lead like that, my curiosity knows no bounds,' Antonia prompted. Her own eyes were shining with something besides tears. That gladdened him. Her grief today had been hard to watch, not because he knew her that well—he'd only known her a week—but because of her strength. What a year she must have endured—a year beyond his imagining. Perhaps she needed to hear a story as much as he needed to tell one.

'If you're certain you want to hear it? Don't say I didn't warn you. Prepare to be scandalised.' He teased a smile from her before he dropped his opening line. 'We met in a brothel in Wapping. We were both there on business, but different kinds of business, you might say. This was before he'd met you.' He gave her a wink. 'Don't worry, Keir was there to try to persuade the owner to sell. It was down in the London Docks area and Keir wanted a place he could use as an office and a kind of club where his buyers who came to warehouses could retreat to, a place where he could meet with his shippers and Captains without having to go very far.'

'I know that place. He told me about it. His acquisition was successful. Now it's the Captain's Club.' She cocked her head. 'And what were you doing there?' she enquired with mock solemnity. 'Distributing religious tracts?'

'Of course,' He grinned. 'Should I be hurt that you assume I was up to no good?'

She gave him a sly look, proof that she was feeling better. 'A young man in a brothel? You forget I had a London Season. I know what young men get up to.'

'I was half shot on gin and on my way to being entirely squiffed. I ran into a man and spilled my drink on him. Fisticuffs ensued. I won the brawl, but ended up being tossed out on my backside into the alley. I was too drunk to realise the danger of that. I ended up dozing off, only to be awakened by street thugs going through my pockets and none too gently.

'Let's just say, there were knives involved. One of those knives might have been more "involved" if Keir hadn't come along and taken the pair of them on. He chased them off and sobered me up. But the thugs had my money, my watch, anything of value. He'd seen me fight and offered me a job as a night watchman at one of his warehouses.'

He smiled at the memory and spread his hands on his knees. 'And that was the beginning of our friendship.' He hoped there wouldn't be too many questions. Like what had he been doing at the brothel? Why hadn't he simply gone home after the incident in the alley? He just wanted her to focus on Keir. His own past needed to remain there for as long as it could.

'You didn't stay a watchman for long, though, did you?' That was a safe question and he was glad to answer it.

'Keir was smart. He'd made me a night watchman to keep me out of the brothels. I didn't have time to visit such places, working nights. But being a night watchman gave me a lot of time to study what he did there and a lot of time to think. He also saw that I was good with people.

'Soon, he asked me if I wanted to work the warehouse, unload fabrics, assist with some sales. Pretty soon, I took over the sales and I saved my wages until I had enough to go to Keir and ask to buy a small share in one of his cargoes.' That had been the beginning of his own fortune and their partnership.

'You are exactly the kind of person Keir liked to help, someone who needed their potential polished, who just needed a chance. You are a credit to him.' Her green eyes were shining and Cullen felt a twinge of guilt. What she said was true. But he knew how she viewed it—that Keir had taken a young man with limited prospects because of his birth to the lower orders and made him into something. But this didn't seem the moment, after all they'd gone through today, to redirect those assumptions. His prospects had been limited by birth, he'd argue, but just not in the way she thought.

'You're a credit to him, too,' Cullen said, changing the conversation. 'I'd left to handle the South Seas venture before he even met you.' The less said about why he'd left for the South Seas the better. He quickly directed the conversation towards her. 'But when he mentioned you in letters, it was clear marriage made him happy, that *you* made him happy. I'd not seen many happy marriages in my lifetime, so I was doubly pleased for him.'

Perhaps even jealous that Keir Popplewell, self-made man, had the one thing that Cullen Allardyce, son of a marquess, born to have access to all nature of worldly riches if he wanted them—which Cullen did not—would never have. Love and loyalty could not be bought, not really. 'You are everything he said you were.'

Part of him had to admit that if it was possible to be envious of a dead man, he was—envious of what Keir had had. Objectively speaking, Antonia Popplewell was a rare gem, not that such a moniker worked in her favour. London often didn't know what to do with rare gems that didn't fit into the niches carved out for them.

'I'm hungry. That roll didn't last long. Why don't we find some lunch?' His stomach rumbled as if on cue. He laughed at the intrusion. 'I confess I miss Tahiti when it comes to food. It literally just hangs on the trees, waiting to be picked at leisure. When I was hungry, I picked a breadfruit, a banana, or a lime and just like that I had a meal. But here…' He rolled his eyes. 'Here, I have to really look for it and think ahead.'

'Tahiti sounds wonderful. Food at your fingertips instead of wondering if a restaurant will serve a woman without ruining her reputation.' She gave a wry chuckle. 'Lunch sounds good, though.' She rose and brushed at her skirts. 'We can discuss the foreclosure over warm soup.'

He put a hand on her arm in polite correction, a gesture he found himself making often where she was concerned. There were definitely rough edges between the two of them, each of them preferring their own ways of doing things. 'No, not today. No business. Let's have lunch, take a walk in the park. You can show me what's new in London since I left. No business today, just… friendship. I think Keir would have wanted that: for you and me to be friends.'

She put a hand over his and offered a soft smile. 'I think he would have wanted that, too.'

Chapter Eight

They dined at the Bristol on Prince's Street, savouring the quiet atmosphere and the warm soup after the briskness of the cemetery. She laughed as Cullen surreptitiously glanced at the nearby tables to be assured no one noticed them, then quietly put his hands about the curves of his bowl. He closed his eyes and gave a pleasant sigh.

'Is London so cold you're reduced to stealing the heat of a soup bowl?' she asked with a smile at this little slice of vulnerability he displayed.

'Yes, it absolutely is. I don't think I've been warm since the ship put into Marseilles and it's only got colder, greyer, damper and wetter ever since. The weather is more miserable than I recall.' He gave an exaggerated shudder. 'How *ever* do you endure it?'

'The promise of an English summer springs eternal.' She laughed at the doubting look he gave her. 'Have you forgotten how lovely June and July can be with strawberries to pick and wildflowers in the fields?' The memory was enough to make her smile and her words ran away with her before she realised where they were headed. 'We have a small estate in Surrey, not far from Emma and Garrett's.'

She paused, realising what she'd said. Her tone quieted. There was no 'we' any more. The estate was hers now, just hers. She reached for a smile to cover her gaffe. 'I should have you out when the strawberries are in bloom.' That only made it worse. An unmarried woman had just invited an unmarried man to her summer estate. She was making a hash of this. First, she'd invoked memories of Keir and then she'd invited a man to visit her.

Cullen looked uncomfortable, further proof she was making a hash of this. He shifted in his seat. 'June seems a long way from now when one looks out the window and sees all this rain.'

She drew a deep breath and made an ungainly about-turn in the conversation. She tried for some teasing of her own. 'Tell me about the weather in Tahiti. It must be outstanding indeed if it can erase the pleasures of an English summer. Perhaps talking about it will warm you up.'

As hungry as she found herself for soup and fresh bread, she was hungrier still for some piece of him, this man who'd met her husband in a brothel, whom her husband had lifted up and made into a successful business partner. The longer she was with him the more of a mystery he became or perhaps it was the more intrigued *she* became.

He gave her a grin and she wondered if the grin was for her or for his memories. 'The sky is impossibly blue. It's the colour of the deepest, brightest sapphire you've ever seen. The clouds are white, fluffy pillows. The water is a hundred shades of blue, green, teal, turquoise and aqua.' He leaned forward as if to impart a secret, tawny eyes dancing. She couldn't help but hang on his every word, and every picture those words painted. 'And it's warm. The water is warm, the beach is warm. But there's coolness, too. There are lush teak forests in the hills and mists in the mountains.'

'And food hanging from tree limbs?' she asked. 'What does breadfruit taste like?'

He gave a low chuckle. 'Would you believe me if I said it tastes like bread? It's not untrue. I think it tastes like a cross between bread and potato.'

'What do you do all day?' Her soup lay cooling and untouched, forgotten.

'Our days are busy, but not busy like here. There are no appointments, no bustling around. There are canoes to make, food to gather. People to meet with it.' He gave a grimace. 'European presence has politicised the clans, but that's a story for another time, not today.'

'You mentioned that you swim?' she prompted, unwilling to break the spell that wrapped their little table.

'Every day. We snorkel and dive, too.'

We. She noted that. It was the second time he'd used the term. She was curious. Who was we? She noted the presence tense as well. It was not 'we snorkelled and dived' as if those were activities relegated to the past, but activities in the present, activities he might resume shortly. But like the politicising of the clans, that, too, seemed a topic for another time.

'There are some divers who can go to extraordinary depths, down into the ocean where the sun doesn't reach. Pearl divers,' he said admiringly. 'There are others who are cliff divers, who jump into the ocean from great heights.'

'Did you? Jump off cliffs? Or dive deep in the ocean?' She couldn't resist the question.

He shook his head with a laugh. 'I don't do the deep-sea diving. That is a dangerous art. I do enjoy cliffs, though.' He grinned. 'It is like flying. But it's the water I like best, the canoeing, the swimming, the snorkelling. The fish are beautiful. They're blue and yellow and orange, such vibrant colours. Not like here where all the fish seem grey and silver. Some of the fish are very small, they're for beauty, not for eating. The tangs and the angel fish are too tiny for anything more than ornamentation. It's a beautiful world under the sea.' His wistfulness was obvious.

'You miss it.' Antonia said gently.

'Yes, I do miss it.' Their eyes met and held for a long moment, breaking only when the waiter came to remove the cold dishes.

Antonia looked around, realising for the first time the restaurant was empty. 'Oh, dear, I'd not realised it was so late. I fear we're on the verge of wearing out our welcome.' The waiters lined the wall, trying to hide their impatience over their two lingering guests, no doubt eager to get ready for the dinner guests.

'Perhaps it's a good time to take that walk we talked about.' Cullen rose and held her chair, offering her his arm, his gestures natural as was her own response to them. They'd not started this morning with such ease, but that ease was there now, a product of good food and even better conversation between them. It was something of a surprise to realise over the course of the day, they had become…amicable.

The optimist in her found the concept pleasing even as the caution she'd been forced to adopt over the last year warned her to be wary of amiability. He had more to gain from it than she did. But optimism won the day. Today there was no harm in walking beside this man who'd known her husband and enjoying his stories, enjoying his company. There would indeed be time to consider the foreclosure matter tomorrow.

They strolled Prince's Street on the way to the park at Hanover Square near the town house. He turned the collar of his coat up against the chill and she laughed, remembering his descriptions of the warm weather and the turquoise waters. There was nothing warm about a damp February afternoon in London.

'We don't have cliff diving, but we do have Berlioz,' she offered as they passed the rooms at number four Hanover Square. 'He performed last year and he's likely to direct something again this spring. England seems to agree with *him*.' The emphasis implied that she'd been keeping track of all of his dissatisfaction. He didn't like the food—it wasn't readily available; he didn't like the clothes—there were too many of them; he didn't like the weather—it was too cold. She slid him a sideways look, braving another question.

'Does *nothing* in London agree with you?' It was hard to imagine someone not finding *something* to like about one of the greatest cities in the world. She might not like the fog and soot, but she did love the fashions, the theatre, the balls and parties. At least she'd used to when Keir had squired her about.

He did not answer her directly. He favoured her with a thoughtful smile. 'Perhaps it is that I like Ha'apape more. I left behind a whole life in Tahiti to come here. I left a way of living that I appreciated, I left behind friends who are as dear as family to me. I left behind who I was to become someone I haven't been for a very long time.' He cocked his head to look at her. 'I even left behind my name.' She gave him a considering look, not quite following the last comment.

'In Ha'apape, I was called Kanoa, the Seeker,' he explained.

'Because you travel between the islands seeking goods or because you were looking for something more, ah, philosophical?' she ventured, intrigued by the idea of having a new life, a life apart from the one she had now, of having a different name.

'That's very astute. Both, I think. Rahiti's father gave me the name when he claimed me as an adoptive son.' She could see that pleased him, that he took pride in being this man's son. 'Rahiti is my best friend in Ha'apape. He's my brother in all ways but blood. He was married right before I left. There were canoe races to celebrate the wedding.'

The canoe races fascinated her and it took two rotations of the Hanover Square park to exhaust the topic. It was interesting to hear about the different positions in the boat, the importance of the tempo, of reading the waves and the tide. She'd never considered such things before. But the real treat was in watching his face light up as he spoke, the quickened cadence of his words as his own excitement grew.

This was *his* world and he was giving her a rare glimpse into it, into the things he did, how he lived, and the people he lived with, the *people* he cared for. Rahiti, Rahiti's mother and father. There'd been his words: '*I left a whole life behind.*' He certainly had. It begged the question of who else had he left behind? His friend had married. Had Cullen left behind someone who mattered to him in that way?

She did not dare ask for fear of having to examine her reasons for wanting to know and because it seemed too private, too personal of a question to ask despite the progress they'd made today. Or perhaps it needed to be asked for that very reason, because of the events of today.

He'd held her in his arms. He'd offered her his strength when she had none. He'd offered her physical human comfort, the one thing she'd craved in this year of loneliness; to be touched, to be held, to be comforted with another's body and not just empty words. And now a deep part of her didn't want to share that comfort, didn't want to think of others he might have comforted in the same way. That part of her wanted those moments to belong to her, to them, alone.

The more rational part of her said it didn't matter. If there was or had been someone, that person was thousands of miles away and he was here, her business partner now. Part of *her* world.

Your world is a place he despises, the voice in her head prompted unkindly. *He is here under duress, out of loyalty to Keir. Don't forget that. And don't forget your-self. You have a business to protect and sustain. Just a few days ago you were worried he might want to usurp you and now you're thinking the two of you might be-come friends.*

They reached the park gate and he ushered her out on to the pavement beyond the park. She felt deflated at the realisation their afternoon had come to an end. 'I'll see you to the town house, Antonia. I've taken up enough of your time this afternoon with stories of home.'

'I enjoyed the stories very much.' She wanted to pro-test. An evening of loneliness stretched before her, stark and empty—emptier than usual when compared to the company of today. 'Today started badly, but I think it's ending very well. Thank you.'

The town house was not far from the park and they reached her steps quickly. 'I want to thank you again for today.' For a moment she thought of inviting him in. But to what end? Her motives seemed amorphous and yet concerning to her. She had no business-based reason to invite him. A woman simply did not invite a man in without creating the wrong impression. There was an awkward pause while she looked for the right words to express her appreciation. 'Thank you most of all for your friendship, today.'

He bent over her gloved hand and kissed her knuckles in a show of gallantry that was only half playful. 'The pleasure was all mine.'

Then she climbed the steps and faced the long eve-ning ahead, already counting the hours until nine o'clock the next morning, when she could be with him again.

Chapter Nine

The offer of friendship to a woman was always a reckless proposition even when offered with the best of intentions. To offer friendship to a woman who was also one's business partner *and* the widow of one's best friend was perhaps dangerous living in the extreme. It combined proximity with memory and the combination evoked that most deadly of ingredients: emotion.

Cullen rolled to his back and tucked his hands behind his head, looking to the dark ceiling of his room for answers, for sleep, and, if neither of those were available, solace. He was used to dangerous living. Taking risks was what he did best. It was the feelings that came with this particular risk that he was not ready for. His risks were usually calculated with a clear understanding of what he stood to lose or gain. But this risk was neither calculated nor clear. This risk was motivated solely by emotional factors, all of which could be summed up in the phrase: this is what Keir would have wanted.

Now, he was lying here, unable to sleep because the driving force behind his reckless offer today was leading towards costly consequences. Everything he offered to do for Antonia came with complications. First, it pushed his return to Tahiti back, which led to the second complication: the longer he stayed in London, the more risk there was of his presence here becoming known to certain circles.

For himself, he did not care one iota if the old scandal was unearthed, but there would be consequences for those associated with him. He had to consider the potential damage it might do to Antonia and to the business.

That was *not* the sort of help Keir would want him to provide. Yet Keir would not want him to abandon Antonia or their venture. Keir would want him to see that the business they'd put in place to help victims of colonisation survive economically in a world that oppressed them politically was taken care of, too. That venture was as much Keir's legacy as the department store was. To abandon it would be like abandoning Keir himself and their friendship.

Returning to Tahiti before everything was settled was not the way to repay that friendship. Yet he wasn't sure that staying was appropriate repayment either. But perhaps Keir hadn't realised those two goals might well prove to be mutually exclusive. If Cullen wasn't in Tahiti the latter would suffer. In the immediate future, the solution was obvious. He needed to remain in London. If he wasn't here in London, Antonia and the business would both suffer. He couldn't be in both places at once.

The trick was in deciding how long he could stay here without undermining the good his presence could do. Part of him was relying on the old scandal as an escape route. He could use it as an excuse to leave, but what happened if it could be quelled? Or if it didn't surface?

Would the 'foreseeable future' become a slippery slope towards never being able to leave? Antonia needed him here whether she wanted to admit it or not.

The events of the last week had shown her strengths as well as the chinks in her armour. She was being asked to do the impossible—to run a business she had little experience with, to undertake a project where she was learning as she went and adjust to life without her husband. Any one of those items would be a tall order. But for her, impossible included futile. Yesterday's ultimatum from the bank suggested that no matter how hard she tried and no matter how much success she had, it would never be enough to satisfy banks and investors.

If there was one thing Keir had taught Cullen about business it was that successful businessmen had networks. No one went it alone. Yet Antonia was being forced to take that route. It was a route destined for failure at worst, limited success at best. It was not a route that could sustain the holdings Keir had put together. But that did not mean he was the man to hold it all together. If the old scandal surfaced, if it still had teeth, he would not be an asset to Antonia.

Cullen sighed and slid his gaze towards the long windows he'd left uncovered. Outside on the street, he could hear the early morning noise of London waking up—milk wagons rattling with their tin cans, vendors trundling their carts towards the markets. If he got up now, he could go for a run, something the hotel staff thought he was crazy for doing, but something he needed desperately. He and Rahiti used to run the beaches together and, since there was no place to swim in the middle of

London during winter, he had to settle for running the dark morning streets in a pair of loose trousers. He'd come back and do his exercises in his room.

He didn't want to return to Tahiti softened by city living. He'd lose his tan while he was here—there was no real sun in England to speak of—and he'd already cut his hair, but he was determined not to lose his strength. Perhaps it was vanity, but he was quite proud of the body he'd acquired while abroad. Swimming, running, canoeing in the outriggers, had all left their mark for the better on him.

There were, of course, places a gentleman could join that featured opportunities for fitness, like Jackson's boxing salon—if it was still open. Keir had mentioned in one of his early letters that Jackson had died. But Cullen was not interested in blatantly announcing his return to all and sundry. He'd avoid that as long as he could. Which might not be very long. Still, he took comfort in knowing that bankers and merchants didn't run in the same circles as peers. He had some anonymity yet.

Cullen levered himself out of bed with a grunt and reached for the trousers he liked to run in, a specially made pair out of flannel. The tailor had thought him crazy.

Being back in London had personal implications as well for him aside from the scandal. The longer he was here, the less likely it was that he could avoid his family. His father *would* hear he was in town, as would his mother, and they'd want what they'd always wanted from him: to settle down, to take his place in the marquessate beside his brother, the heir, do his duty to ensure that old, antiquated traditions were preserved. Especially now that his brother was still childless.

Cullen reached for his shoes. They were difficult to run in, but there was no question of running barefoot any more than there was the possibility of steering his mind away from thinking about the scandal that had earned him the appellation of notorious and had been responsible for sending him to the South Seas. London had a memory like an elephant. If he was in town, the scandal was in town. He'd prefer that scandal not to surface just yet.

Outside, he shivered in the cold. That wouldn't last long. He'd work up a sweat soon enough. He broke into a jog up Brook Street and headed towards Hanover Square, then over to Hanover Street. He'd made it a habit to run past the store. His mind plotted his route and ran through his day. After exercising, it would be time for breakfast and then Antonia would call for him.

They were visiting the warehouses today, his old workplace. That would be safe enough. He'd only ever been Cullen Allardyce there and no one in the warehouses read Debrett's. But soon they'd have to meet with the bankers and they knew who he was, who his father was. Before then, he'd have to tell Antonia who he really was so that she wasn't ambushed. But in the knowing, she might be disappointed.

His feet pounded the pavements in time with his thoughts. Why did he care what Antonia thought of him? He was her business partner. She need not like him. True, but *friends* usually liked each other. That's how friendship worked. It was something of a point of interest to him as he ran to realise that he *wanted* her to like him, that her esteem mattered. Perhaps it was only that she was the one person he was in contact with, outside of Bowdrie, who also knew Keir. If Keir cared for both of them, it stood to reason that they should *like* each other.

Yet he worried that she wouldn't like him when the whole sordid truth of his story came out. He wasn't exactly the protégé she thought he was. He turned up Hanover Street and focused his thoughts on his morning outing, which was a far more comfortable direction instead of wondering why it mattered to him if she liked him or not. After all, what difference did it make if he was just going to sail away again? But it continued to bother him that he wasn't the man she thought he was.

Cullen wasn't the man she'd thought he was. Or perhaps what she meant was that Cullen wasn't the man she'd drawn in her head all these months waiting for him to arrive. This was the theme of her thoughts as the carriage headed to Mivart's to collect him. She ought to be thinking about the foreclosure, about her strategy with the bank, but her thoughts had gone a different direction entirely.

When she'd begun the search for Cullen, he was nothing but a name. She'd thought only about getting that name on all the right papers, then he'd be more than welcome to go back to Tahiti and they would spend the rest of their association communicating with bi-annual letters. In her mind, she'd created a two-dimensional image. The man she'd imagined was nothing more than a place holder whose signature she needed. He was not a man with a story, or a past, or feelings.

But yesterday, he'd been all three of those things; he'd become not just a man her husband knew, but now a man she knew personally, a man who loved beaches, who swam in turquoise waters and paddled outriggers. In her time of need, he'd offered friendship and comfort, and, in his own way, he'd offered the protection of his name—to the business, of course, not to her especially.

The carriage turned on to Brook Street and she felt her stomach give a flutter of anticipation. What would he offer her today? Who would he be? The business partner or the friend? Or perhaps something in between? Being friends with a man was tricky business. Other than her brother, she didn't think she'd ever been just friends with a man.

Yesterday, they'd done well together, taking lunch at the Bristol on Prince's Street before strolling the park at Hanover Square. She'd hung on every word of his stories about Tahiti. They'd talked the afternoon away. It had furthered the ease between them, there was a comfort in being together. It no longer seemed odd to take his arm as she walked beside him. As a result, the earlier stiffness between them had softened.

By the time he'd bent over her hand at the townhouse steps, the stiffness had vanished entirely, replaced by something else. She called it friendship because that seemed appropriate and convenient. To call it something else would be less appropriate and certainly less convenient. For now, she would take the newfound ease although the question remained: ought she trust that ease? Was she being foolish? Was she putting aside too soon her earlier concerns about his presence?

The optimist in her always pursued potential when it came to people but being an optimist didn't mean being naive. He'd leapt to her defence yesterday, wanting to put himself forward as a means of discouraging the foreclosure and she was grateful. Having him here would quash the bank's misgivings. But what motivated his offer? Was this a way forward for him taking over the helm? Would he use the hand of friendship against her? Was it only a strategy? Or had his offer been genuine?

He was already outside waiting for her, dressed in a long wool coat, top hat and gloves when she reached Mivart's. He got in quickly, the wind blowing the carriage door shut behind him. He flashed her a smile and she had to remind herself how it would be easy, too, to forget that for herself, she knew little about him despite yesterday's stories. It would be a dangerous assumption to think she knew him well when she did not. It would be easy to let down her guard, to be ambushed by his kindnesses, by his handsomeness, by the quality of his relationship with Keir.

They worked the warehouse from the bottom up. The London Dock warehouses featured underground wine vaults and Keir had made good use of them, using them to store the red wine much beloved by the Duke of Cowden and the hard-to-come-by Archambeau *coteaux champenois* from Emma's new husband's vineyards, although Keir and Garrett Luce had been importing the wines for years. The wine steward Keir employed offered them a taste of a new barrel that had come in.

'Cheers,' Antonia offered as they each took a sip. The wine was good, it was an excellent *coteaux champenois*, sent no doubt courtesy of Julien Archambeau, but she must have grimaced unconsciously as she swallowed.

'Do you not like wine?' Cullen enquired.

'I do. This wine is quite good and somewhat rare.' She set her glass down on a nearby barrel.

'Then why the frown?' Cullen asked.

'This wine is from my friend Emma's husband's vineyards. Emma's *second* husband's vineyards.' She sighed and tried to explain. 'Emma was married to Garrett Luce.'

'Ah, I see,' Cullen said quietly, setting his own glass down next to hers. 'Garrett Luce, Keir's friend who also drowned. And Emma has remarried already.' He gave her a long look until she confirmed it.

'Yes. She married last summer, six months ago.'

'And you think it was too soon? You don't approve?' It was quiet and dim down in the wine vaults, just the two of them. The space invited intimacy, an exchange of confidences.

'I suppose so,' Antonia admitted. 'Emma was madly in love with Garrett. The night of the flood we had to hold her back so that she wouldn't rush out into the night. She *loved* him.'

'And you wonder how such love could be replaced so quickly.' This came as a statement, followed by a low-toned, private question. 'Do you think you will never love again, Antonia? Do you think you will be alone for the rest of your life? Do you *want* to be?' His tawny eyes gleamed lion-like in the dimness, the atmosphere charging like an electrical storm. 'The question makes you uncomfortable. Why?'

Antonia swallowed. 'Because we're supposed to find our soulmates. Soulmates implies there is just one person for us and when that person is gone...' She couldn't finish the sentence.

'We are humans, Antonia, not swans.' He gave a low chuckle, but she knew instinctively he wasn't laughing at her.

'Maybe some of us are, though. Perhaps it's possible that some of us mate for life and others do not. It's the only way I can explain it.' She picked up her wine glass and took another sip, suddenly finding she needed to wet her dry throat.

'Maybe not all of us are made for monogamy either.' He tossed the challenge out casually. 'Have you ever thought that monogamy goes against human inclination? If it weren't for missionaries, I think much of the South Pacific would be polygamous. Monogamy has always struck me as something socially enforced, but not naturally prescribed, a torture we give ourselves.'

Antonia nearly choked on her wine. She'd never had such a conversation before, not even with Keir. 'You are a scandal, Cullen Allardyce. Do you really think about such things?'

'Yes. It's hard not to when one reads travel accounts of other explorers.' He leaned close with a wicked smile. 'And what becomes clear to me from those gleanings is that an enormous number of indigenous cultures were not originally monogamous.' The smile faded to a hard line, his words wry. 'It's just one of the many consequences of European conquest. Europe has not been good for a large part of the world.'

'You don't agree with monogamy?'

'I don't agree with conquest, with oppression,' Cullen replied. 'People ought to be left to decide for themselves what behaviour best suits them.' She'd wanted to get a rise out of him, to see something finally get under his skin, and here it was. There was passion beneath his words. She'd never heard anyone speak like this, not even Keir, who held similar opinions.

Antonia met his gaze over the rim of her glass. 'How did we get from Emma's husband's wine to empire building?'

'It's entirely your fault.' His gaze did not waver and her stomach gave a little flip of awareness. Some women must find him absolutely devastating. 'You didn't answer my question,' he drawled. 'Do you want to remain alone? And if so, do you think that is what Keir would have wanted for you?'

This was getting entirely too personal. It was time to put a stop to it. She gave him a sobering stare. 'What I *think* is that it's complicated and we have the main part of the warehouse to explore yet.'

She headed for the stairs, aware of Cullen close behind and aware that he didn't find her answer satisfactory. Neither did she. But an answer was far *more* complicated than it might have been six months ago, or even two weeks ago when her answer would have been a resounding yes, she *did* see herself spending her life alone.

She could not imagine another's companionship in Keir's place.

But then *he'd* come and his coming was changing everything: the store, the company, even her. He infuriated her and challenged her. He challenged her decisions about the business and about herself. He made her feel and made her face all she'd lost, not just Keir, but also the loss of the life she'd had. Being with him for hours every day forced her to acknowledge how lonely she was and how long she'd be alone with nothing but work for companionship, an arrangement that was entirely antithetical to the social creature she was.

In the past, she'd been with Emma and Fleur every day and the six of them had been out together most evenings, taking in the theatre, concerts, or dining with friends and playing cards. Even before that, she'd enjoyed the formal events of the Season—the concerts, the Venetian breakfasts, the balls—even if not the people. This past year, though, there'd been no entertainments, none of the social life she'd once enjoyed.

She'd not thought she'd missed it, but Cullen's question was prompting her to rethink her answer. Apparently, she missed it more than she'd realised. It opened the possibility that perhaps Emma didn't have it wrong after all. Which led to a host of other new and confused thoughts that formed an inconvenient tangle in her head, no matter how hard she tried to push them away.

At the top of the stairs, Cullen came up close behind her, his voice a whisper at her ear, private but with an unmistakable undertone of decadence that set her stomach to flipping yet again. 'Just so you know, Antonia.

I'm not a swan.' Dear heavens. With the amount of flipping her stomach was doing this morning, maybe it *was* something she'd eaten after all. Perhaps her stomach had finally rebelled against eggs for breakfast because the alternative explanation available was unthinkable.

Chapter Ten

Directly paying the loan in full was unthinkable for reasons both of principle and practicality. They had to talk about it. It could not be put off any longer. Cullen sighed and sat back in his chair in the private office of the Captain's Club. They had retreated there after touring the warehouses instead of going to the town house—a place she seemed to seldom go unless she must. She slept there. That was all. The rest of her days were spent elsewhere—in warehouses and various offices Popplewell and Allardyce Enterprises kept around town. He could guess the reasons why.

He tucked his hands behind his head and watched the flames in the fireplace, mentally sorting through what he knew. He'd gone over the accounts again to be sure, hoping he'd missed something the first time that would allow them to pay the loan in full without damaging other aspects of the company. He had not. His conclusions were still the same.

It would dangerously deplete their liquid capital to pay that loan, which in turn would impact the payment of wages and the outlay of cash to pay for cargoes before the resale profits came in. Those expenditures would further shrink the ready cash in their accounts. Yes, Keir had a fortune, but it was locked up in property and ships, and cargoes that were somewhere in the various stages of being readied for resale. It was not what Antonia wanted to hear.

As if on cue, Antonia spoke from the desk across the room where she sat working through correspondence and invoices. 'I want to pay the loan in full. It will make us independent of the bank. They won't be able to harass us again.'

At least not until the next time they needed funds. Cullen pushed a hand through his hair. 'I advise against it. It's the riskiest choice you can make. It puts the company in a cash-poor situation, which, on the surface, sends the wrong message to investors. They will see the company as struggling. If they sense a struggle, they'll pull back on their investments and take a wait-and-see attitude that *will* truly put us in a struggling position.'

He rose and stood with his back to the warmth of the fireplace. Dear Lord, had London always been this cold? His bones were starved for Tahitian sun. From there he could see her, could watch her expression from behind the big desk as he continued his lecture.

She had a glass face that worked in her favour. When she was charmed, a man knew it. When she was vexed, a man knew that, too, her green eyes narrowing to sharp jade slits of displeasure. No wonder she'd taken London by storm during her Season. Her expressions were a source of encouragement and discouragement. A man could plan a courtship according to those glances, always knowing where he stood. That openness could do in a single honest glance what coy, hidden messages attempted to do in many.

At present, her face remained relatively neutral, except for her eyes. She was waiting, her clear green gaze resting on him, sharply alert in anticipation of his verdict. She looked good behind the desk in her high-necked white blouse, her jacket long since discarded, a loose golden tendril of hair curling softly against her cheek, the perfect combination of intelligence and femininity.

The sight of her stirred something primal and masculine in him. He wanted to be her…warrior. To fight for her, protect her. She wouldn't like that last part. She didn't think she needed protection. But she needed it all the more because of that. He'd been a warrior in Tahiti. He'd stood with Rahiti and his clan against the French.

But here, he needed to be a different kind of warrior in a different kind of fight that would require different weapons. Spears and outriggers could not help him here and the tools that would be of use were tools he was loath to employ. He was not in the habit of throwing his family connections around. It was antithetical to his personal beliefs about equality.

'With the exception of property, everything we do is based on a joint venture system,' he explained, unsure how much she knew about the inner workings of the company. It was one thing to read ledgers, it was another to understand the nuance behind the numbers. 'Our investors pool their funds in order for us to afford the voyages and the cargoes. It also protects each of us if the ship is lost. No one loses everything, as would be the case if the voyage was sponsored by a single individual. Fewer investors, however, means our burden and our risk increases as we shoulder what investors have left unfunded.' This had been one of the first lessons Keir had taught him when he'd invested his hard-earned savings in that first voyage.

Usually patience was a virtue, but not in Antonia's case. He'd learned that, for her, patience was simply a way of waiting him out until she could have her say. She gave a nod when he finished. But the nod did not signify agreement, only understanding. 'Perhaps I should have chosen my words more carefully. What I meant to convey is that we *can* pay the loan. Whatever their motive is behind issuing this foreclosure, we *can* call their bluff and we should. It will be difficult, yes, but it can be done.'

'And the danger, the financial insecurity we face if we do?' Cullen queried. Had she heard all of what he'd said?

She rose and came around the desk, the wide sweep of her blue skirts swaying gently. In general, Cullen found the current fashion for the wide cages women wore beneath their skirts the height of foolishness, but the style suited her. The fullness of her skirts emphasised the slim circle of her waist, her trim torso, the round, feminine curves of breasts beneath the pleats and tucks of her white blouse. Cullen gave himself a scold. These were hardly seemly thoughts given the context of conducting business and he forced himself to focus on her words.

'The danger you speak of is not the only danger, though.' She crossed her arms and fixed him with one of her hard stares. 'The other danger is what happens if we don't pay the loan. The bank will take the store and all the money that has been put into the building will be lost. We will lose money either way. But at least *my* way, we get to keep the store and we can recoup our investment over time.'

Cullen leaned against the oak mantel and gave a dry laugh. 'Is that what you're worried about? That the solution best suited for the company won't be *your* solution?' He paused. 'That's rather disappointing, Antonia. I thought we'd moved past that. I didn't expect you to be so petty as to risk the financial well-being of the company for your own territorial wars.' If that was the case, he truly was disappointed. He'd thought her capable of much better.

Those green eyes flared and he barely finished his set-down before she replied in clipped tones, 'How dare you think I would risk Keir's store and the business he spent his life building simply because I want to be "right".'

This was progress. He'd made her mad. Good. He preferred her mad, or sobbing, or arguing—anything but the brisk efficiency she usually evinced. She needed to *feel*. There was a reason she didn't spend time at home, a reason she worked without ceasing: so that she didn't have to *feel*. She'd *felt* at the cemetery and she'd *felt* in Bowdrie's office. She thought it made her weak, she despised it. He did not. He appreciated it was in those moments that she showed her real self. And it was in those moments that he understood her the best.

She was close to feeling something right now. What would she reveal? His curiosity wanted to coax that next revelation, wanted to push her for both their sakes. 'Well? Have you asked yourself the hard question? *Would* it be better in the long term to let the store go rather than put the rest of the business at risk?' Even as he made the suggestion aloud, he knew he spoke heresy and yet he wanted her reaction even if it came with a storm. Perhaps especially if it came with a storm. He was not disappointed.

'You have insulted me twice in two minutes. I will *not* give up the store.' Her tone was hot and insistent.

He pushed again. 'Even if the numbers suggest it's the better decision? Even if your business partner advises it?'

Green lightning flashed in her eyes. 'Is that what you're suggesting? If you were any kind of friend to him, you wouldn't even think it.'

'If I were "any kind of friend" I'd do my best to make sure his wife didn't bankrupt his business within the first year.' He was pushing hard now and she was pushing back with equal force, unguardedly and with brutal honesty. 'You have lost your objectivity, Antonia.'

'No, I have lost my *husband*, Cullen.' There was a bite to her words. 'I have lost my life, my love, my hopes and my dreams.' Her voice rose to a near shout, her hand making a fist at her side, eyes blazing. 'All I have left of him and our life together is that store. I will not lose that, too!' Her words ricocheted around the room in the silence that followed.

There! That was what he wanted, this admission of what drove her and why. His heart hurt for her, for the depth of grief that she carried even after a year. He would free her from it if he could. 'Even if it drags you down?' he persisted.

'It does not drag me down. It sustains me—' She stopped suddenly, perhaps realising how much she'd given away in the heat of disagreement.

'Gives you something to get up for in the morning?' Cullen finished for her, watching some of the anger leach from her.

'You make me say all sorts of things,' she accused.

'I make you say the truth,' Cullen clarified, gesturing for her to take the chair across from the one he'd vacated. Standing was confrontational. Sitting was conversational. Rahiti's father had explained that to him. The time for confrontation had passed. Now it was time to talk in the space that confrontation had created. 'I wanted you to *hear* the way you're approaching your decision from your own lips.'

She sat on the edge of the chair, the anger leaving her. 'So I am hoisted by my own petard?'

'Not hoisted. Aware. I want you to be *aware* of what is driving your thinking. You will not listen to me, but you will listen to yourself. You heard yourself, you are too emotionally attached to the project.'

'It's Keir's legacy,' she said, more quietly this time. 'The one thing I have left I can do for him.'

There was guilt in those words. He'd heard it before at the cemetery: guilt for family she'd not given Keir, the guilt for surviving, for having been at a whist game, for laughing with friends when the river had swept him away. This store was more than a legacy, it was a bid for absolution. What would she do when she realised it wouldn't work? That the store was only brick and mortar? That it wouldn't raise the dead or heal her self-inflicted wounds.

'It won't bring him back, Antonia,' he cautioned. She was on dangerous ground here, teetering on the brink of throwing good money after potentially bad.

'No, but in its own way, it will help him to go on and me, too.' There was a need for atonement in her words. 'I am not ready to give up, Cullen, simply because the bank has thrown a wrinkle in the plans.'

He nodded. Despite his arguments, which had been to push her to acknowledge her highly personal stake in the store, he'd like to see the store go forward. Keir was right, department stores were the new wave of shopping. Eventually, the store would make money as long as they could get that far. It was the in between he was worried about and the emotional toll it was taking on Antonia. 'Here's our situation then. The bank wants to be paid and we want to pay them without harming ourselves. Where does the money come from?'

'We need someone else to pay the bank,' Antonia said, half joking. She added more seriously, 'Unfortunately, my father doesn't have that kind of money.'

His did. But he'd crawl on his belly and beg in the streets before he asked his father for anything. Anything he took from his father would negate all the reasons he'd left in the first place. However, there was someone else who could help. 'I think we go to the Duke of Cowden and the Prometheus Club. We ask them to loan us the money to pay the loan. That way, we satisfy the bank, we keep the store and the company's cash flow isn't jeopardised.' Meanwhile, he'd devote his resources to determining who on the bank's board of directors had prompted the foreclosure.

Antonia nodded and some of the tension eased that had stalked her since Bowdrie had given her the letter. 'It's not how I'd prefer my first meeting with Cowden to go, but it's a good solution.' She smiled. 'For Keir.'

'For Keir,' he echoed, but he wondered how true that was. He was rogue enough to admit his motivation wasn't entirely for Keir. It was for her, to see her smile, to see her happy, this woman who loved with her whole heart. He would help her secure the store, although he wondered how happy the store would make her in the long term. No happier than he could. The store might help assuage her guilt in the moment, just as he might help her in the immediate future, but his presence here was not, could not, be permanent. He would leave. He'd promised himself he would. He didn't belong here.

Besides, if he stayed long enough he would disappoint her, just like the store would inevitably disappoint her. No matter how much money it made, that store could not be what she wanted any more than he could be. Only, she didn't see it yet. He hoped she would see it before it was too late, before the realisation destroyed her in a different way. But in the interim, perhaps he could help her move on and perhaps that would be held in the balance and weigh the scales in his favour when judgment came.

'I'll send a note and set the meeting up. Cowden is usually in town. If not, there's a train that runs near his estate at Bramble.'

'I want to be there, Cullen. You're not to go to that meeting without me,' she instructed.

'Of course, we are partners,' he assured her even as he felt the sting of her words. He was expected to treat her as a partner, but it was obvious she didn't see him in the same way. She still believed the decisions regarding the company were up to her. He was merely a counsellor, not a partner. One had only to look at her use of pronouns to see it. He couldn't help her if she didn't untie his hands. It was time to start working on those knots. 'Now that's decided, I must insist that I meet with the bank alone.'

'Why are you meeting with them at all?' she asked, instantly sceptical. 'I think a snub might do them good.'

'I want to figure out who pushed the idea of foreclosing on a loan against a reliable customer and I want to know why.' He wanted to confirm Bowdrie's suspicions that the bank was nervous with a female at the helm. 'I think it would also be *helpful* for them to see me. I can be more effective alone.'

The bank had treated her shabbily. They needed to understand this was his company, too. Treating her poorly was tantamount to treating *him* poorly, something he was sure they would think twice about if given the right inducement, if for no other reason than that he was a wealthy *man* with a proven track record of success. He would do his best to ensure it didn't happen again. As much as she wouldn't like it, this had to be handled man to man. Warrior to warrior. He would be her champion. Because it was what Keir would have wanted.

And it's what you want, whispered a little voice he was finding more and more difficult to ignore.

Keir was gone and he was here, and Antonia needed a man whether she wanted to admit it or not.

Chapter Eleven

Antonia did not like how things were being handled. It was Cullen who'd met with the bank, who'd brought home the dismaying news that the bank had foreclosed because it was uncomfortable with a woman being in charge of all that money, and it was Cullen who'd been in contact with the influential Duke of Cowden. It was Cullen who'd arranged the train tickets to Cowden's Sussex estate, Bramble, when the Duke proved not to be in town after all. But what she liked least of all was how she *felt* about it.

She *liked* having things handled. She told herself it was because it meant there was one less thing for her to worry over, but she suspected it was more than that. There was comfort in Cullen's competence, in letting him handle these things and knowing they would get done. Even more disconcerting was that there was comfort in his company. In the weeks he'd been here, she'd come to look forward to picking him up each morning and spending the day going over business with him. She could admit to that. She told herself liking his company was *not* the same as liking him, a condition that would require much more reflection should that ever become the case.

Even such a tempered admission, however, came with the classic tension between dependence and independence. By the time they made the all-important trip to Bramble, she was feeling distinctly *de trop* and worrying that her usual optimism had played her false. Cullen had done exactly what she hadn't wanted him to do and he'd done it exactly how she'd feared from that very first day at Verrey's Café: by making himself indispensable, by acting as if he was serving her interests, when in reality he was serving his own. He was being nice because it benefited him.

She stared out the window of the coach that had met them at the station, a coach sent by the Duke and arranged by Cullen—yet another result of how he'd inserted himself into her life.

He is a partner. He is doing no more than what a partner would do, the voice of optimism in her head reprimanded. *You've merely been alone too long. You are not used to sharing responsibility.*

She was making too much of his assistance. But that scold was always followed with a dose of self-doubt—he was doing all of this because she could not. The business with the bank's foreclosure proved it. She'd fallen short. She had not been enough on her own. Never mind that Keir had always depicted business as something best done with a small group of trusted participants, or that Keir had always collaborated with Luce and Griffiths, and Cullen. For her it was different, though. She had something to prove.

'You're troubled,' Cullen interrupted her internal monologue as the red-brick architecture of Bramble came into view. 'We're nearly there. I don't want to arrive with you angry. Cowden is sympathetic to us and he is a friend to Popplewell and Allardyce Enterprises, but he is also an astute man who is careful with his funds. If he senses there is dissension in the ranks, he will not put his money behind us. This visit is not a *fait accompli*.'

'Of course, my apologies.' Antonia pasted on a smile. She didn't need him to tell her how devastating Cowden's refusal would be. They'd be back to where they'd started: making a difficult decision about how to handle the loan payment. 'You needn't worry, I'll be on my best behaviour.' This was no time to let emotion interfere with decisions.

His tawny gaze rested on her. 'I know you will. You would never do anything to jeopardise the business.' He smiled and she was struck by how utterly devastating he looked today in a dark blue jacket and jade-green waistcoat paired with charcoal trousers. An emerald stick pin winked in his neckcloth, its gem matching the one set in the heavy gold ring on his little finger. 'Do I pass inspection?' he enquired when her gaze lingered too long.

She laughed. 'I was just thinking that for a man who a few weeks ago had only two changes of clothes to his name and preferred to wear as few clothes as possible, you go well-heeled.'

He leaned forward conspiratorially. 'Don't worry, I still prefer to wear as few clothes as possible, it's just so bloody cold here.'

He had to stop saying such things. It certainly wasn't

cold in the carriage, not after that remark. Antonia smoothed the wide skirts of her red and black tartan ensemble, casting about for something to say. She very unoriginally came up with, 'Do I pass inspection as well?'

'You always pass inspection.' His words sent her stomach flip-flopping. He reached for her hand as the coach rolled to a stop in front of the steep-roofed façade of Bramble, his touch sending a warm thrill up her arm. Drat, she should be more resistant to such things. Those stomach flips and warm thrills were two recent developments since the day they'd gone to the cemetery. She did not need any added complications. He squeezed her hand in assurance. 'Everything will be all right, Antonia.'

And it was. The visit went well. The Duke received them in his oak-panelled office with its view of Bramble's parklands and listened intently to their situation, something Cullen let her take the lead on explaining. She tried not to resent him offering input at key parts in her telling. 'I think it is important the bank understands that treating her shabbily with this arbitrary demand for payment in full is inappropriate,' Cullen shared when she finished.

The Duke nodded in assent. 'It's the principle I don't agree with. If they foreclose at will, then they cannot be trusted.' The Duke neatly flipped the situation. This was no longer about the credibility of Popplewell and Allardyce Enterprises, but the credibility of the bank. 'They make themselves no better than the moneylenders in St Giles. I'd be more than glad to have the Prometheus Club offer you backing.'

Antonia felt as if she could breathe again. They'd done it! The store was safe, their funds were safe, the business was safe. She schooled her excitement into professional gratitude lest her excitement indicate how desperate she'd been. 'Thank you so much. This means a great deal.'

'I am pleased to help, my dear.' Cowden's eyes lingered on her and she braced herself for the inevitable. The last time she'd seen the Duke and Duchess had been at Keir's funeral. She waited for *the* question. 'How are *you* doing, Mrs Popplewell? I thought of your husband the other day. He is missed.'

'I am doing well. I am very busy with all of my husband's holdings.' Antonia gave her standard answer and then deflected. 'I hope you and Her Grace will visit the store when you're in town. I would be proud to offer you a tour.' She had to stay strong. She could not let kindness undo her as it had in Bowdrie's office.

The Duke nodded and turned his attention to Cullen. 'And you, welcome back. It has been a long time.' Cowden gave Cullen a fatherly smile. 'Frederick is here with his wife and his children. I know he'll want a good visit with you.' Cowden rose, indicating the meeting was over. 'My wife has a luncheon planned for us and she won't forgive me if I monopolise your company. I hope we can talk later, though, Cullen, before you leave.'

'I hope we can, too.' Cullen smiled warmly at Cowden, and she gave him a long considering look, surprised at Cowden's use of his Christian name. She'd not realised he was so personally close to the Duke's family. She'd assumed his connection was simply through

Keir and the Prometheus Club. How interesting that he was friends with the Duke's oldest son, Frederick. It raised questions though, like: how did a man ditched in an alley know such people?

Luncheon was an enjoyable affair. It was hard not to like the Duke and Duchess of Cowden, both of them heading towards the end of their middle years. They were affable and considerate hosts. Within minutes of sitting down for lunch, Antonia felt at home. Of course, she knew them both socially and had met them briefly on several occasions. She and Keir had been regular attendees at the Duchess's annual November charity ball in town, which kicked off the holiday season. She hadn't attended this year because she'd been in mourning.

Even more compelling was the easy affability of Cowden's son Frederick and his wife, Helena, who took turns eating lunch with a toddler on their laps instead of sending him off with the nurse. Helena was so engaging, Antonia almost didn't mind when it was time to leave the gentlemen. Cullen tossed her a smile as she followed the Duchess and Helena from the room that said he knew what she was thinking—that they'd discuss business without her.

Outside, the day was fair, teasing the unsuspecting victim with the temptation of spring and the Duchess opted to walk in the garden. Helena set the toddler down where they could keep an eye on him as they strolled. There would be plenty of rain and mud, damp and cold, between now and the first blooms, but for today Antonia was determined to enjoy the country air and the rare sunshine. And the company. She'd not had feminine company since Holmfirth. She missed Emma and Fleur furiously.

'Frederick has told me all about the store. It sounds marvellous. You even have a children's department and a sweets counter. How exciting.' Helena looped an arm through hers with easy familiarity. 'You must start thinking about publicity if you mean to open in April. I had an idea. You must have a grand opening for the public, but also a private affair, something invitation-only for customers you especially want to cultivate. Something with champagne and cake.' Helena laughed. 'I'll go anywhere for champagne and cake.'

'It's actually a good idea and champagne will be easy. Emma Luce can supply it.' Antonia laughed with her, caught up in the idea of a party for the store. She was already making plans in her head before she recognised her error. 'I mean, Emma Archambeau now. She has remarried.'

'Ah, yes, to the man who ensures my husband has his red wine.' The Duchess joined them, coming up on Antonia's other side. 'I was so happy to hear of the marriage.' Her blue eyes sparkled, but her smile softened coyly. 'What about you, my dear? Will you be next to wed? Is there anyone special in your life at present?'

'Oh, n-no,' Antonia stammered, the bold question catching her by surprise. 'I am happy for Emma, but it is much too soon for me to think about such things.' It was a bald-faced lie. Ever since Emma had married, she'd done nothing but think and rethink such things. Cullen's presence had forced her to reframe those thoughts yet again as she grappled with her growing attraction to his…companionship.

'Too soon with the likes of Cullen Allardyce lurking nearby? That's hard to believe.' Helena gave one of her light, bubbling laughs. 'He's a handsome fellow. Most women would do nothing *but* think about remarriage with him nearby. Although I'm not sure that's a two-way street.'

He was indeed handsome, and he did raise…*feelings*… in her that she'd thought had died with Keir. But he was also dangerous to her position in the company. It would be all too easy for him to see her relegated to a back role. She might be an optimist, but she was not naive.

'If not Allardyce, perhaps we could suggest some other fine men,' the Duchess offered. 'With the Season just around the corner, we could have a list drawn up.'

Absolutely not! Antonia moved quickly to squash the idea. 'I don't think remarriage is for me,' Antonia said firmly.

'Perhaps an affair, then?' Helena said mischievously.

'That is not what I meant,' Antonia stammered, blushing furiously.

Helena patted her hand. 'Our apologies. We are making you uncomfortable. Her Grace and I misread the situation.' She slid a sly look Antonia's way. 'At lunch, we thought perhaps there was something between you and Allardyce.'

'There is.' Antonia maintained her firmness. This was her chance to dispel the notions of these two match-makers. 'It's business. We are partners whether we like it or not. Circumstances have thrown us together.'

Helena gave a light laugh. 'I didn't get the impression that Mr Allardyce minds being thrown together with you too much.' Helena leaned close in feminine confidentiality. 'No man looks at a woman the way he looked at you when he "minds it".' She made an airy gesture. 'I remember when Frederick and I were courting. I could feel his eyes on me from across a ballroom, any ballroom, it didn't matter where we were. I always knew when he was watching me. I still do. Now look at us. Married with four sons.'

Married *and* happy. One could not be in Helena Tresham's presence to know the future Duchess of Cowden was a woman exceedingly pleased with her lot. It made Antonia's heartache just a bit. She'd been that woman once. To be with Keir, to believe in the potential promise of children had filled her with an unmatchable joy. She would be lying if she said being with Helena this afternoon didn't make her yearn to have that joy again. Emma had found such joy, could she also? If she would just look for it? If Helena was right, would she even have to look any further than Cullen Allardyce with those piercing tawny eyes and delicious touches?

Oh, this was madness! What was she thinking of? Certainly not thoughts of marriage to a man she'd just met. An affair, then? A toe dipped in the pools of romance before taking the full plunge?

'I think it would be good for Cullen to settle down,' Helena was saying when Antonia finally corralled her thoughts. 'Frederick might have worn off on him a bit better if he'd stayed around. They've been friends for years.' She sighed. 'But *things* happened.' She said it as if Antonia knew what those 'things' were. 'Then Frederick got married and Cullen went to the South Seas instead.' Instead of what? Instead of marrying as well?

What a set of loaded comments that was, both of them so casually dropped into the conversation. Antonia's curiosity was notably pricked, especially after her earlier realisation that Frederick and Cullen had been friends before Cullen had met Keir. She'd not imagined it. Helena's comment confirmed it. What secrets lurked here? It was a rather vivid reminder that she knew very little about Cullen Allardyce. But there was no time to ask her questions. The garden gate opened, and the nurse bustled in with Helena's other three sons.

'My boys!' Helena beamed at the sight of them. She tugged Antonia along with her. 'Come meet them.'

The boys were charming, two years apart and replicas of their father, although Antonia thought if one looked closely, they were a fine blend of both their parents. They were full of energy, excited by the good weather and a chance to be out of doors. The rest of the afternoon was taken up with play. The boys had brought a small ball and a tag-style game, where the object was to keep the ball away from a designated player, soon ensued.

Everyone played, even the toddler and the adults. Her Grace the Duchess was promptly transformed into 'Grandmama' and the elegant Helena was simply 'Mama'. Antonia found herself rather quickly reduced to 'Toni'. No, not reduced, she thought, finding herself tagged and declared 'it'. Elevated. For a few hours she was elevated to 'Toni', to the status of a child's friend, and she loved it.

All of this laughter, the running and playing together, *this* was what it meant to be a family like the one she'd grown up in. *This* was what it meant to be alive. But if this was what it meant to be alive, what did that make her these days? She caught one of the boys and swung him around until he laughed. She laughed, too, because it was better than thinking about the answer.

Laughter floated through the open windows of Cowden's library where the gentlemen had adjourned after luncheon to talk some more business. But that had quickly degenerated into catching up. Ten years was a long time to be gone and, for the first time since he'd returned, Cullen was actually glad to be in England. He'd missed Frederick, and Cowden had always been a father figure and father fixture in his life since he'd been of school age.

'The boys are out,' Frederick commented with a chuckle as a particularly loud hoot penetrated their conversation. 'I don't remember us being that noisy growing up.' Us, being Frederick, his two brothers and their friends—Cullen, Conall Everard and Cam Lithgow.

Cowden laughed. 'At least you know where they are,' he commented sagely to his son. 'It's when you don't hear them that you should worry.' The two men chuckled, a warm look passing between Cowden and his grown son. Longing stirred in Cullen. What a wonder it was to see such a relationship, to see what was possible between a father and a son who cared for one another.

Frederick had shared that he and Helena spent most of the year living with Cowden and the Duchess in residence at Bramble with their sons, coming into town only for his politics during the Season. There were other ducal estates and Frederick could have raised his family on any one of them, but this had been their choice. There was genuine affection between the foursome despite the shared roof. Cullen couldn't imagine deliberately choosing to live with his parents. He'd gone as far away from them as he could.

There were shouts of 'Toni! Toni! Throw it here!' and Cullen's eyes went again to the window. The boys had roped Antonia into playing, it seemed. He couldn't help himself. He rose, unable to resist. He had to *see* what was going on down there. The sight that met him was glorious. The women had joined in the game, all concern for propriety having been set side. Antonia's hair was loose and, even at a distance, he could see her cheeks were red with exertion and laughter. She was carrying the youngest Tresham boy piggyback and helping him tag his brothers.

It might have been better if he hadn't looked. Cullen found he had to swallow around a thickness in his throat. This was a scene rife with potent images of family and love and of a life he'd never had, but one that he'd once craved, a life that had always been out of reach for him. The closest he'd ever got to it growing up was with the Treshams, then as an adult there'd been first the connection.

But a part of him had still been on the outside of that, belonging but not completely. Now, seeing Antonia playing and laughing, setting aside concern about the store, setting aside her grief and *living*, brought the need rushing back: a family of his own where no one worried about birth order and heirs, where there was only love. A family with a woman like her...

Eventually, Cullen was aware of Frederick standing next to him. How long had he been there? 'I could watch Helena play with them all day. She is indefatigable for her boys,' Frederick said softly. 'They are my greatest joy.'

Cullen slid a look at his friend. Pure love shone on his face, love and pride, and contentment. Frederick Tresham was a man at peace despite being a busy man who balanced his political responsibilities with the responsibilities of being a landowner and heir, father and husband. But it was easy to see which roles he treasured most.

'They are my great joy, too.' Cowden joined them, standing on Cullen's other side. He gestured to the play on the lawn. 'That is my greatest legacy, right there. What the Prometheus Club does for England's economic well-being, whatever I do to improve the land here at Bramble, all of that is worthy, but it pales compared to the people I leave behind to carry on.'

Cowden gave a nod towards Antonia. 'She's a natural with the little ones.' She was, Cullen agreed. She should be a mother. She *wanted* to be a mother. He recalled their conversation at Kensal Green and the disappointment in her eyes. Fate had been cruel there. Keir had been able to give her everything but a family. She felt the loss of it keenly, the incompletion of it.

They were both incomplete when it came to family. They had that in common. But they were incomplete for different reasons. He didn't dare reach for his dream for fear of attaining it only to ruin it. What did he know of creating a family like the one Frederick had when he'd not been raised to it himself? What did he know of being a parent when his own had, in his opinion, failed him? He would not father a child simply to revisit the mistakes of the ancestors on them.

'Thank you for this. She needed to get out, to enjoy herself,' Cullen offered as the men watched the children play.

'What she needs is a husband and children, a chance to have her life back. She tries to hide it, but anyone can see how empty she is and how much she has to give,' Cowden replied with a pointed stare.

'She says she's not ready.' Neither was he. He was certainly not ready for this conversation. Cullen was growing exceedingly uncomfortable with the direction the conversation was heading. Surely they didn't think *he* should be that husband? Frederick and Cowden of all people should know he wasn't marriage material and why. Now, bedroom material, that was different. He did have a certain prowess there. But marriage? No.

'She's young and she's had a year to grieve. If she was an equestrian who'd fallen off a horse, you know what I'd tell her to do,' Cowden mused. 'Losing Keir Popplewell was a blow to all of us. He was a good husband, a good friend and mentor and a man with sound social values. There's no question that his absence has left a gap in the many lives he touched. But the longer she waits, the harder it will be for her to let go.' Cullen could feel the older man's eyes on him. This message wasn't solely about Antonia. It was about him, too. He'd had ten years away, ten years in which to make his own peace with his family and with the scandal. But he hadn't.

'I am happy to back the store,' Cowden continued. 'Keir Popplewell knew a good investment when he saw it and I have no doubts the store will be a money-maker, but I am not convinced the store is good for *her*.'

A little trill of vindication flowed through Cullen. He'd thought the same thing. 'She sees it as Keir's legacy.'

Cowden nodded. 'Such a vision is worthy and ambitious, but she needs more.'

Frederick elbowed him in the ribs. 'She needs you and I think you need her. I saw the way you looked at her during lunch.'

'I was hardly ogling her.' Cullen felt suddenly defensive, trapped on all sides by Frederick, Cowden and feelings he hadn't quite sorted out. He knew what Antonia needed, but should he be the one to provide it? He thought of Cowden's endorsement of Keir earlier. He would never measure up to that.

'Of course not. It was the solicitude in your gaze. You were concerned about her comfort, her well-being. You were checking in with her with your eyes and she with you. There was that last look you gave her when she left the room, a private joke just between the two of you, perhaps? You've become close. There's no shame in that. It's a good start. There's something between you even if you haven't explored it fully yet.'

Did Frederick know how tempting his words were? How often had he thought the same? How he'd wondered what would it be like to reach over and stop her mouth with a kiss when she worried? Or to do more than take her hand and offer reassurance when what she needed was more than words to move past her grief? What she needed was a lover, someone to bring her back to life, to show her how to live again.

'Don't send an announcement to *The Times* yet, Frederick,' Cullen offered wryly. 'She needs to lean on someone at the moment while we straighten things out. Once I have her settled, I need to return to Tahiti.' Because Tahiti needed him and he needed Tahiti and while Antonia needed him, too, for the short term, he could not be what she needed in the long.

That got Cowden's attention. He raised a greying brow. 'You don't mean to stay?'

'No. I can't sustain the relationships we've grown in the South Seas if I'm here. I need to be on location.' It sounded logical, objective, when he said it that way.

'Surely you have an assistant, someone who could do that who is already in place there?' Cowden cleared his throat. 'I assumed that you were back permanently.'

Cullen felt distinctly uneasy. He feared for a moment that Cowden would rethink his support of the loan. Antonia would have his head if that happened. 'I don't think it's necessary and my life is in Tahiti now.'

'I think it could become necessary.' Cowden speared him with a hard stare. 'What happened with the bank could happen again and probably will. Whether it's right or wrong, Antonia Popplewell at the helm makes men nervous. Let me be frank—it will make even some men in the Prometheus Club nervous despite my endorsement.

There's a reason the one woman in the club is a silent investor and has an alias,' he said pointedly. 'If you're half a world away, you will be of no use to Mrs Popplewell. She needs you right here and that will not change, not in her lifetime.'

Cowden's words left him with a sinking feeling.

You can't go back.

All those promises he'd made himself about returning by September were useless in contrast to reality. He didn't want Cowden to be right, but he knew truth when he heard it. For the first time since receiving the news about Keir, he wasn't sad, he was *angry*. What the hell had Keir done to him? The feeling of being trapped persisted, all his freedom stripped away, everything he'd fought to achieve for himself lost.

'You know I can't stay. The longer I am here, the more likely it is I'll be a hindrance instead of an asset to her.' Even as he said the words, he felt the prick of guilt. His anger was selfish. Perhaps it was even cowardly. He'd left ten years ago, but what had he changed? What had leaving achieved?

Cowden's voice was quiet. 'I know very well why you left, Cullen. But perhaps it's time to face the fight, time to make your stand here where it can matter most. And time to make your peace before it's too late. Trust me, time will slip away and you don't want to regret it.'

'It's a lot to take in.' Frederick clapped him on the shoulder, intervening with an easy smile. 'Nothing has to be decided in the moment. Let's go down and join the women. They're having more fun than we are and I want you to meet the boys before you have to catch the train. Now that you're back, we can spend more time together.'

Now that he was back.

Cullen wasn't sure he liked the sound of those words. They were in fact downright ominous. Almost as ominous as the words, 'Antonia Popplewell needs a husband and children'. What made those statements ominous was that both of them were true.

Chapter Twelve

That sense of foreboding followed Cullen back to London. Clouds heavy with rain hung low in the soot-dark sky of the city, welcoming them back shortly after seven o'clock that evening. Even Antonia seemed to feel the effects. The positive energy and crisp country air of the afternoon seemed to belong to another day. It hadn't helped that the train had been delayed at one of the stations, turning a journey of less than an hour into two.

It had meant an extra hour trapped in a train compartment with his thoughts *and* the object of those thoughts. Far too much time to think. For her, too, he'd wager, based on the amount of time she spent staring out the window. Although he wasn't sure if her thoughts were driven by the meeting with Cowden, by plans for the store or by something the Duchess and Helena had talked about. Knowing Antonia's penchant for efficiency, it could very well be all three.

By the time they reached London Bridge station, lunch at Bramble seemed a lifetime ago. Both of them were tired and irritable. They'd set out early and the day had been long even if the results had been good. At least the coach was still waiting for them. He was thankful for that little luxury as he hustled Antonia through the crowd and into the carriage just in time to escape the first raindrops.

The storm didn't wait. Hard rain pelted the carriage roof before they were halfway to the town house. The loudness of the rain made it difficult to talk. But perhaps that was best. They might be better served with silence until they'd each had enough time to sit with the thoughts in their heads.

What would he say if she asked? That he'd spent the train trip back thinking of old hurts, old dreams and new acquaintances? That he'd been thinking of *her*, of how she'd looked in the garden with the children, how it had made his heart ache not just for himself but for her and how that ache had led to other more provocative thoughts. How might he comfort her? How might they comfort each other? How might he help her step out of the aloneness?

He could not save himself, but perhaps he could save her, show her that the time for her dreams was not yet past? Cowden said she needed a husband, but before that, Cullen thought she needed a lover. Someone just for her. A lover could be a bridge between the old world and the new, between loss and rediscovery, if she would allow it. Every day, he thought she grew closer to allowing it, every day the aloneness weighed on her a little more. He could be that lover. A lover needn't measure up to Keir. Only a husband needed to do that. A lover could be a fleeting fancy.

Cullen studied her in the dimness of the interior, her face turned in profile to see out into the evening streets.

There was a sadness to her gaze tonight and, despite his earlier advice to himself about silence, he could not let that sadness stand, especially if he had contributed to it in some way. 'Penny for your thoughts?' he ventured, aware that he might have left it too late. They were close to Mivart's. There was little time left for talk.

She flashed an apologetic smile. 'I'm not sure they're worth a penny. I was just feeling sorry for myself. I was thinking about how I'd given the staff the day off since I was gone and how quiet the house will be. Eating alone has little appeal.'

Especially after the Treshams. Cullen could guess what she was really thinking. What a stark contrast her evening would be compared to her day. 'If I go back to Mivart's I'll have to send out for something.' A thought that didn't appeal to him any more than her thoughts of eating alone. But finding a restaurant in this weather wasn't appealing either. 'May I make a bold suggestion?' He laughed to underscore that his use of the word bold was intended hyperbolically. 'Why don't we eat in? Neither of us needs to eat alone. I'm sure between the two of us we can put a meal together from whatever is in your pantry. Ham, toast, eggs.'

Antonia wrinkled her nose at the mention of eggs. 'All right, no eggs, then,' he amended. 'We'll improvise. As long as there's cheese and bread, it will be a feast.' He tapped on the carriage roof and gave the driver new instructions.

Cullen had never been inside the town house. Keir had purchased it as a wedding gift for his bride. Cullen had been gone two years by then. It was a three-storey home with pristine white trim about the door and windows. It was intentionally impressive on the outside and unintentionally oppressive on the inside. It was a mausoleum at worst, a museum at best, everything neat and orderly, all things in their places—places Cullen thought those objects had occupied for years. This house was not lived in any more. She was hardly here, hardly had the time to mess anything up. It reminded him of his parents' home. Elegant and empty. Soulless.

'It's beautiful,' he lied.

She tossed a doubtful glance his direction. 'Is it? It was when Keir was alive. I hardly notice it any more. The kitchens are this way.'

He followed her through a darkened dining room and down the stairs. The kitchen *was* better. It was clean, but obviously a lived-in, active place. Pots and pans stood at the ready for tomorrow's breakfast and the larder was stocked. Cullen gathered up a loaf of bread, a wheel of cheese and thick sausages. He slipped a bottle of wine beneath his arm. Out of the corner of his eye he watched Antonia tie on an apron and tuck up her hair as he deposited his finds on the long work table.

She handed him a knife. 'If you slice the bread for toasting, I'll slice the sausages for frying.' She paused and cocked her head. Domesticity suited her, he thought. 'You're smiling, I see it in your eyes. You're surprised I can cook.' She playfully brandished the knife. 'Well, I can, but don't tell anyone; it's my dirty little secret. Emma can cook, too. We used to sneak downstairs and make breakfasts for everyone when we were together.

Cook hated it, thought we were usurping his authority, but we loved doing it.'

'Yes, I *am* surprised.' Cullen picked up the knife and began slicing bread. 'You are a baronet's daughter. I thought such tasks were beyond a lady.' Surprised, but pleasantly so. She'd known struggle and difficulty and had overcome it—something else they had in common.

She gave him a long look. 'Before I married Keir, my family was struggling financially. We had to let our cook go. My mother and I spent a whole year cooking for the family and on a budget, too.' She laughed. 'I can make mutton taste like a four-course meal.' But there was seriousness as well. She'd not been pampered all her life.

'I approve.' Cullen reached for the wheel of cheese. 'Rank should not limit our need for basic life skills.'

She piled the sausage rounds into a skillet and gave him a soft smile. 'Keir rescued us both. You from the alley and me from genteel poverty. He rescued my family, too.' She set the knife down as if she had something important to tell him. Cullen waited. 'I loved *him*, though, not his money. It was never about the money. You might hear otherwise once the Season starts. It's a lie. I did need to marry well, but I loved Keir.'

The desire to be her warrior stirred once more. He knew too well how cruel *ton* gossip could be. If anyone dared to slander her, he would deal with them. 'I appreciate your honesty.' He was jealous of it, too. If only he could be that honest with her. Was that why she'd told him? Was she looking for him to reciprocate with a confession of his own? His confession would make hers pale by comparison. He moved to the stove to start it up and her next question caught him off guard.

'Keir *did* save you from the alley, didn't he?'

He nearly burned his finger on the matches. 'Yes.' Why would she question that?

'But you knew Frederick Tresham before you met Keir. Helena said you'd gone to school with him.' He could feel her eyes on him as he lit the stove.

'Even a poor gentleman's son attends school.' He knew where this was headed. It had always been the risk in taking her to Bramble, but there'd been no choice. She'd insisted on it and now she'd noticed certain things. He had to be careful. 'Your brother went, no doubt, despite the family straits,' he pointed out, taking a calculated guess.

'He did.' She nodded and went back to slicing sausages. Perhaps her curiosity was appeased. He hoped so. There were things he wasn't ready to explain. But his hope was misplaced. The afternoon had made her curious. She fixed him with a too-casual stare. That should have warned him. 'You're a gentleman's son, then, not a street rat.' There was no condemnation in it, but it was still a scold. 'When you said Keir rescued you from the alley, I assumed you'd been brought up in St Giles or something similar.'

'You never asked for clarification,' he answered.

'I was the one making assumptions. I will own that, as I will own there is always a certain danger with assumptions.' Her green gaze was intent and steady. 'But perhaps I was also deliberately led to those assumptions. You knew what I would think and you let me think it.'

The sausage began to sizzle, a rather apt physical metaphor, he thought, for the trill of tension buzzing between them.

'You never talk of your family,' she probed. 'Are they still alive?' She turned to the stove to move the sausage around the skillet and perhaps to give him some privacy in which to answer. He sensed he'd better make the answer good, or she'd just have more questions.

'Yes, they are. But we are not close. A gentleman isn't pleased to have his son in trade. My choices did not endear me to my father.' All true. He could say quite a lot about that relationship without naming names.

She turned from the stove for a moment. 'Then why did you do it? Why did you choose to enter trade if you didn't need to?'

He held her gaze as he answered, 'I do not think one man above another. To me, it is wrong to live off rents and the efforts of others while doing nothing. That is feudalism at its core and that social structure has outlived its usefulness in this new world where we tout equality and promote reform,' he said quietly. 'My father can't see that any more than he can see that his way of life is antiquated and on its way out, whether he believes it or not.'

'I'm sorry,' she said softly. 'Families should be close.'

'I'm not sorry,' he assured her. 'Families aren't always blood. I have the Treshams and in Tahiti I have Rahiti's family and I had Keir.'

'Father figures to stand in the void?' she said astutely. 'And Frederick? Does he stand in place of a brother who sides with your father?'

'Yes, I suppose he does.' He was a bit unnerved that

she saw so much, understood so much, and yet to be understood in that way was comforting. 'Frederick is a great champion of reform. He ran for his own Parliament seat in the House of Commons so that he could serve the interests of the masses and not the aristocracy.'

She smiled at that. 'And the South Seas? Is that about equality and reform, too?'

'Yes. Keir and I believe that economics is one way to foster equality across the empire.'

'That's what you're doing in Tahiti? Fostering equality?' She bent to put the grilled cheese in the oven, hips swaying.

'Yes. I do covertly what the French do overtly, only I offer a choice. The French offer only the illusion of choice.' That was all he wanted to say about the South Seas at present. It would be best now to direct the conversation elsewhere, preferably towards her. If today had raised her curiosity about him, it had also raised his curiosity about her. He leaned across the worktable and gave her a grin. 'Since we're talking about past lives, how is it you're so good with children?'

'I helped with the little ones back home. I taught reading at the church school in the village and I was always helping out with children's activities like the Christmas pageant.' She gave a little shrug. 'It just comes naturally. I like children. They're interesting and clever and so much more observant than people give them credit for.'

'You should have your own.' It was a bold statement. He watched her blush before she could turn away and put the skillet on the stove. 'Do you still want a family?' he pressed. 'You mentioned before that you and Keir had hoped for one.'

'I think that's out of the question now.' She checked the bread and cheese in the oven, suddenly busy. She rummaged a blue-checked cloth for the worktable and spread it over one end. She laid out pewter plates and found two wine glasses. He ought to help, but it was too much fun to watch her avoid the question or maybe it was the images that question conjured she was trying to avoid.

Within moments she'd transformed their corner of the table into a cosy eating space. She reached for a bowl on a high shelf and couldn't grasp it. 'Let me get that.' Cullen came up behind her, breathing in the soft, floral scent of her, an utterly feminine scent, the very promise of spring itself. Spring was nothing if not the season of hope.

He did not step back. Instead, he kept his voice at her ear. 'Why is it out of the question, Antonia? You are young. You have time.' Surely, an afternoon with the Treshams had reminded her of that, had brought such a thought to the fore. One could not be with the Treshams and not think about family, not hunger for a family of one's own.

'Because it would require remarrying and I don't think… Oh! Please back up. Hurry, we're burning the grilled cheese.' She bent swiftly to retrieve the rack with their melted cheese and bread from the oven. Cullen retreated to the table and retrenched, popping the wine cork and lighting a thick tallow candle. When she turned with the platter of sausages and grilled cheese in her hands, her eyes lit with pleasant surprise. 'You've made our table look lovely.'

'I think it's you who makes it lovely. Good meals start with good company.' He took the platter from her and set it down between their plates. He passed her a glass of wine. 'Here's to today. A long day, but a good day.'

'Thank you for this.' She took a sip of the wine.

'You did most of the work. I should thank you.' Good lord, she was beautiful by candlelight in her apron. No ballgown could look finer.

'I mean for the meal, for eating together. I did not want to eat alone.' She paused, looking thoughtful, as if she were about to tell him something important. 'It's dinner time I miss the most, and breakfast. Keir and I made every meal a celebration. Now, meals hardly mean anything at all.' Beautiful *and* lonely, Cullen amended. He would chase that loneliness from her if she would let him.

'You are alone, too much.' Cullen took a bite of juicy sausage, his eyes resting on her, forcing her to look back at him. 'In all seriousness, have you ever thought of taking a lover?' He barely got his question out before she spit her wine all over the blue-checked cloth.

'I beg your pardon?' she managed between gasps.

He had to stop doing that—saying such audacious things. *Do you want children? Have you thought of taking a lover?* How was a person supposed to respond? With the truth? Hardly. The truth might send him running for the door, might jeopardise the business partnership he hadn't quite signed for yet. She couldn't afford the truth. He had to stop looking at her the way he was right now, with the full intensity of those lion eyes. And she *had* to stop looking back or the truth would tumble out, that, yes, she would consider it if the lover was him.

'Truly, Antonia. Why not take a lover? It would be good for you.' He took a sip of wine and she remembered too late it wasn't his drink of preference.

'Would you like cider instead? We probably have some.'

'No, I would *not* like cider. I would like an answer to my question.' How could he sit there and discuss lovers so casually? 'A lover makes perfect sense, the best of both worlds.' He carried on the conversation calmly. 'You can have companionship, you can have physical intimacy without needing to give your heart.' He helped himself to a cheese sandwich. How could he eat when he'd managed to tie her stomach into knots with such a decadent discussion? 'That's what's holding you back, isn't it? The idea that you have to love someone again?'

Dear lord, he read her like a book. 'Am I that transparent?'

'Only in the best of ways, Antonia.' He leaned across the table, his thumb dabbing at the corner of her mouth in a gentle motion. 'You had a bit of cheese there. I got it.' He smiled, the casual intimacy of his touch easy and natural. 'I didn't mean to upset you, but I did mean to make you think. What are you going to do for the rest of your life? Keir died, not you, but you've buried yourself along with him. You can still have a life if you would just claim it.'

'I do have a life. I have the store, the businesses. I am very busy,' she reminded him.

'Busy isn't the same thing. I saw you today on the lawn. You were *happy*.' He moved his head to catch her gaze, to bring it up to meet his, his eyes boring into her, into her soul. 'Don't you want to be happy?'

His warm hands closed around hers as they rested on the table and she thought, *I want happiness. But not the consequences.* How did she explain such a thing to a man who feared nothing?

'I cannot risk it. Happiness has its costs. *I* simply can't be hurt again, I'd never survive it.' She feared not being whole, but she wasn't whole now, with all of these protections she'd mentally put in place. She was empty. She was realising belatedly that part of being whole was being filled.

'Let *me* fill you.' He came around the worktable in a slow movement, his eyes never leaving hers, his intent written openly in their tawny depths. 'You needn't marry to not be alone.' He pushed an errant curl back behind her ear. 'Tell me you're not tired of being alone. Tell me you don't want to be touched and I'll stop.'

But she did not stop him. She could not tell him a lie. He bent his mouth to the space below her ear, pressing a kiss to her skin. Her breath caught; her pulse leaped. She *did* want to be touched and she wanted *to* touch. To have and to hold.

'Yes, I want those things,' she breathed her confession into the candlelit darkness. She was tired of being alone, of not feeling for fear of what would happen if she did. Today had driven it home to her just how alone she was.

'You can have them,' he murmured against her skin, his mouth kissing the corner of her lips. 'I can give them to you. For a night, for a week, for a month. It needn't mean anything; you needn't attach your heart.' It was the perfect temptation—all the benefits, none of the cost.

It would mean something though, it would be a step back towards living, towards feeling, and it beckoned like the light beyond a dark room. Oh, this was a wicked lure. To take what he offered required a certain bravery. 'This is not as easy as you make it out,' she whispered her resistance. She should step away from him before this went too far. But, in truth, she didn't want to step away, didn't want to stop this.

'It can be.' His eyes were half lidded as his hand cupped her jaw, his mouth inches from hers. 'Let me show you. Let me be your lover, let me bring you back to life.'

'Yes,' she whispered, reaching for his mouth with hers.

Chapter Thirteen

⚜

He tasted of sharp tannins and cheese. He smelled of vanilla and spices and exotic places she'd only dreamed of until she'd met him. This was madness, delicious, outright madness, and she was wilfully drowning in it after treading water alone for so long. She gave her mouth to him, her neck, her throat, a little moan escaping her as his teeth nipped the tender skin just beneath her jaw, the rough pricking defining the rules of this engagement. This would not be gentle. It would be fast and cathartic.

Her mouth sought his with a hard kiss to seal the contract of his teeth. She'd given her consent with a single word: yes.

Yes, kiss me in the kitchen, yes, wake me from this half-life, show me how to live again. Yes, touch me. Yes, take me. Yes, tear my clothes, exorcise my ghosts. Set me free.

From here on out the pace would be fast, the passion fierce and given free rein to consume them at need.

He lifted her to the worktable, his body finding its way to her, amid the volume of skirts and crinolines, to stand between her thighs, to press proof of his own want against her, the hardness of him straining and evident even though layers of fabric separated them.

It was evidence, too, that this was not all for her, that he needed, wanted, this, as well, for himself. An afternoon at the Treshams had shaken something loose in them both. Their mouths sought each other, tongues tangled, lips devoured. Her breath caught, her hands fisted in his hair, anchoring her to him in a swirl of passion's torrent.

'Too many damn clothes,' He swore against her mouth, his hands seizing the bodice of her gown and ripping— freeing. Yes! Her blood pounded in primal joy.

Take them all, she thought. *Take every last petticoat, untie every ribbon, set me free.*

Her own hands tore at his neckcloth, fumbled with the buttons of his shirt, of his jade waistcoat. Clothes piled on the floor, desire riding them hard, leaving her only in her chemise and he in his trousers. She made short work of those trousers, feeling his eyes on her as she freed him, baring the hot, long length of him as he'd bared her. His voice was a growl at her ear. 'Shall I take you upstairs?'

Her resolve wavered, passion cooling for a moment as rational thought asserted itself. Not upstairs. Not in Keir's bed. She drew him close, defying the ghosts that pressed hard. 'No, here. This cannot wait.' She would not survive stairs. Her passion was like lava, burning fast and hot and just as quick to cool. She needed this, but she didn't trust it to last, not quite yet.

'Here then it is.' His own breath came ragged. His hands gripped her hips and pulled her to the edge of the table until she would have fallen if not for him. He was her strength, her pillar, her arms wrapped about his neck, her legs wrapped about the lean muscles of his hips, their bodies perfectly aligned for intersection.

The first thrust took her hard and she gloried in it, her neck arching back while a primal groan climbed her throat. Release stalked her, she wanted to explode, wanted to shatter into a million pieces. He came into her again. She would get her wish. It would not be long now. Her hands dug into the muscles of his bare shoulders, feeling the tension of his body as it gathered for its own completion.

Then completion was upon her and he left her with a force equal to how he'd entered her, his own satisfaction occurring against her thigh, both of them sagging against one another, sated and exhausted, the sudden fury of their want spent, the storm blown out. She leaned into him, her head against his chest, marvelling that he could keep his feet at all. She could barely stay upright. For the first time in ages she felt as if she could sleep the night away, so complete was the sense of peace that flooded her.

Despite her surroundings, she must have drowsed any way, her body vaguely aware of being lifted, of being carried and then laid down, of Cullen's weight beside her on a mattress, of being drawn into his arms, the murmur of nonsense words at her ear until sleep claimed her entirely.

Watching her sleep claimed the attentions of both his body and mind. His body could relax at last, the tension within him satisfied. Peace was not something he experienced often, but it was here with him in this big bed, with this woman. His mind, however, did not share that same peace. As much as his body wanted to join her in slumber, his mind had other ideas. The heat of the moment had passed and he was left with the reality of what he'd proposed—that he'd be her lover—and the consequences of what he'd done.

The proposal had been intended solely for her and yet that had likely been a lie from the start. He'd wanted her for himself, this brave, beautiful woman, who'd taken on the world, who fought for those she loved even at the expense of herself. And so he'd persuaded her that she needed this when in truth he'd needed it, needed *her* just as much. It was poorly done of him. He could offer her nothing. Whether he stayed or left, he would disappoint her on all fronts—as a business partner, as a friend and as a lover.

She stirred and he gently pushed back a strand of hair from her face. Her eyes opened and for a moment she tensed and looked about the room. He heard her exhale. 'Ah, good. A guest room.' She closed her eyes with a sigh heavy with relief.

'*Our* room,' he murmured in understanding. 'Our place.' He'd had enough wits left after their explosive lovemaking not to take her to the main bedroom, but was that because he was a coward, afraid of offending Keir's ghost where it was most likely to linger? A thought intruded. What would Keir think of what he'd done? Was this the action of a friend? He pushed the thought away.

Antonia snuggled against him, her breasts taut against

the fabric of her chemise as they pressed to his chest, her hand tracing the curve of his shoulder, slipping around to his shoulder blade. Her fingers traced and stopped. 'What is this? I feel something.'

He chuckled. 'My tattoo.'

'Tattoo?' She sat up and tugged him upright so she could study it in the lamp light. He felt her fingers trace the dark ink of the bird in soft, gentle strokes. 'Were you a pirate?' she teased as they settled back down beneath the blankets. Her drowsiness was gone and her eyes caught the light, glinting like emeralds hiding in the dark. She was doubly charming like this, alive and curious and unguarded.

'A warrior,' he corrected, wrapping a long gold curl around his finger. 'In the South Seas, the bird is a messenger from the gods. Some even believe that the bird has its own powers. The bird on my back is a tern. One island I visited, the elders said terns are symbols of safe return because they never spend a night on the water.' He propped himself up on one arm, his hair falling to one side. 'It's more than a symbol. It's true. If you're at sea and you see a tern, you can follow it. It will lead you to land.'

'So, you're a messenger?'

'Yes, I thought it was rather fitting given the job Keir sent me to do, which was to establish trade relations between our company and the island clans. Twice a year, I journey between the islands collecting cargo and then I ship it back here out of Papeete. Tapas cloth, necklaces and bracelets made of shells, pineapples, coconuts, teak, handwoven baskets, vanilla, seeds of exotic plants to be grown in English greenhouses—' He broke off with a chuckle.

She ran a hand down the length of his arm, the stroke of her fingers pleasantly rousing him with their warmth. 'What a life you must lead. It sounds…wonderful. Different beyond anything here. I think I might be more than a little envious.'

'It is different.' He gave her a soft smile. 'And I am a different man there.'

She laughed. 'Ah, yes, the man who wears few clothes.'

'That's right.' He grinned. 'In Tahiti, I wear a *malo* around my hips and it's very freeing. I can run, swim, climb, without restriction. A good English jacket would rip at the seams the way these tailors sew them to be skin-tight.'

'Form-fitting, I believe that's the word you're looking for.'

'Ridiculous is what it is. A man can't move in these clothes.'

'Try a corset and crinolines.' She slid him a teasing look. 'Sometimes there are doors I can't get through all in the name of fashion.' Then she remembered the original thread of the conversation. 'How else are you different in Tahiti? You have a tattoo and wear a *malo*, what else?'

'I am barefoot. I hardly ever wear shoes when I'm not in Papeete. I go everywhere in an outrigger.' He did his best to describe the canoe to her. He dropped his voice to low conspiratorial tones. 'I used to have hair down to my waist.'

'No!' Her eyes were wide in disbelief.

'Yes, it's true. I cut it when I came back.'

She threaded her hands through his hair. 'That makes me sad somehow. It must have been magnificent. But this is nice, too. You look like a lion.'

He laughed. 'How so?'

'Your eyes, your hair like a mane and you're large, quite intimidating really. The day I met you it was your height I noticed first, and I thought to myself, "He's a big man."'

'The first day I saw you, I thought, "There's a beautiful woman, she's everything…"' He stopped himself. He was going to say she was everything Keir had said she was, but they were doing so well, making such progress in bringing her back to life, moving her forward, he didn't dare risk it. There was no place for Keir in this particular bed just now. So he said instead, 'Lovely. I thought you were everything lovely.' He kissed her softly and whispered against her mouth, 'This is good, Antonia, us, together. *We* are good.'

'We are,' she whispered back, her hand seeking him beneath the covers, his phallus rising at her touch. 'What if we try it again, this time more slowly. I want to savour you.'

He smiled against her mouth. 'And I want to savour you.' Good lord, but this felt right. Too right, truth be told. There was no way he could hold on to it. Eventually he would disappoint her, but before he did, the interim would be glorious.

Chapter Fourteen

She had a lover.

It was the most glorious, most decadent thought to wake to and she held it close as she drifted slowly to the surface of consciousness. The day would come with its challenges and inevitably tarnish these moments, but for now she floated in pure bliss. Her body bore witness to the truth of it from the exquisite, sated lethargy that kept her in bed long after the usual time she rose to the delicate soreness in the most private of places, reminding her she hadn't dreamed it, but lived it, *felt* it to her bones—all of it: the heat, the passion, the overwhelming, reckless desire to throw caution aside. Last night she'd done just that—on her kitchen table no less.

Oh, no, the kitchen! Her eyes flew open, last night's fantasy connecting to this morning's reality. Her clothes were still down there. So were his and it was too late to do anything about it now. Cook would be here, would have seen the clothes, the two place settings. Cook would tell the housekeeper. The housekeeper would tell her maid, Randal.

Antonia let out a groan. She could not hide this. Or him. Which raised the question, where was Cullen? Had he gathered his clothes and gone home before dawn? If so, perhaps she could cobble together some sort of explanation that might appease Cook's curiosity. Her brain began to work. Perhaps she could say she'd been caught in the rain and left her wet clothes downstairs. That wouldn't explain the two place settings, though.

The jingle of approaching china in the hall broke her concentration. Her door opened and she braced for Randal with tea and questions, but it was not Randal who slipped inside. It was Cullen, bare chested *and* bearing morning gifts with delicious smells, a feast for the senses on all levels. 'You're shirtless.' She was at once aroused and horrified by the sight of him. 'Did Cook see you like that?'

Cullen grinned and carefully set the tray on the bed. 'She did.' He gave a playful waggle of his brows. 'Don't worry, I'd got my trousers on before she arrived. I don't think she minded.' He gave a casual shrug to indicate it was of no import. She disagreed. As for the not minding? Probably not. One could do worse than to start their day with a half-naked Cullen Allardyce in one's kitchen. But there'd be no hiding it now.

'I told Cook I stayed over because you weren't feeling well last night.' He reached for a slice of toast and buttered it. She watched the butter melt on the heated bread, her mouth watering. The explanation wouldn't hold for long, but at the moment she was too hungry to worry.

'I'm starved.' There was a sense of wonderment to that. How delightful to be ravenous in the morning, to crave food. How *different* after a year of lacking real appetite.

He tore off a bit of the toast and fed it to her, his fingers brushing her lips. 'That's what an active night of lovemaking will do for you, my dear. Restores your appetite like that.' He snapped his fingers and laughed.

'What else did you bring?' She glanced at the tray.

'Sausage, toast, tea. No eggs.' He fed her another bite and set about buttering his own toast. 'Why don't you like eggs?'

'I like eggs,' she clarified, 'they just became symbolic, that's all.' She reached for a sausage link. This was how breakfast should taste: hot and delicious with a touch of spice. Not unlike the man who sat cross-legged on the bed wearing only trousers, stubble lining his jaw, waiting expectantly for her to continue. 'When I came home from Holmfirth, I thought everything would change, but it didn't.' She tried to make light of it, but couldn't quite pull it off. '*I* had changed. A terrible tragedy had happened to me. *My* world would never be the same, so why was everyone else's?'

She played with the toast, sorting through her thoughts before she spoke them. 'Every day was the same, the same thing for breakfast, the same things needed doing—menus, instructions for the housekeeper. I thought—how was it possible those things still needed to be done? How could things be the same after what had happened? I wanted to move on and I couldn't.' She gave a shake of her head. 'Am I making any sense?' He probably thought her a raving lunatic.

He offered a disarming smile. 'You make perfect sense.'

She looked down at her toast. 'I was mad at you. It

was easy to blame you, to make you the embodiment of my inability to move forward. I needed your signature and without it everything was held up.'

He took another sausage. 'Yet you found a way to muscle through that detail until I arrived. I disagree. Everything *had* changed. You had new responsibilities with the businesses. You've done marvellously.'

'I've made mistakes Keir would not have made. Mackleson, for instance.' If she was confessing her faults, she might as well confess all of them.

Cullen grimaced. 'How were you to know? That's why I am here. That's why we have partnerships—to fill in each other's gaps. No one person is good at everything. No one expects it.'

'I do. I expect it of me.'

'Then you expect too much. It's a sure path to disappointment,' Cullen warned. He rose and moved the tray to the bureau. He turned and stepped towards the bed, his eyes burning hot, his voice a low husky drawl. 'What shall we do today?' He took another step, stalking her, intention in his gaze that made it apparent this was a rhetorical question only. A trill of anticipation rippled through her. She could do a little teasing of her own, too.

'We need to meet with the designers for the ladies' department to go over the plans for the displays,' she said, as he took another step closer. She wet her lips, teasing him. 'Then we need to oversee the transporting of goods from the warehouse so those displays can start being set up. Then—'

'Stop it, Minx,' he growled, putting a halt to her list of tasks with a kiss that was soft, playful, a gentle invitation to sensual exploration and she took it. Making love in the morning, surrounded by daylight, was a new delight. The mystery and shadows of the night were gone and in their place was a quiet open honesty, one's body entirely on display, entirely at the mercy of daylight, and Cullen was taking full advantage.

She stretched beneath him, giving a small moan as his lips pressed kisses down that body, raising heat and desire in their wake. This was a delicious, wicked worship and she wanted more, more of this play, this pleasure, this slow burn that would sear her as assuredly as the wildfire of last night had seared. He reached the juncture of her thighs and there *was* more, a whole new level of desire unfolding as his mouth sought her innermost source of pleasure, ratcheting her need from languorous satisfaction to the active seeking of fulfilment.

He licked at her core, she arched her hips upwards, anchored her hands in his hair in a desperate attempt to be closer, to push the pleasure further, all gentleness gone from the interaction now, replaced with a need to seek and find completion. He knew her need and he answered. She could feel the heave of his shoulders, hear the panting of his breath as the shudder of her own release claimed her with no small sense of awe. She'd not known it could be like this, that lovers could lay abed fully naked in the morning light, doing wondrous things to one another's bodies. What a discovery…about lovemaking, about herself.

Cullen stretched beside her, his eyes half-lidded. 'Did you like that?'

She gave a throaty laugh that hardly sounded like her.

She was becoming wanton. 'You know I did.' A wicked idea came to her. What was good for the goose… She slipped her hand beneath the sheet and flashed him a coy glance. 'Perhaps you'd like a bit, too?'

Cullen grinned and rolled on to his back. 'I thought you'd never ask.'

It was her turn to explore with her mouth, her teeth, her tongue. Not only his body, not only this new passion between them, but her own power. To know that she could rouse and control, that in this bed without the world between them, they were true equals. It was a heady realisation indeed, one that excited her as much this passion play did. When his release came, she took him in hand, revelling in the pulse of his pleasure. His eyes were the colour now of rich amber, dark with his desire, proof that he, too, was pleased by the power politics in this bed.

'We are good together.'

Yes, they were.

She sighed, curling up against him. 'I don't want to leave this bed.'

'We'll come back, I promise.' He laughed and pressed a kiss to her hair, but neither rose from the bed with any haste, in no hurry to move on with their day.

Last night she'd taken the next step in moving on and she'd been floating on air all day. It was, perhaps, inevitable that she would crash. One could not float on air for ever. The guilt came late in the afternoon as she climbed the stairs to change for dinner. The work of the day was done, the goods moved from the warehouse to the store where workers could begin the long process of unpacking and arranging, Cullen had returned to Mivart's to change as well. Now she was alone with her thoughts, which were not only reflections about last night, but also about the guilt.

A whole day had passed. Should she have felt guilty sooner? Was it wrong that she only just now contemplating that guilt? She passed by the door to the room, *their* room, guilt pricking at the sight of that closed door, the chamber of their secrets. Was it wrong that she'd enjoyed herself so thoroughly? That she'd not thought about Keir in those moment of extreme pleasure, but rather of the man she was with? Of herself? Had it been wrong to live in those moments and let them consume her?

She wished heartily that Emma was here. Would Emma tell her she had also felt guilty at first with Julien Archambeau? But Emma was across the Channel and even if Fleur was in town, Antonia saw little of her. Between her own commitments to the store and Fleur's commitments to the newspaper and the publishing house, there was little time for social visits and in the beginning there'd been too much grief, both of them hiding away, burying themselves with work in their private sorrows as they mourned. She would have to come to terms with this latest development on her own.

He had come to terms with last night, and with this morning. Cullen gave his neckcloth a final tug and inserted a topaz stickpin. They were dining out tonight at the St James's, then perhaps taking in a play, but Cullen could think of other things he'd rather be doing with her than sitting in a theatre box risking potential notice by early arrivals in town and wasting time that could be better spent in bed. He was hopeful he could change her mind.

The anticipation of changing her mind made him smile. Antonia was a passionate lover. She'd thrown herself into lovemaking with an abandon that had matched his own. He'd meant it when he'd said they'd been good together. Not just physically good, but there'd been a mental, emotional connection as well that belonged just to them. Not to Keir. He was no part of it.

That had been the piece he'd had to come to terms with. There'd been moments last night when he'd felt like a cad. The question that had guided his decisions to date had reared its head: what would Keir want him to do? It had been the question he'd asked himself upon leaving Tahiti, certain that Keir would want him to come back to England and ensure the company's survival. It had been the question he'd asked himself in regard to the decision made since then, too. What would Keir expect of him when it came to the business? When it came to watching over Antonia?

Answering those questions had come with sacrifice— leaving the life he'd built in Tahiti. Now with developments at the bank and Cowden's warning, another sacrifice loomed—that of being unable to return. To save the business might require him permanently staying in England as might watching over Antonia. Was it fair to ask that much of him? Perhaps he ought to stop asking the questions what would Keir do? What would Keir want? In the quiet of the late afternoon in his rooms, Cullen had decided he could not let that be the sole criteria of his decision-making. It would lead both him and Antonia to leading lives lived for a dead man instead of themselves.

Cullen checked his pocket watch. Antonia and the carriage would be pulling up to the kerb soon. He gathered up his long wool coat, slipping it on as he headed out the door. The decision had given him perspective on the affair with Antonia, but by no means did that decision make anything simpler. The affair itself had its own complications.

What did she expect from him? By necessity, it needed to be short term if he stood any hope of returning to Tahiti. Would that be acceptable to her? Perhaps he might suggest that once the store opened they would ease their need for daily contact. After all, Keir and he had not seen each other every day even when he'd been in England. Business partners needn't live in each other's pockets. That would give them this month to enjoy one another.

It seemed a good plan, one that made sense for five minutes, right up until he climbed into the carriage and saw Antonia dressed for the evening. Then, all rational thought fled. She'd chosen a gown of midnight-blue velvet with a sweetheart bodice, a thin, sparkly silver belt at her waist, a wrap of soft white fur about her shoulders, her blonde waves done up high in an elegant coiffure that exposed the slimness of her neck—a neck his mouth knew very well the heat in his blood reminded him. 'You are stunning,' He reached for her hand, encased in long white gloves, and kissed her knuckles.

She laughed. 'You look well yourself considering you were hauling crates and entirely dusty a few hours ago.'

'And loving every minute of it.' He grinned. 'It brought back old times, old memories of working in the warehouses. It felt good to do manual work. On the island, life is full of exercise. We're always fishing, swimming, sailing, hauling, hunting, building. I worry about growing soft here. I don't know if calisthenics in my rooms and running the streets before breakfast are enough to keep me in shape.'

'Running the streets?' She gave him a glance that was part worry and part curiosity. 'Where do you run? Wherever it is, I hope you run fast. London streets are not the safest even in good neighbourhoods.'

'Yes, I run fast.' He smiled at her concern, aware of how that concern made him feel—cared for, included, as if there was a place for him here in a city where he'd never quite felt at home.

'I wouldn't want to lose you,' Antonia offered softly, barely loud enough to be heard. Perhaps she hadn't meant for him to hear it.

What could he say to that? He could not say 'you won't' because that implied promises he was not comfortable making and it implied a permanence he wasn't willing to contemplate. Yet for her, something deep within him yearned to say those exact words, yearned to be a man who could stay, who'd want to stay, who could tolerate London and its hypocrisy. So he said instead, 'I hear St James's has a spectacular steak.'

St James's was empty given that it was the middle of a week in winter. A few year-round politicos dined at various tables, too busy with their discussions to notice them. Cullen preferred it that way. It wouldn't be long before he'd have to tell her…something. London would slowly start filling up. Someone of import would notice him and word would get back to his father. That would lead to a confrontation he'd rather avoid because it couldn't change anything for him, but it could make things worse for Antonia.

Perhaps things were already worse? Other than the little bantering exchange in the carriage, Antonia had been quiet. Something had dampened a bit of her joy. Not second thoughts, surely? Not after her remark about not wanting to lose him. Guilt, then? Perhaps she, too, had spent some time this afternoon grappling with the terms of their relationship.

He did not broach the subject until after their meals came—steak for him and fresh, grilled trout for her. 'What's on your mind, Antonia? Are you not having a good time?' He could not bring himself to use the word 'regrets'. He didn't want her to have regrets—regrets about what they'd done, what they wanted to do, or regrets about him.

She put down her fork and gave him a solemn look. 'I think the problem is that I *am* having a good time. I am, perhaps, enjoying this too much.'

Ah, so it was the guilt then. He had felt some of that, too, and found a way to dispose of it. 'You are entitled to happiness. You do not owe the dead your life.'

She shook her head, the diamond earrings sparkling in the lamplight. 'It's not that. It's more that I have guilt *about* the guilt. Primarily, I feel guilty because I didn't feel guilty at all until much later.' She played with the stem of her wine glass, her voice low and private. 'You should know that being with you was unlike anything I'd ever experienced before.' She glanced up at him, her green eyes shimmering. 'It both thrills and frightens me.'

He imagined those fingers doing to him what they were doing to the wineglass. They should have stayed in. 'Frightens you? How so?' Having such a discussion in public was its own aphrodisiac and it ratcheted his desire to be home with her early tonight. Time was wasting indeed.

'Because all good things end. I know that now. I also know they end sooner than one would like. I don't want to wake up one morning and suddenly learn that you're gone. If you're going to leave, I at least want to prepare myself for it.' There was a sharpness added to her gaze now that had him alert, his steak forgotten. 'You *are* going to leave, aren't you, Cullen?' It was more statement than question. They'd never spoken of it aloud, but it had been implicitly hinted at in his comments and she'd noticed.

'That hasn't been decided.' And it was much harder to decide staring at the decolletage of her blue velvet gown.

'There's no need to prevaricate, Cullen.' Somehow this had gone from a pre-seduction dinner to a business negotiation. He did not like this one bit. It was starting to look as though he might not get a second night, let alone a month.

Antonia responded to strength and truth, so he would give her that. He sat back in his chair and fixed her with a stare. 'I would *like* to go back to Tahiti. My life

is there. But you are here and my obligations are here.
It is not clear to me that I can leave without jeopardis-
ing the company.' Only that he must leave at some point
before his past caught up with him. Leaving her would
be far more difficult than he'd anticipated.

'Things will not always be unsettled. The company
will not always need you so close at hand.' That was
debatable according to Cowden, but Cullen would not
argue that point with her tonight when there were other
battles to win. 'Let me ask you point blank, Cullen. If
those are the only things holding you here, how long
do we have?'

'If those are the only things...'

He'd caught the phrase. They most certainly weren't,
but they were the only things they'd discussed. They'd
tacitly avoided renegotiating their affair.

Well, so be it. He'd given her truth. Now he'd give her
honesty. 'We have until the store opens. We have March
and a couple of weeks beyond.' Even if he stayed, they
wouldn't have any more time than that before someone
unearthed his scandal and trotted it out. Town would be
full of aristocrats by then. He'd need to have his defences
in place so that the scandal didn't hurt the business.

He had become a silent partner and gone to Tahiti in
order to disappear the first time scandal had reared its
head. Disappearing had worked wonders. People had
forgotten him. But this time he was no longer a silent
partner. This time he was the one standing in the breach,
convincing investors and banks their money was in good
hands.

'A month and change.' She nodded slowly, thinking.

'I won't trap you, Cullen. You needn't stay here. I won't steal your life. We have a month to open the store and a month to ensure you can return to Tahiti, to the life you want. I promise you, when the time comes, I *will* let you go.' That promise should have thrilled him more than it did. Her voice took on a coy edge that pleased him far better. 'But if time is of the essence, I might recommend going home. Now.'

'I couldn't agree with you more.' Cullen signalled for a waiter. 'The bill, please.'

Chapter Fifteen

Time was indeed of the essence—the essence of life, the heartbeat of the living and Antonia's pulse beat in time to its rhythm in the heady days and weeks that followed. Antonia felt as if the world around her was signalling spring. The long winter of both season and soul was giving way to better days, darkness giving way to light, grief giving way to joy, death giving way to life.

Her cup was running over with happiness. The store was coming together brilliantly. Cullen had replaced Mackleson with a new foreman by the name of Maxwell and things had run smoothly since. Each day the departments took further shape, displays were finished and more shelves were stocked until one could see the store come alive. It was rich and vibrant, the merchandise visually appealing, and it exceeded her expectations.

Her days were spent at the store while Cullen divided his time between the store and the warehouses, having taken over the office at the Captain's Club down on the docks. She loved the days best, when they worked side by side, solving problems and making plans. But nothing topped their nights.

The nights were just for them. They made a pact not

to bring work home and their evenings were spent dining in or out as the mood struck them. If they stayed in, they spent the post-dinner hours playing two-handed whist or backgammon before heading up to bed. If the staff was scandalised that Cullen spent more time at the town house and only the guest room gave signs of being used, no one said a thing. She liked to believe everyone was simply happy for her, that no one was judging.

That guest room had indeed become their place. Cullen had a few items stashed in the bureau drawers and she had a dressing gown in the wardrobe. But it wasn't the things in the room that made it theirs. This was the place where they made love, where she lay in his arms listening to stories of far-off Tahiti, falling in love with the South Pacific, its sandy beaches, turquoise waters and sunshine, as much as she was falling for the man who told those stories. Her happiness would be complete if not for the reminder that time was passing.

As plans moved forward for the grand opening of the store, an unexpected anxiety gripped her. Instead of feeling a sense of accomplishment in knowing that she'd preserved Keir's legacy, she was filled with dread. Dread about what to do next. The store was complete and she could manage it as she'd suggested to Cullen. But that did not fill her with the same anticipation it once had. It was simply more work to get up and do in the morning. Something to fill her days with until… until what?

Did she really want to spend her days with ledgers and accounts and contracts? But if she didn't, how would she fill those days? She needed purpose. She needed *something.* There was dread, too, in knowing that the completion of an old dream also meant the ending of a new dream, a dream she hadn't even known she wanted until six weeks ago. Despite her promises, she did not want Cullen to go.

She'd hoped having time to prepare for the loss of him would offset the hurt, that it would give her a way to protect herself—if she needed it. She'd hoped to not need that contingency. She'd not begun this affair with the intent of indulging her heart. She'd meant to believe Cullen's wicked promise that first night in the kitchen—that physical intimacy, physical satisfaction, didn't require the engagement of emotions. But it had followed none the less.

She often wondered if it had happened for him, too, or if he was just counting down the days, filling them with a trifling affair? There were times when she'd catch him looking at her with intense longing and she would think that he'd fallen, too, that he was no longer keen on leaving, that he might stay, that they might have more of these early spring days together when anything was possible. But at other times, she wasn't so sure. His gaze seemed far off as if part of him was already in his canoe paddling his blue waters. How she would love to see that sight in person!

She would remember him that way, she'd decided, imagining him in his *malo*, out on the waters he loved, his hair growing back to its former length, his deep tan returned, and she would know he was happy, that she'd been right to keep her word. To keep him here was tantamount to the keeping of the lions she'd seen as a girl in the cages at the Tower of London menagerie. He was not meant for town.

There was still time, though. The optimist in her wouldn't let her dwell on such sweet sorrow for long. There was still the now. She wouldn't ruin the present by looking too far ahead. Although every day, the increasing quantity of mail in the silver salver reminded her that time was running out. Invitations mounted. The Season was nearing and with it the end of her affair. The store would open and Cullen would leave, his promises fulfilled. The way that made her feel inside was worrisome indeed.

'You seem pensive.' Cullen rolled the dice and moved his pips on the backgammon board.

'Why would you say that?' She rolled and grimaced. A two and a three would do her no good. She had a pip on the bar and Cullen had all his home points blocked out except the sixth. She couldn't get in.

Cullen grinned and rolled again. 'Because we're a week away from our grand opening gala and you've missed three opportunities tonight to put me on the bar.'

'That is all true.' She laughed and rolled again, a six and a five. At last, a roll she could use. She moved her pip in to play. 'But to be honest, that's not the whole reason.' She rested her elbows on the game table. 'An invitation came a few days ago. I've been thinking about how best to approach it with you. Lady Camford is hosting a ball and I'd like to go.'

She paused and then continued, launching into her carefully crafted list of reasons. 'It should be a small event, not a lot of folks have come up to town yet for the Season. It's meant to be a practice ball of sorts for her goddaughter who came out last year. Apparently the girl is a bit shy and Lady Camford wants her to have a bit of a warm-up before the larger affairs.

'Lady Camford is a friend of my parents, which is why I've been invited,' she explained the connection. 'I thought it would be good practice for me, too. Perhaps I need a bit of a warm-up after a year out of society. I thought it would be good for the store as well, a chance for me to promote it, to encourage people to come by.' She clasped her hands together, readying herself for the larger request. 'Would you come with me?'

Come with her? He'd like nothing more and yet it was the thing he should do the least. Who would have thought six months ago he'd relish the idea of a ball with an English woman on his arm? That his body would thrill at the prospect of seeing her in a ballgown, of waltzing her across a crowded floor. Yet, giving in to the prospect tempted fate when he'd nearly fulfilled his promise, when he might be able to leave England undetected and without doing harm.

But one look into the emerald eyes, sparkling with hope and even with nervousness as if she were a young girl putting herself on the line for a boy she liked, when they were neither, had him rethinking the wisdom of refusal. On what grounds could he refuse, though, without exposing himself? If she knew everything about him, she might decide he was not the escort she needed, or even the partner she needed. 'I appreciate the offer,' he said gently, 'but perhaps you should think about what it might mean for us to be seen together socially. Lady Camford is a family friend, so your parents will be there, yes? Are you ready to explain me to them?'

'I will tell them it's business.'

'Do you think your mother obtuse enough to believe that?' Cullen asked bluntly. 'In my experience, mothers are endowed with a sixth sense when it comes to their children's romantic inclinations.'

She laughed a bit at that. 'It sounds like there's a story there, something you know first-hand?'

'Yes, and it's a story I'd rather not tell if you don't mind,' he answered soberly. He wanted to make it clear he could not be teased about this, that this was not a topic open to probing.

'All right.' She reached a hand across the table and placed it on his, her touch warm and encouraging. 'I won't push you on it. I will, however, push on the ball. It is my first social appearance since coming out of mourning. People are going to speculate no matter what. Have I come out because I am looking to remarry? What kind of situation did Keir leave with me? Am I a wealthy widow? The fortune hunters will be on their game. Having you with me will spike their guns for a while even if I proclaim it is strictly business between us.

'Think of it as your civic duty to me and to the store. While I don't like the idea that a male presence at the head of a business steadies investors' nerves, I understand it is an unfortunate truth in our present world. With you beside me, we can bolster confidence in Popplewell and Allardyce. Peers may not dirty their hands in the daily running of companies, but they *do* invest. The Prometheus Club is proof of that. And their wives shop. I want their patronage.'

'You are far too persuasive for your own good.' Cullen shook his head in defeat. If he didn't go now, she'd ask again later when it truly was out of the question. His father was always in town for the Academy art show and his mother made appearances at all the balls.

It was not that he was a coward. He'd gladly face his father in a crowded ballroom, but now he had someone to protect, someone who could be hurt by that relationship and the old scandal, and that someone was her. And, perhaps, that someone was him. It would hurt him to cause her pain after she'd already endured so much. It was unlikely anyone of note would be at Lady Camford's. This might indeed be fortuitous, after all. If not fortuitous, then certainly the lesser of two evils.

'If you think you're up to it, then I am up to it.' He smiled. 'I would be pleased to stand beside you as you make your return.' He gripped her hand in a supportive squeeze. 'You will dazzle them as always. Perhaps so much no one would look twice at me.'

She laughed. 'If you think that, you underestimate your appeal. Every woman in the room will notice you.'

'Perhaps the appeal you underestimate is your own.' He rose and raised her with him. 'I seem to have lost all interest in this game when another, more enchanting game awaits me upstairs.'

She gave him a flirty look of mock bashfulness. 'But, sir, you were winning,' she said coyly.

He stepped close, letting his mouth hover tantalisingly near her own and whispered, '*Now* I am winning.' He claimed a kiss and all thoughts of ballrooms fled in exchange for bedrooms.

Ballrooms had not changed much in the ten years he'd been away. Cullen had not expected they would. The aristocracy didn't like change much. They clung to their traditions, their rituals, and both were on intentional and unintentional display in Lady Camford's ballroom. The parquet floor was polished to a walnut sheen, its soaring Doric columns that lined the room, separating the dance floor from the perimeter and supporting the soaring ceiling, were draped in pale pink silk swathes and baby-pink rosebud garlands in honour of her goddaughter who was dressed to match in a white gown and pink sash. The six-piece orchestra was sequestered in a musicians' balcony that overlooked the top of the ballroom.

In an adjacent room, the usual refreshments were laid out—orgeat in a giant silver punch bowl, trays of prettily iced biscuits done in pink and white, lobster patties and finger sandwiches. In his younger days, he and his friends would bet on who would eat the most lobster patties. The one saving grace was that footmen were circulating with glasses of cold champagne—a drink that was always in season, not that Cullen intended to partake of it much. Still, it would be better than warm, watery punch if a man needed a drink.

'Nothing has changed,' he whispered at Antonia's ear as they passed through the ballroom, looking for her parents. Lady Camford had mentioned in the receiving line that the baronet and his wife had arrived earlier.

She gave a light laugh over her shoulder. 'Did you think it would?' No, he hadn't and in that moment he keenly felt the comment Antonia had made to him that first night together—that she'd thought the world would change because she had. He supposed part of him felt that way, too, hoped for that, too. But the broken system seemed to find a way to limp along, outliving even itself.

'Have I mentioned you look stunning tonight?' He had his mouth close to her ear, using the crowd and the noise of conversations as an excuse to keep a hand at her back and his body near. She smelled of vanilla and flowers and he wanted to breathe her in, the scent a reminder of the freshness of spring, the infinity of hope and possibility. She wore emerald-green silk tonight, a shade that brought out her eyes and drew attention without being ostentatious. A diamond choker sparkled at her throat, matching earrings sparkled at her ears and a wide bracelet sparkled about the wrist of her long white gloves.

'Perhaps you are biased,' she demurred with a private smile that said she was remembering how long it had taken them to get dressed and why they'd arrived later than planned. He thought the late arrival might work to their benefit, though—there would be fewer people to notice them. People were already partnered off into their preferred groups of friends and acquaintances, immersed in catching up after a winter apart.

He growled. 'I am not biased. Every man we've passed has looked at you.'

'Don't be jealous. Every woman we've passed has

looked at you,' she parried with a laugh. 'I don't mind. Because I know a secret.'

He gave a low chuckle, liking this flirty game of hers. She was happy tonight, joy spilling out of her. She was made for this, to be among people. 'Tell me,' he cajoled. He was already glad he'd come if being here gave her such joy. He'd promised to bring her back to life and this evening was proof that he had. Truth be told, as long as she was beside him, the evening was enjoyable for him, too, something he'd not expected. He'd not realised how much of a difference her presence made to him.

'I get to go home with you. No matter how much they flirt with their fans and flutter their eyes, you are mine.'

Her confidence aroused him. What a spark she was! It was a treat to see that spark unveiled in surroundings outside of business. 'Maybe we don't have to wait until we get home.' His gaze was already quartering the ballroom, looking for an alcove, old habits dying hard, or not really dying at all.

'Look! There are my parents.' She shot him a teasing look.

'Minx.' He groaned. 'You are a such a tease.'

'And you are wicked. Now, be on your best behaviour,' she scolded with a laugh.

He would be, for her, because tonight meant so very much to her personally and professionally.

Her parents were delightful as far as parents went. Antonia had her mother's looks, which had aged well, and her father's charm. But Cullen didn't think he and Antonia were fooling either of them no matter that Antonia introduced him as Mr Cullen Allardyce and emphasised repeatedly his role as Keir's partner in the company. He'd hoped to escape any further inquisition when the music began, but Lady Lytton was too quick. 'Perhaps you might do me the honour of a dance? I am afraid my husband doesn't dance as often as he used to.'

Cullen bowed and offered his hand wryly. 'How can I refuse?' The baronet and his wife were much cannier than he'd given them credit for. He should have known better. Antonia had to have come by her talents somehow. Years of watching them had no doubt rubbed off on her in some degree and she'd merely refined them. In anticipation of the evening, Cullen had been prepared for the potential of interrogation, but in his imaginings it had always been man to man. He'd not anticipated the interrogation coming from her mother, that was his fault, his oversight. After experiencing Antonia's bluntness, he should have known better.

The music began and he led Lady Lytton through the opening movement, but she led the conversation. 'You and my daughter are having an affair.' She smiled as he tried to hide his surprise. 'I see you're the one who is used to doing the shocking. But let's not have any coyness between us. My daughter has had a difficult year. The world is not kind to widows, especially young ones. I see her sparkling tonight and if you are the reason for bringing her back to life, than I don't much care how you've done it.'

'Yes, ma'am.' What else could he say? He was entirely off script here, feeling his way. Usually these sorts of conversations ended in duels.

They began the next pattern, Lady Lytton as sharp on her feet as she was on conversation. 'I wonder though if my daughter knows who you are?' Her smile was a little colder now and his own was more formal, more guarded. 'She made much of your partnership with her late husband, but does she know you? I admit my husband and I did not. It was not our business to poke into Keir Popplewell's business. However, now that his business is our daughter's business and there's a silent partner that's surfaced, we did our research, Lord Cullen Allardyce, second son of the Marquess of Standon.'

He'd been braced for that. He was ready. 'That ought to please you. Even a marquess's second son is quite an elevation for the daughter of a baronet.'

She shot him a sly look. 'Only if you marry her. Is that your intention? It was not my understanding that you were a marrying man, that you had no interest in the trappings of the peerage and that was the reason you went abroad.' She speared him with a hard stare reminiscent of Antonia on her mettle, challenging him about the store.

'My husband and I go about society only a little. We prefer our life in the country with our horses and innovating around the estate.' She arched a blonde brow. 'Perhaps I do not have the story correct? I do understand society can get the facts wrong on occasion.' The overture was skilfully done. She was giving him a chance to correct the narrative attached to him. He also wondered how much she knew? Or if this was a veiled request for information? Was she inviting him to spill the whole sordid tale?

'I do not think your daughter is looking to remarry,' he offered diplomatically.

She gave a short nod. 'How convenient for you, then. But that's your business, that's between the two of you. Frankly, I do not care if you're a marquess's second son, or a duke's heir. What I am most concerned about is, you do not immerse her in scandal now that she's clawed her way back to the land of the living.'

She paused and leaned close as the dance ended. 'Mr Allardyce, if I know, others know. I just want my daughter to know before it comes back to haunt her. I am sure you can imagine the damage it would do her and I hope we agree that neither of us wants to see her hurt.'

'Of course, my lady. I appreciate your candour.' He gave a short bow and escorted her back to Antonia and Sir Jonas. The next dance was a waltz and he led Antonia to the floor, desperately wanting these minutes with her, fully aware that everything between them was about to change and he'd be the one to change it for better or worse, although he wasn't sure at present what the 'better' would be. Right now, he could only see 'worse'.

Chapter Sixteen

He would find a way to make it better, Cullen vowed. He would give her this moment, he would let her shine, he would let London see her sparkle. Cullen placed his hand at the small of her back and positioned them for the dance. She looked up at him in anticipation as if she'd been waiting all night for this one dance. He would not take that from her even as his mind was already rife with all the ways in which his scandal could do exactly that.

He moved them into the dance, unable to look away from her and she from him. 'People will talk,' he warned.

'Then let them. It would be a waste to spend this dance staring into the blank space over your very broad shoulder,' she bantered in private tones.

At the top of the ballroom the tempo of the music picked up and he accelerated coming through the turn, the pressure of his hand at her back urging her closer, giving him better control over the dance until they were flying, soaring, together without their feet leaving the floor.

Exhilaration glowed in her eyes, there was exquisite joy in her smile and he savoured it. If London was look-ing, so be it. There was just this moment and it was his, theirs. He would remember it long after he returned to Tahiti: the night he'd held the most beautiful woman in his arms, a woman who cared for him, and he'd given her the waltz of her life, the perfect bookend to the promise he'd made her—that he would bring her back to life. Now his work was done. He could leave in good conscience, his debt to Keir paid. There was no longer any pretence of a grey area there, nor any hope that they might choose to renegotiate that departure.

After speaking with Lady Lytton, it was clear that the hurt he would inflict would not be just the social fallout or the ways in which his past could hamper the department store. One might be able to ride out those particular storms. But there would be internal scars, too. She had not undertaken their affair lightly. She'd battled guilt and grief for this, and she'd be repaid with scandal if he stayed any longer. He was risking much even now.

She would feel betrayed, misled and she'd blame herself. She'd think she ought to have known better, just as she felt she ought to have known better about Mackleson. To stay would risk destroying her confidence. He would not be responsible for that. Her optimism was one of the things he loved about her best. It was an integral part of who she was, a part of her charm, what set her apart from others.

He leaned close to her ear. 'Did you know the waltz was a metaphor for sexual congress? The man in pursuit of the woman, the closeness of our bodies, the heightened risk that your breasts might brush the lapels of my coat, or that our bodies might touch below the waist,' he whispered naughtily.

'There's little chance of that, not with crinolines. A man can't get within twelve inches of a woman in petticoats and hooped skirts.' She gave a low, throaty laugh. 'And I dare say that's still six inches too far for most men.'

'What a vixen you are.' He grinned at her bawdy humour and suddenly wished they were anywhere but a public ballroom for what he had in mind. 'I'd like to dispense with those petticoats and crinolines forthwith,' he growled.

'And I'd like to dispense with your jacket, your waistcoat, your shirt…' She laughed up at him. Was she aware of how lovely she was? 'Based on all this naughty banter, I'd say the waltz is not a metaphor for sex but foreplay.'

He grinned down at her, taking a final turn. Soon the magic would be over. 'What do you know about foreplay?'

She was up for the challenge. 'I know your nipples are sensitive to tongues. I know—' Her eyes broke from his for a moment and when they returned there was shock in them. 'Cullen, everyone is watching us.'

That was unfortunate. There should have been anonymity on the dance floor. He'd meant for this dance to be for them, for her, not for public display. And yet it had become that. He leaned close once more. 'We can't stop them from looking, so we might as well give them a show. Eyes on me, love, and keep smiling. They can look, but they can't come into our world.' Not yet. He wouldn't be able to keep them out for ever.

'And then?'

'And then we'll go home and finish this.'

She gave a mischievous smile. 'Ah, so I was right. The waltz *is* foreplay.'

She'd not been this glad to get home in quite a while. They'd finished the waltz with a flourish amid applause from the perimeter. Cullen had taken a bow and she a curtsy. Never, even at the height of her debut, had she cleared a dance floor. It had made leaving a little more difficult than she'd have liked, everyone wanting an introduction as they made their way through the ballroom to make their farewells to Lady Camford who was certain they'd made her early pre-Season ball the talk of the society pages. Antonia had laughed, saying, 'As long as they also mention the department store', but Cullen had been surprisingly reserved or perhaps he'd just been wound tight with desire and eager to be away.

Subsequent events certainly bore the latter out. They'd been halfway undressed by the time they were halfway home and they only made it halfway up the stairs in the empty town house before all restraint was lost with the rest of their clothes.

He took her there on the staircase, balanced between his body and the wall, her legs wrapped about his hips, her hands tangled in his hair, her pleasure a gasping chorus of sobs, so great was the release that swept her when climax shuddered through them both. It had been rough and glorious and fulfilling. And yet, something was off because when something was too good to be true, it usually was—even an optimist knew that.

He lifted her in his arms and carried her the rest of

the way to what was now *their* bedroom. He laid her down and stretched out beside her in what had become his usual post-coital pose—his long body on its side, his head propped in his hand. 'An amazing night,' he murmured, his voice still husky.

She pushed a length of his hair back behind his ear, giving his jaw a soft caress, and gently ventured her theory. 'It was. I will not forget that waltz. Nor will anyone else who was there, I dare say. Are you all right with that?' It had seemed that he was. After all, he'd suggested finishing up with a show for the onlookers, but afterwards, he had been tense. She'd not misread that. Some of the unease she'd noted in him then was still there, lingering in his eyes.

'You were dazzling. People will always notice a beautiful woman.' He smiled, but it did not convince her. A thought occurred about the source of that unease.

'How was your dance with my mother?' Perhaps she had said something to upset him? 'She can be rather headstrong at times.' And protective of her only daughter.

That earned her a chuckle. 'Like her daughter? I see where you get your personality. Your mother loves you, she cares about you. I cannot fault her for that.'

'That sounds suspiciously like another way of saying she was hard on you.' Antonia raised up, mirroring his position, her head on her hand. 'Tell me what she said.'

'She wanted to make sure I didn't hurt you.'

'You won't,' Antonia assured him. She saw now what it was. He, too, had been thinking about the timeline they'd laid out. The store was set to open within days and she'd made a return to society. His promises were fulfilled. All that remained was to ensure the company was able to function with him halfway around the world without investors panicking. She and Bowdrie had been working on that. She would keep her promise, too, and let him go.

'We knew this was coming. We never meant this to last for ever, only to enjoy it. We've had our time. I admit it will be hard to let you go and perhaps I would choose differently, but we made promises and we will honour them.'

It took all of her courage to say those words. She did not want to let him go, but it was the honourable thing to do. He'd come halfway around the world for her and now she had to let him go back. His part of the deal was fulfilled. But she was touched that he was worried about hurting her—perhaps it proved that this had meant something to him as well, something more.

He shook his head. 'Leaving you will indeed be hard...'

'Leaving can be renegotiated,' she said, but he pressed a finger to her lips.

'It's not that, Antonia. I could not stay even if I wanted to. I left the first time so that I would not be a liability to Keir and I will leave again so that I am not a liability to you. You will have my money and my name, and I hope it will be enough to see you through. But you cannot have me—indeed, you do not want me anywhere near.'

She stared hard at him, trying to understand. His tone sounded ominous, not unlike Mr Dyson's quiet tones when he'd come to tell her that Keir was dead. 'What are you talking about, Cullen?'

'I am talking about the scandal that comes with me and the fact that after tonight you and I are living on borrowed time before the Marquess of Standon comes knocking.'

'I don't even know him. What does he have to do with you? With us?' Her stomach tied itself in knots.

'He's my father and I am a stain on the family name and, by association, you will be dragged into it, too. He's been wanting his revenge for quite some time.' She understood now. The marquess would go through her to get to his son. She and the store were at risk. She reached for patience, for steadiness in the face of her anger. How dare he hide this from her, how dare he drag her into this? The little voice in her head asserted itself. This wasn't solely about her, but Cullen, too. He was hurting.

She got out of bed and fetched their dressing robes. This was not a conversation to have naked. She slid her arms through hers and tossed his on the bed. 'You'd best tell me everything if we're to figure a way through it,' she said calmly, but inside she felt as if her world was about to fall apart just when she'd put it back together.

She sat in the chair beside the bedroom's small fireplace, watching Cullen pace the length of the chamber, his robe open, offering tantalising glimpses of nakedness every few steps. She did not rush him. He was choosing his words, perhaps considering where to start. Her eyes never left him. Her own mind was a riot of thoughts. How was it possible that they'd been so happy a few hours ago? The ecstasy of the ball seemed far away. But only for her, came the sharp reminder. Whatever it was he was about to tell her, he'd known all of it the entire time and he'd withheld it. At some point, there'd have to be an accounting for that.

'I find it best, Cullen, to start at the beginning,' she prompted after a while. 'Tell me why you went to Tahiti. It wasn't only for the promotion of trade, was it? Not only because your principles demanded it?' She did not doubt they were part of the reason. But neither were they the entire reason as he'd implied that night they'd fried sausage and eaten grilled cheese. 'What was so awful that you had to leave England?'

'Are you sure you want to know?' He turned from the window. 'Once you know, it will be the beginning of the end for us.'

'We were always going to end, Cullen.'

'But not like this, not with you hating me. Tonight, your mother insisted that I tell you before you heard it from someone else, somewhere else.'

She nodded, her heart twisting. She detested seeing him like this, tortured and troubled. Even more, she despised the idea that he thought her hate was so easily acquired, that she had no tolerance for error. 'Cullen, I care for you. I have given you my body, my heart, and you have brought me back from the dead. Nothing will put you beyond my love.'

He gave her a hard look. 'Are you sure about that, Antonia?'

'Whatever it was, it couldn't be that bad. You had a wild youth, many young men do. My own brother had plenty of scrapes before he joined the military. If it was gambling, or drinking, or lightskirts—' she thought of the brothel and the night he'd met Keir '—or brawling, it is not so terrible.'

He faced her squarely and the rest of her assurances died on her lips. 'Antonia, it was murder. I killed a man. Illegally. In a duel. He was the brother of the woman I was supposed to marry.'

There was nothing to say that wouldn't make a mockery of her words. She'd asked him to trust her love. She couldn't back out now because the words were frightening or because they held heinous connotations and she would not do him the disservice of trying to mitigate them with platitudes like 'I'm sure you had good reason'. Was there ever a good reason to take a life, let alone to take it on the duelling ground in the heat of misunderstood honour? But she could do him the service of listening. She settled deep into the chair, her feet curled under her. It was going to be a long night.

Chapter Seventeen

He'd given her enough to go running from the room or to send him out of the house or both. Perhaps that's what he'd been hoping for. It would make things easier for him if she were angry, if she simply banished him. He wouldn't have to explain the whole sordid mess to her, wouldn't have to see her face fall in shock and horror when she heard the truth about the man she'd let into her life, into her bed. But if that was what he'd hoped for, he was sorely disappointed. Antonia's optimism was made of sterner stuff.

'There's certainly a lot to explain to me, Cullen. A duel, a death and a debutante,' she said solemnly. She looked so damn serene, so beautiful, sitting by the fire, her hair loose, her silk robe flowing over curves, and it hurt to know that the serenity was a hard-won façade. It was an illusion only and it was his fault.

A man had to know where to look to understand that: in her eyes where anger and worry sparked like embers; at her hands where they lay tightly clenched in her lap. No, she was not calm. Right now she was probably wrestling with her anger and with her need for self-preservation. 'I suppose, though, the only question that matters is why? Will you answer it?'

He would answer it if for no other reason than the truth was all he had left to give her. But where to begin? With his father? With the marriage? He gave a short nod of his head and opted for the latter. 'I didn't want to marry her. I made it clear to her, to her father and to mine that I found the match unsuitable and I had no intentions of honouring it no matter what inducements it came with.' He grimaced in remembrance. It had come with several inducements: two estates in the country, a home in town, a carriage, horses, a significant allowance from his father.

Antonia looked thoughtful. He knew what she would ask before the question came. 'Many men would find those inducements sufficient to overcome marital reservations. Is it wrong of me to ask why you refused?'

'They assumed my integrity was for sale. Only my father and I disagreed on what a man's integrity ought to consist of. I felt integrity lay in being true to my own personal beliefs and he felt that a son's integrity lay in being loyal to his family, to his family's line, especially when that line came from the peerage.'

He stopped before the window and stared out into the dark garden behind the house, remembering those difficult days. 'It was complicated. I can't explain why I refused the marriage without also explaining my father. He and I were always at loggerheads. He is a Tory to his core. Traditions, family lines, rituals—those things matter to him. They are worth fighting for, sacrificing sons for. Change concerns him, change undermines the things he treasures, the things he protects.'

Antonia cocked her head to one side, considering.

'But not you. Change excites you. New places, new people, new ideas. It's why you like Tahiti so much.'

'Because it's new to me, not because it has no traditions.' He chuckled. 'Sometimes I think Rahiti's father would get along well with mine. He and his clan have their rituals and traditions, too, and they are as equally important.'

'But they're new to you and that's why you love it there,' she surmised.

He nodded, some of his anxiousness easing. He couldn't spare her the consequences of his tales, but it felt good to be understood as he told it, a reminder that she understood *him*. 'My father felt it was within his rights to arrange a marriage for his second son that would benefit the marquessate. He wanted the alliance that would come with me married to the Earl of Southberry's daughter.' He shook his head. 'Selfishly, I didn't want to be married yet. I was only twenty-five, I'd been working for Keir for two years and loving it.

'My father spent those two years ignoring me, ashamed of what I was doing—working in trade and supporting reform wherever I could. I stood against everything he stood for. To him, it was worse than whoring and running up gambling debts. Those at least were a gentleman's vices. He could understand them. What he *couldn't* understand was the pleasure it gave me to work in the warehouse, to talk with captains, to meet people from all over the world.'

He diverged for a moment. 'The docks *are* dangerous, but they are also full of ordinary people having extraordinary adventures, everyday sailors making modest wages, but who speak two or three different languages not because they've been to a fancy school, but because of the experiences they've had. It's amazing to me, but men like my father don't see the value in it.'

He shrugged. 'Anyway, my father felt this marriage was a way for me to redeem myself and come back into the family fold. He told me, "You've had your fun, now it's time to come home and serve the family. I need you and your brother needs you." What he really meant was that the marquessate of Standon needed me. My brother had been married for five years and had not produced a child.'

He studied her for a long moment, gauging how she was taking the news. This was the good part. It was going to get worse. 'Perhaps you think it was indeed selfish of me? After all, you were much younger when you came to town looking for a husband and a way to save your family.' She'd not flinched at the sacrifice while he'd baulked entirely.

'I don't think that at all, Cullen. I made my choice willingly and no one was forcing me. My whole family was in on the plan together and I don't think it occurred to any of us that I would fail to find someone who was both acceptable to me and to our needs.' She gave a soft chuckle. 'We Lyttons are like that. Optimists to the core.'

She was encouraging him with those words, he realised. Encouraging him to go on with his tale, letting him know that she was listening to understand, not to judge, that his story, no matter how terrible, was safe here in this room, with her. He hoped she wouldn't regret those very generous offerings.

212   *Alliance with the Notorious Lord*

'Was your freedom and your disagreement with your father the only reasons you didn't marry her?' Antonia prompted gently.

He blew out a breath. 'I was suspicious of just how sweet the pot was. I was getting a lot for doing what my father classified as my duty, as what was expected of me. It wasn't like him to be so generous. So I started digging. I discovered that the generosity was prompted by the Earl. I also discovered his daughter was pregnant with another man's child, a reprobate of an officer in the army who'd made false promises and left, but not before damage was done.

'The Earl was willing to offer my father votes and seats in the House of Commons and to promote my father's political ambitions as well as setting me and his daughter up with considerable wealth if I took her off his hands and claimed the child.' He gave a short huff of dry, wry laughter. 'Of course, I wasn't supposed to know about the child. I was supposed to think the child was a wedding-night conception and an early birth.'

'That's terrible.' Antonia wrinkled her brow. 'I am surprised a man like your father who is so concerned with his line would tolerate an illegitimate child as heir.'

'My father felt his odds were fairly well hedged. My brother might still have a child, the child my bride carried might be a daughter. Any son that came afterwards would be mine and we had proof that this bride was fertile, if nothing else. Of course, the plan was that I was not to know any differently. Appearances are everything to men like my father, the Earl and the Earl's son.'

He watched her thoughts work behind her sharp eyes.

'That's why there was a duel. Word got out you'd refused the marriage, but once the child became apparent, everyone would assume it was yours. The dishonour of abandoning her would be yours, too.'

'I was a convenient target. To be fair,' he said solemnly, holding her gaze, 'I don't think the brother knew what his father was up to. My biggest regret is that the brother believed he was defending his sister's honour.'

'You were both victims then,' she offered quietly. Then anger got the better of her. 'Men and their stupid culture of honour. I didn't think anyone duelled these days. It's a ridiculous way of settling things.'

'In 1840 the Earl of Cadogan killed a fellow officer. In 1845 two men named Seton and Hawkey duelled fatally. Last year, apparently, two French émigrés, Barthelemy and Courmet, also duelled,' he recited in rebuttal. He'd just heard about the latest from Frederick during their visit. Duelling might be less fashionable than it once was, but it was not *out* of fashion.

'I don't excuse what I did,' Cullen said sombrely. 'I am not telling you any of this for absolution or in hopes of you softening it for me. I simply want you to know why I can't stay, why there must be distance between us. Death by duel is murder even if the courts are not likely to apply the term. I won't sugar-coat it. I murdered the Earl of Southberry's heir in order to save myself.' His throat tightened. After all these years he still couldn't talk of it, think of it without emotion. 'If I could take back those seconds, if I could stop my hand on the trigger, I would.'

Antonia came to him, not with her body, or her touch.

Perhaps she knew physical contact would bring him to his knees. She came to him with her eyes, those green flames locked on him, her words soft but stern with the command, 'Tell me.'

Cullen closed his eyes, but it didn't stop him from re-living every moment as vividly as if it were yesterday. 'He was nervous. I'd seen his hand shake when he'd picked up the pistol. He was younger than me by a couple years and in over his head. When it came to worldly living I definitely had the edge. But when it came to righteous indignation, he had me there. He was furious about his sister and what he perceived was my despicable behaviour towards her. If he could shoot me, he would. The real issue was the question of his talent. Did he have the skill, the cool hand and head to make the shot? Or would he delope and feel satisfied? He was an unknown commodity to me and I wasn't sure what he'd do.'

He paused and opened his eyes. 'Keir was my second. When step nineteen was called, Keir saw him turn. He cried out a warning. I pivoted on my heel, and let in-stinct, let self-preservation take over. I fired. The shot took him in the thigh and, two days later, he died.'

'Keir was your second?' Antonia's eyes had widened.

'Keir saved my life that day and in the days that fol-lowed. He was the one who got me on a ship and out of the country before anyone might think to arrest me. He was the one who sent me to the South Seas.' He gave a short chuckle. 'Even in the midst of crisis, he believed in me. He turned that crisis into an opportunity. It got me through the shock of what had transpired, of what I'd participated in.'

'Thank you for telling me,' was all she said for a long while. When she did speak again, it was out of concern for him. 'Can you still be arrested?'

'Technically, I suppose so, but I doubt anyone has that kind of interest in the event. Southberry cannot push any legal claims without risk of exposing himself or his daughter. Legal claims must be investigated and proven with incontrovertible evidence. Southberry would not risk it. Nor would he risk standing up publicly against the Marquess of Standon and the Duke of Cowden.'

'Then what is there to worry about?' Antonia asked bluntly.

'Gossip. Rumours. This might not be tried in the court of law, but it most assuredly will be tried in the court of scandal where things need only to be spoken of to be breathed into being. They don't need to be proven. Keir and Southberry's heir might be dead, but there are others: the other second, the doctor, the house servants at Southberry House, the gentlemen at the club the night the challenge was issued.

'It was no secret we were going to duel. Plenty of people knew. Twenty men must have heard us, but they were only party to the public story: that I was refusing to marry an honourable earl's daughter. I was already the villain, having eschewed *ton*nish life for life with Keir in trade. I was only at the club to meet with my brother in some attempt to negotiate a way out of the situation. I was already "the Notorious Lord Cullen Allardyce"—this just added to my notoriety.'

He took the chair across from her, slouching. Telling the story had come with its own mental exhaustion and there was still the fallout to deal with. 'Do you understand now why I can't stay? How I have put you at risk? Once that story starts to circulate, reminding people why I've been away, you will be attached to the scandal, too.'

'It has not hurt business before,' Antonia was quick to point out and his heart swelled at her effort to protect him when he was the one who ought to be protecting her, had in fact been sent for to do just that. Now the shoe was on the other foot.

'Then, Keir was the face of the business. I was a silent partner and the *ton* does not pay much attention to trade. Keir handled the bankers, so I was of little consequence except to him. It was very much a case of out of sight, out of mind. You know how society works, a scandal only lasts until the next one rolls along. But now I *am* the next scandal. Notorious Lord Cullen Allardyce, too wild for London, raking around the South Seas half-naked with long hair and a tattoo.'

'I see. I can't be at the public helm of the company and neither can you. I am scandalous because I'm a woman in business and you are scandalous...'

'Because I am me. Yes, your analysis is correct.'

He watched her think for a moment. 'I've heard it said that any publicity is good publicity. Perhaps this works in our favour. We open the store, the story gets around about your return and people flock to the store to get a look at you. And then once they see that you're not so notorious after all and once they see that a woman can run a department store, all this will be forgotten.' It sounded overly optimistic, even for her. He wished it could be so, but it was too much of a fairy tale to hope for. Some day a world where such an ending was possible might exist, but not yet.

She rose. 'You've given me much to think about, but not tonight.' She extended her hand. 'Come to bed, Cullen. I do my best thinking in the morning.'

He took her hand and let her lead, but not before their eyes met, communicating silently what they refused to say out loud, but what must be mutually understood. This would be the last time. The end had come.

Chapter Eighteen

Antonia had known he'd be gone in the morning. It had been implicitly agreed upon and the knowledge had underscored the slow, savoured lovemaking that had lingered through what remained of the night. But knowing had not prepared her for how it felt to wake up without him. He was not in her bed, his warm body wrapped around hers, nor was there any sign of him in their room, no reminders that he'd ever been here. His clothes were gone, the trifle dish where he kept his cuff links was empty. It was like waking from a dream one had thought was real, only to discover it wasn't. Had he even been here at all?

It was for the best that he was gone. This was only ever meant to be a fling, a chance to put mourning behind her, to prove to herself that she could move on. She rationalised it all as Randal helped her dress. She'd known it would hurt, she'd been aware that she'd engaged her heart despite her best advice to self that she not do that nor was she required to do that. She'd done it anyway.

If she felt sadness over the end of the affair, she had only herself to blame. She'd been warned. It would pass.

The affair had been temporary. She would get over it. She *would* get over him. In the long run she would be glad for the distance. She understood the reasons for it. It had not been done unfeelingly, but out of a need for protection so that Keir's legacy could go forward untarnished.

All of this excellent, logical reasoning got her downstairs, but it was no match for the newspapers that waited beside her breakfast plate. The society pages had not wasted a moment picking up on Lady Camford's ball. *Waltzing into Scandal!* declared one page. *An Alliance with a Notorious Lord!* another touted. They would have made her laugh if they hadn't been about her.

Antonia scanned each of the articles. That beautiful waltz, those precious heady moments, had been reduced to gossip fodder. But it could have been worse. Neither story had brought up the old scandal. There was no mention of the duel, of jilting Southberry's daughter. There was only the mention that Lord Cullen Allardyce, known for his notorious exploits about town and his scandalous tendency to work for a living, had been spotted at Lady Camford's ball after a ten-year absence from English shores where it was posited that he'd lived and traded among the indigenous peoples of Tahiti.

She took a swallow of hot coffee. Yes, it could have been worse. There was hope in the fact that it wasn't. An idea came to her. What if she could keep the newspapers' attentions turned on other issues besides Cullen? Idle hands were the devil's workshop, as the saying went. Perhaps the same could be said of idle minds in the press. If she could keep those minds full of other things, they might overlook pursuing more about Cullen.

Antonia read the articles again, something else striking her. The articles had mentioned her only once as Cullen's dance partner and had said nothing about the store. That was where the attention ought to be. They'd attended the ball to promote the store. If she could get Fleur to help, her idea might help them both.

She sought out writing materials and dashed off a quick note to her friend, asking for an appointment later that morning at the *Tribune* where Fleur had taken over in the wake of her husband's death. Fleur might not have time to socialise, but she always had time to discuss business.

'Antonia! It is so good to see you.' Fleur came around the desk in the editor-in-chief's office to envelop her in a hug. 'Look at you! Yellow was always a good colour for you. You look wonderful.'

Fleur smiled, genuinely pleased to see her. Fleur was always authentic, she never faked emotion even when she should. She was dressed in grey serge with white cuffs, an apron over her bodice and skirts. For half-mourning or out of workplace necessity? Antonia wondered.

'Come in, how can I help you? You must be swamped with the store getting ready to open. I have reporters assigned to the gala tomorrow night and to opening day.' Fleur was a whirlwind, hardly drawing a breath.

'You are a marvel, Fleur. Editor of the newspaper? Head of the publishing house? Two jobs in one. I'm impressed,' Antonia complimented, looking around the cherrywood-panelled office done in deep greens and cream with its polished bookcases, plaques denoting accolades hung on the walls and long windows with a view of the street. It was a professional, masculine domain. But it was a woman who sat behind the desk these days. 'Do you ever sleep?'

Fleur laughed and tucked an auburn curl behind one ear. She flashed a smile. 'That's rich coming from you, the business magnate running an import-export company, overseeing property investments *and* opening a department store.' She paused for a rare moment. 'And yet you went dancing last night. Is that why you're here? Do you need me to investigate your mystery partner?'

It took Antonia a second to realise Fleur didn't know she'd not met Cullen at the ball. She glanced down at her hands briefly. 'It wasn't the first time we'd met. He's not a mystery to me.' She was fumbling for words and making a hash of it as she tried not to give too much away. 'He's been here since February. He was Keir's silent partner. We've been trying to sort some business things out—contracts, things like that.' She was talking too much now, overexplaining and overjustifying.

She stopped and clenched her hands together in her lap. She drew a deep breath to reorientate herself. 'I am here because I am wondering if you could run a story tomorrow about me. Perhaps a human interest story about me and the store. You already know me so it would just be a matter of writing it up. I know it's short notice, but it would focus everyone on the gala tomorrow night.'

Fleur leaned across the wide desk, reaching for her hands and taking them in her own. 'Of course I'll do it. We've been friends a long time. I'll do anything I can to help your endeavour succeed. What good is it to run a publishing empire if you can't use it to help your friends? But will you answer a question for me in return?'

Antonia hesitated a moment too long. 'It's just about publicity for the store.'

Fleur gave her a strong stare. 'Not deflection? You want this story to draw people's attention away from the notorious Lord Cullen Allardyce waltzing you about the ballroom last night? Deflection would be good for both of you.'

Antonia sat up a bit straighter, feeling put on alert. 'You'll have to explain that to me, I'm afraid.' She'd not been ready to discuss him with anyone. She'd rather liked having him all to herself. He was her secret.

'You're mixing business with pleasure. How long do you think it will be before someone figures out what you just told me—that he is your deceased husband's business partner? Waltzing is not signing contracts.'

'We were at the ball to promote the store. We thought it might be a good idea to be seen together for business reasons,' Antonia explained.

Fleur nodded. 'You were thinking that his face and his name would shore up any questions about the company being in good hands. It's a sound strategy even if it's unfortunate we have to take such measures at all. Or it would be sound if he was the partner you needed. Is that it?'

Antonia said nothing, not wanting to impugn Cullen. Fleur gave a dry laugh. 'He's a walking scandal, isn't he? When a man is gone for ten years without a word, there's a reason, usually a pretty big one. So now, here you are, with a silent partner who cannot publicly be of

use to you, and you cannot get the credit you deserve.'
In more ways than one. Antonia thought of the bank
and their attempt to foreclose on her early.

'I think it will help if people are reminded that the
store is Keir's legacy. That I am finishing this for him.'

'And Allardyce? Where will he fit in to all of this?'
Fleur persisted.

'He will go back to Tahiti once the store is open and
our new partnership agreement is signed. Society will
forget about him.' But she wouldn't.

'Will the company survive once your investors realise he's gone?'

'Will it survive once they realise the depth of his
scandal if it comes out?' Antonia countered. Fleur had
already guessed there was one, she needn't go into detail.

'You're damned if you do and damned if you don't.'
Fleur gave a sigh of sympathy.

'I did meet with the Duke of Cowden and I do think
I'll have some support for the company from the Pro-
metheus Club even if Cullen is a partner only on paper.
I am optimistic,' Antonia said.

Fleur smiled. 'Of course you are.' Silence stretched a
bit too long. Fleur played with a paperweight. 'You called
him Cullen,' she said quietly. 'You've become close? Is
there a chance that waltz was more than a waltz?' Fleur
stared and Antonia knew her face had betrayed her.

Fleur nodded in realisation. 'Dear Heavens, Antonia,
you've taken a lover. Well, that explains the glow.' Then
she gave a heavy sigh. 'You could have chosen a more
discreet lover. You don't want word of this to get out. It
will destroy whatever bit of credibility you have—sleep-

ing with your husband's business partner who comes with his own full-blown scandal already included.'

Antonia chewed her lip. 'I know it sounds bad, especially when you put it that way, but it won't get out. He's leaving. He'll be half a world away. I'll likely never see him again.' The enormity of that finally swept her. She'd been ignoring it all morning, all last night, burying the realisation with practical concerns like the gala and Cullen's revelations. It was not, she realised, unlike the way she'd handled Keir's death—burying it beneath work, burying it so deeply she didn't have to face it. But now, Fleur was forcing the issue.

Fleur's face softened. 'Oh, my dear girl, you love him.'

'Yes, yes, I think I do.' Antonia swiped at her tears. 'But it doesn't matter. He has to leave. He can't stay.'

'Do you think he feels the same way about you?' Fleur asked hesitantly. 'I know it's a delicate question. Sometimes love only runs one way in these affairs.'

'You mean when a woman loves a rake?' Antonia gave a watery smile. 'He has not said as much, but I do think he cares for me, deeply.' She thought of the many things he'd done for her since his arrival. He'd delayed his return to Tahiti, he'd fired Mackleson for her, he'd helped her through her grief when she could not help herself. Sometimes actions spoke louder than words.

She'd seen the genuine look of regret and hurt on his face last night as he'd shared his scandal. He'd not wanted to tell her, but telling her had been done out of love, out of a desire to protect her so that she was not ambushed by it, so that she understood what needed to happen next and why. But she did not tell Fleur that.

Last night was still too new, too private, and it was not her story to share.

'If he feels the same way, why not go with him?' Fleur posited. Fleur could not know how those words gave life to her own nascent fantasy. She'd been captivated by Cullen's stories of Tahiti, of the sun and sand and white beaches of palm trees and fruits she'd never tasted, of turquoise waters, waterfalls and warm lagoons, a place where cold winters and soot-filled skies became fictions. To be in such a place with Cullen would be Paradise. But Paradise had a cost.

She shook her head. 'It's impossible, Fleur. There's the store to think of and the company. I must be here to oversee everything.'

'If it's an anchor about your neck that is keeping you from happiness, then perhaps you should sell it. Sell it all, Antonia.'

The thought bordered on heretical. 'I couldn't. Keir spent his life building all this.' She couldn't even begin to wrap her head around the idea of selling the company, the ships, the warehouses, the property spread around town, the town house, the store she'd just fought so hard for.

'Are you to spend your life being a dead man's caretaker?' Fleur did not mince words. 'Who is this legacy for, Antonia? There is no son or daughter you are holding this for.' Antonia heard the anger and the truth in Fleur's words. There'd once been hope that Fleur might be carrying Adam's child, someone to take over Adam's empire. Sadly, it was not to be.

Antonia looked about the office. 'Would you sell the newspapers, the publishing house?'

'I think it is different for me. I am not in love and facing separation, risking a second chance at happiness,' Fleur said honestly. She steepled her hands. 'I'm sorry. I've made you uncomfortable. I'll write up the story immediately and make sure it runs in the evening edition. I'll talk about who you are and remind people of all of your and Keir's philanthropic work in the city. It will do what you hope. And I'll see you tomorrow night at the gala. We can drink Emma's champagne and celebrate your success.'

Antonia rose. 'Thank you, Fleur.' She smiled and hugged her friend goodbye. It had been good to see her, good to talk to someone at last, but it had not given her the clarity she'd been hoping for. She could not be distracted by such things at the moment. She had a heart to mend. She'd best mend it by tomorrow night when she saw him again. People would see them together and she couldn't afford to give anything away. She had a store to open.

Chapter Nineteen

She was at the store helping with last-minute displays in the ladies' department when the evening news came, delivered in person by Cullen, which was a surprise in itself. She had not been expecting him. After last night, she'd not thought to see him until the store gala tomorrow and, even then, she'd only thought to see him here-after in a professional capacity. From the stormy look on his face, something more had happened. She tried not to panic. It could be anything—a problem at the ware-house perhaps? But in the back of her mind, she knew the look on his face was not commensurate to a prob-lem at the warehouse.

She set aside the lacy underthings she was folding and went to him, drawing him aside before he could draw too much attention from the other clerks working nearby. 'What is it? What's happened?'

Cullen slapped down the papers beneath his arm. 'This is what has happened, what I told you would hap-pen. Someone has dug up the scandal. The society pages are full of it. Except the *Tribune*, which had the good sense to cover the real story.'

Antonia flipped through the *Tribune* first, noting the

half-page story about Popplewell's Department Store and the Popplewell legacy, just as Fleur had promised. Then she flipped through the other papers and grimaced.

More than one ambitious reporter had gone straight to work after last night's ball, not content to simply note Cullen Allardyce's return. Three other papers had dragged out the scandal in some part. No one paper had the whole story and none had it right. Antonia tried to look for the silver lining. 'Most of this is just speculation.'

'The average reader doesn't make the distinction between speculation and fact,' Cullen said grimly.

'The *Tribune* has a wider circulation than these papers. Perhaps that story will offset the others.' She said it for herself as much for him. She gave a heavy sigh. 'I know how damning this is, Cullen, for you, for us and for the store, I won't pretend otherwise. But I *will* hope, because what else can I do?' She held his gaze, wanting to lend him some of that hope. He was grimmer than he'd been even last night.

'There's something else.' He reached for her hands—deliberately or out of reflex? Was he finding it as hard as she was to transition back into being partners only? It was difficult being this close to him and not touching him. Only they were touching now and that made it even worse. His touch reminded her of other touches, touches she would never have again from him.

'Have you thought of going with him?'

Fleur's heresy came to mind. She pushed it back and tried to focus on the next crisis. There was a new cut above his eye, she noticed just then, and she wondered if that next crisis had something to do with it.

'I found Mackleson lurking in the unloading yard when I came in. I dispatched him.'

'Violently, it appears. He took a swing at you.' She couldn't help but raise a gentle finger to the cut. 'Does it hurt? Do you need ice?' Then she remembered he was a brawler. It was how he and Keir had met.

'Ow.' He flinched. 'It doesn't hurt unless *someone* touches it. I'm fine. He looks worse.'

'What was he doing here?'

'I don't know. I looked around, I didn't find anything out of order. He's gone now.'

She knew he meant to be reassuring, but it wasn't. 'Gone where, though? Do you think he'll come back? Do you think he'll try something disruptive at the gala? Do you think he'll go to a reporter and tell some story about how you beat him up? That would be damning because it would fit with the apparent history of violence associated with you and it would make the rumours easier to believe.'

Cullen shook his head. 'I don't know. I will tell everyone to be vigilant about strangers though, just in case. The loading bays and the yard will be busy and well populated tomorrow night. It would be easy for someone to slip past unnoticed.'

'That worries me,' Antonia confessed. 'We'll have a lot of important people here. I don't want them to be in danger.' Doubt crossed his face, and she retraced her thoughts. 'Do you think we won't? Do you think the gossip will deter our guests from coming?' It was a horrible thought. To be so close to the finish line and then to falter, to be brought down by rumours before they even had a chance.

She gathered her resolve and every ounce of optimism

she possessed. 'No, I think people can't stay away from a rumour. They'll come to see if it's true, to judge for themselves.'

'You will need more than one night of success.' There it was. *You.* No longer *we.* No longer *us* or *our.*

'When are you leaving?' She swallowed hard. Asking the question made it real, no longer a theoretical date on an invisible calendar.

'I stopped at the ticket office on the docks this morning. There's a ship that sails the day after tomorrow.'

This morning. He'd gone from her bed to the ticket office. Her heart sank. Perhaps she'd been a bit too optimistic when she'd told Fleur she thought he felt the same. 'You wasted no time.' She tried for a smile. 'You did not want to wait until after opening day?' Had he picked that day because he knew she couldn't possibly see him off? She'd be needed here from open to close and hours before and after.

'I thought it best that I be gone as soon as possible.' He gestured to the newspapers. 'I think I was right. The store doesn't need me anywhere near it. I am wondering if I should even come tomorrow night.'

Anger flared. She tamped it down. 'People would be disappointed. You might be the main attraction.'

'If I am, I am sorry for it, Antonia. Sorrier than you know,' he said gently. 'I only meant to help.' He gave a rueful smile.

'You *have* helped, in ways I can't begin to express,' she argued.

'I should go.'

If she didn't tell him now, she might lose her chance.

The ship might not sail until the day after tomorrow, but it was clear that in many ways he was already leaving. There might not be another opportunity to be alone with him without interruption.

'No, you should come with me. We are not done with our conversation.' She drew him into a storage room, the most privacy she could arrange on short notice. The storage room was filled with boxes and she wished she could have done better. She'd never dreamed she'd be having one of the most important discussions of her life surrounded by lacy underthings.

'Antonia, I don't think this is a good idea,' Cullen moved a box of French stays aside and took a seat on the packing crate. He knew what she wanted. It was what he wanted, too. He simply couldn't give it to her. All he could give her was bad news, bad press. Wasn't today's taste of that proof enough? And this was just the start. It would get much worse.

'I disagree. I think it's a great idea. We've talked about what the store needs, but we haven't talked about what I need. I need you. I need you to be here tomorrow night to help me handle everything. I did not do this alone. You helped me finish the store. You fired Mackleson. You got the inventory moved from the warehouse. You got Cowden to manage the loan for us.'

She was making him out to be a hero when what he'd actually done was put her ambitions in jeopardy. Her eyes shone with their green fire. He wished he was worthy of it. She stepped towards him, and his thighs parted of their own accord to accommodate her so that she could stand between them. It was the last thing he should have done. He needed distance, he did not need to be touching her. It only reminded him of all he couldn't have. Her arms wrapped loosely around his neck and he had the suspicion she had already made a decision unilaterally.

'You have been an integral part of this. I can't stand in front of the guests tomorrow night and pretend it was all me, not when Cowden knows the difference. It would make me a liar.' He watched her throat work as she swallowed. 'I promised I'd let you go when the time came, Cullen. I mean to honour that, but I have to ask: do you really believe we are done, that there is nothing more we can give each other?'

He was aware that his own arms were about her waist, that her hips were tucked firmly against his groin and his body did not believe for a moment that this conversation was neutral. 'How am I supposed to answer that, Antonia?'

'Truthfully.' When had their mouths come to be so close that each word was nearly a kiss? That a whisper was all that was needed in order to be heard?

'I need to leave England. I need to be forgotten in order for you to thrive here. I can be the most help to you if I return to Tahiti.'

'And we exchange letters twice a year?' There was some heat to those words. He silenced them with his mouth.

'You'll be fine. I've signed all of Bowdrie's paperwork. My name is on all the financials,' he managed to say between slow kisses. Her hands were in his hair, now, her tongue teasing his lips, making talk more difficult.

Her hand reached for the fastenings of his trousers. It would be tempting to let her have her way, to make naughty, half-dressed love in the storage room knowing someone could walk in at any time—which would put paid to both of their reputations for good—but he couldn't allow it. He covered her hand, stalling her progress. 'One more time won't change anything, Antonia. We decided that last night. We are just prolonging our hurt.'

'Our hurt? Or just my hurt?' She stepped back, but her temper flared. He adjusted his trousers. Maybe a fight was what they needed to establish some distance. 'If you believe in us, why won't you fight for us?'

Did she truly not realise she was breaking his heart? 'I *am* fighting for us, Antonia. I am fighting for you, I am giving you every chance you wanted and I am sorry that I am imperfect, that I'm not Keir. That I am not enough.'

It was the story of his life. He'd not been enough for his father and now he was not enough for Antonia, the woman he loved. The realisation that he loved her was like a thunderbolt and the reality of it sizzled through him, but not the surprise. The reality was that he'd loved her long before this moment. He'd simply not been willing to name it.

He could see she wanted to argue. He moved towards the storeroom door with a shake of his head. 'You don't have to say anything. You don't have to disagree. I don't belong in your world. I belong in mine and after tomorrow night, that's where I'll be.' In Tahiti, where he was Kanoa, the Seeker. The one place in the world where he was enough.

'What if I belong in your world?' Antonia challenged softly, her words stopping his hand on the door. God, he loved her optimism, her hope that somehow all the imperfect pieces of the world could be made to fit together.

He glanced back at her briefly. 'I would never ask it of you.' He slipped out the door, quashing the fantasy that flared in his mind of them on the beach at Ha'apape, her hair down, a hibiscus tucked behind an ear, the warm water gently lapping at their bare feet. There was no time for dwelling on impossibilities, not when there was real work to do.

He had people to visit to ensure tomorrow's gala was a success, starting with Frederick and Cowden and the Prometheus Club members. If they came, others would follow. Cowden would use his leverage to strong-arm attendance if needed and Frederick would know just how much damage the news stories had done to drive away invitees. It was the least and last thing he could do for Antonia.

Chapter Twenty

Cullen checked his pocket watch as he made a surreptitious tour of the exterior of the building. Twenty minutes to go. Popplewell's would open at eight o'clock for the evening gala. A sense of relief filled him at the sight of the front of the building. A red carpet had been rolled out for the occasion and carriages had been delivering guests for the last half-hour. People had come and were coming. Guests stood on Antonia's red carpet, sipping chilled champagne, the party starting even before the doors opened, everyone admiring in advance the giant crystal chandelier that hung in the entrance and was clearly visible from the outside.

Cullen smiled to himself as he went around back for one last check of the unloading yard. His evening visit with Cowden and making the club rounds with Frederick, even though it meant significant personal exposure of himself, had paid off. He'd not been sure it would until this moment. This morning, there'd still been some cancellations. Not everyone had been persuaded to overlook the rumours and still make an appearance.

He'd been partly right that the rumours would put some people off. But Antonia had been right, too. Some people couldn't stay away from scandal. There'd also been others this morning who were jockeying for a last-minute invitation and Antonia had been more than happy to accommodate, or so he'd been told. He'd not seen her since last night. They both had separate obligations to complete today if the gala was to go off well. Separation was for the best, though, if they couldn't keep their hands off each other.

Cullen surveyed the unloading yard, sweeping it with his eyes for any security concerns. He nodded to the men stationed there. 'Anything to report?' he asked.

'No, Sir. There was a bit of an altercation earlier while the caterers unloaded some food, but we sorted it out, just some drivers fighting over who got to bring their wagon in first.'

Cullen used the door at the rear of the building to let himself in. Despite Antonia's insistence that he be here, he'd debated coming tonight all day. Would he do Antonia more harm or good by coming or by staying away? If he came, he might inadvertently reignite the notice he hoped to avoid. But if he didn't come, she'd be on her own.

That had decided it. Who would stand with her if reporters asked tough questions? If one of the many investors with Popplewell and Allardyce voiced concerns about her ability to sit at the helm of the company? Or what if simply one of a thousand things went wrong? She couldn't be everywhere at once, putting out little fires. She had to be the gracious hostess, greeting guests and giving every appearance of enjoying her own party as if she hadn't a care in the world, as if this project hadn't been a year in the making. In the end he decided it would look odd, as if there was indeed something to hide if he was absent from his company's own grand opening. Besides, she would need him for moral support if nothing else.

Inside, it was organised chaos. He strode through the first floor where the hat and glove counters gleamed, their glass-paned display cabinets clear without a smear or fingerprint on them, the merchandise inside them laid out in exacting perfection: gloves were fanned out to show each colour available, jewellery glinted. The displays were captivating, drawing the eye so that each department was a feast for the senses. It had taken weeks to get the goods unpacked and arranged. The time had paid off. There was even a section that showcased the goods imported from Tahiti. It was beautifully done with rattan furniture and tropical fixtures so that shoppers might feel they were in Tahiti itself.

Cullen fingered one of the delicate shell bracelets on display. That had been the dream, hadn't it? To bring the world together—the woman on the beach who'd gathered the shells and strung them with the woman in faraway England who would wear the bracelet and dream of another place. He picked up a carved statue. Or the little boy who might put this statue in his room and be inspired to learn about where it came from, where that place was on a map and perhaps some day he might go there; some day in a future where it didn't take months to make the journey.

Already travel time had dropped from six months to three. Already, it was no longer necessary to go around the Cape. He knew there were plans to make the Steam Route even more efficient. There were men who were dreaming of a canal in Egypt. It would make the process a journey of weeks instead of months. He'd spoken with Cowden about it, last night. He'd like to be part of that process when the time was right. He set the carved figure down. This was how change was made. One generation at a time. Not for the first time, he wished his father understood that. Cowden did.

He moved on to the men's department, decorated like a gentleman's club with its walnut panelling, dark maroon wallpaper and tall leather-covered wingback chairs. Artwork featuring riding to the hunt hung on the walls. He focused on the decor; no detail had been spared. It was better this way, better to keep his mind busy with thoughts of the future—the trip back, the chance to meet with some men in Cairo on the return. A busy mind meant no time to think about Antonia, to think about the things she'd said last night in the storage room.

'What if I belonged in your world?'

But she belonged in this world. This was what she'd worked for.

He stopped to talk with the clerks, dressed in well-tailored suits that complemented the quality of goods they offered for sale. He gave a smile and encouragement, a piece of advice where needed. He'd helped Antonia train many of them. He knew them by name. 'Remember to let gentlemen know they can get all of their wardrobe handled here. We can keep their measurements on file so they can have something made up quickly, or so that we can find something of excellent quality for them already on the rack,' he coached.

'You look sharp, gentlemen. You'll be meeting men tonight who will appreciate that. They don't want to be served by someone who is slovenly—' He broke off in mid-speech, feeling the energy of the department shift. He looked about and found the source of the distraction.

Antonia stood there, dressed in an ice-blue gown whose skirts shimmered when she moved, like light on snow. She wore her diamonds at her ears, her neck, the bangle about her gloved wrist, her golden hair pinned up as it had been at Lady Camford's. Had it only been two nights ago that he'd held this enchantress in his arms on the dance floor? It seemed a lifetime ago. She swept forward.

'Gentlemen, you do us proud. By the end of the week, Popplewell's will have a reputation for the most handsome clerks in the City.' She held out her hand to him. 'Mr Allardyce, it's time. Shall we go greet our guests?'

He tucked her hand into his elbow and felt her tremble. 'Nervous?'

'Yes.' Antonia laughed and then sobered. 'Do you think Keir would like it? Would he be pleased with the store?'

'Absolutely. He'd be so incredibly proud of you, Antonia.' As he was. For the first time in a long while, he thought, everything was going to be all right. The last words he whispered to her before the doors opened were, 'You are beautiful, too.' He would hold this picture of her in his mind, of his lovely, fierce Antonia, when he was back in his world.

They received the guests together as if they were hosting a grand ball, sending each group off with a guide to offer a tour of the building, making sure the guide highlighted departments of special interest to each guest. Cullen made a mental note that several guests were the men he and Frederick had talked with at the clubs. Frederick and Helena passed through the receiving line, Helena gushing over how elegant everything looked, the string quartet playing from one corner so that everyone could shop by music. When Cullen asked about Cowden and the Duchess, Frederick promised his father would be along later.

Eventually, Cullen had to leave Antonia's side. They needed to mingle, he with the men and she with the women. He was in the men's department, shaking hands and keeping an ear out for any conversation he needed to nip in the bud, when a familiar but cold voice spoke behind him. 'So, this is what you've been up to instead of visiting family.'

Cullen turned, stiff and startled, but ready. 'Father, what a surprise. I was unaware you were in town.' It was only a bit of a surprise. With all the newspaper coverage, he'd half expected it, assuming his father was indeed in town, something he'd not bothered to ascertain for himself.

'As I was you.' His father's tones were as pointed as ever, his tone highlighting all nature of disappointment. Cowden was with him and Cullen understood the situation immediately. This was the Duke's doing. This was why Cowden had come late. He couldn't blame Cowden for trying. The man meant well.

Cowden gave a broad smile, purposely ignoring the tension between the two men. 'When a man's son pulls off something as spectacular as this, one doesn't want to miss it.' He extended his hand to Cullen. 'The store is spectacular. The Duchess is going to want to redecorate the town house after seeing this.'

'Well, if she does, our house goods and furnishings department stands ready to assist.' Cullen shook the man's hand. 'Have you seen the teak furniture we have from Tahiti? One-of-a-kind pieces.'

'You've become quite the trader,' his father drawled, his eyes sharp on him. There were wrinkles around those eyes, more than Cullen remembered, and grey hair that went beyond the temples.

'It's the way of the world these days, Standon,' Cowden put in jovially. 'The aristocracy isn't what it used to be. It's the beginning of the end of life as we knew it. Besides, a man shouldn't make his fortune living off the backs of others. It's exciting, too, don't you think? So much potential to explore, a chance to recraft our legacies. Self-made men like your son are the future.'

But not even for the sake of the Duke's approval would his father bend. He merely gave a short nod of his head. 'A gentleman never goes out of style, Cowden.'

'Let me show you the section dedicated to the South Seas and you can tell me how Mother is,' Cullen intervened. 'Did she come tonight?'

His father scowled. 'To something as plebian as this? A merchant's trade show? I should think not. You can dress it up with crystal chandeliers and champagne, but that's what it is. If you wanted to see any of us, you could have called at the house where it is appropriate.'

Cullen exchanged a look with Cowden. He was glad Antonia hadn't heard the remark. It would have devastated her. This was her palace, the place she'd sunk her heart and soul into; her happiness, her grief, all of it had been poured into this and tonight was meant to be her triumph. As far as he could tell, the triumph was well under way. He would not let his father steal that from her all for the sake of their personal feud.

He was showing Cowden and his father a teak desk when he heard the first scream, followed by another. He looked up at the wide staircase leading to the third floor, women spilling down it, awkward in their wide skirts. Someone fell. Good God, there was going to be stampede. Then he smelled it. Smoke! 'Cowden, take my father, get out of the building.' Cowden hesitated, no doubt thinking of Helena and the Duchess. 'If they're upstairs, I'll see to them; if they're not, they're already safe.' He gave Cowden a push. 'Go, please.'

Whatever was happening, was happening on the third floor. Antonia was up there. He knew he'd never make headway on the crowded staircase, so he darted for the backstairs the clerks took when they hauled inventory, taking the steps two at a time. When he reached the floor, shrieking chaos was in progress. Flames raced up the elegant floor-length draperies until they were sheets of fire, rapidly spreading to the wallpaper.

He spied her in the thick of things, helping women to the stairs, encouraging people to stay calm. But it was a losing battle. People were pushing and panicking.

'Antonia!' He cut through the crowd, desperate to reach her. The fire was spreading with alarming speed, the air filling with smoke. A third-floor fire would be difficult to reach with water and hoses. Someone pushed at him in their haste and he nearly tripped. The place was in full stampede now out of fear the fire would chase them down—and the greater fear that the fire would outrun them. He watched in horror as Antonia fell and struggled to get up. She fell again. He clawed his way to her side, shielding her with his bulk until he could get her on her feet. The last of the guests were gone from the floor, the smoke thick now. 'We must hurry.' He glanced around at the destruction—where beauty had reigned just hours ago in immaculate displays there was now only disaster. Flames licked at dress forms, tore through bolts of fragile fabric. The third floor was lost.

'Steady on, we'll get out of this,' he said fiercely, his voice hoarse. 'Whatever you do, don't look back.'

Too late. She glanced over her shoulder and saw it all—the fire eating up everything, the beautiful, carefully arranged floor where a woman might shop and find feminine sanctuary burning with abandon. Whatever might be saved, it would be nothing here. Fabrics were incinerated, the creamy fixtures marred with ashes and soot and the ravages of flames, a dream going up in smoke.

Her eyes stung with smoke, with tears of loss. She never looked back and tonight she'd broken her cardinal rule. That was when she stumbled, her ankle twisting in her skirts before Cullen caught her. She hobbled once. Cullen swore and swept her up into his arms.

'Turn your head into my chest, you'll be able to breath better,' he instructed as he descended the staircase. But she couldn't look away, her gaze riveted on the conflagration burning over his shoulder.

There was only smoke on the second floor and Antonia thought there might be some hope, after all. If the fire brigade came quickly enough the fire might be contained. They might save something. Empty of people, the floor was eerily quiet as if it was already resigned to its fate, all the beautiful furniture prepared to be sacrificed as kindling to the fire that raged above. But then came a crack and the roar of flame as the ceiling began to falter, flame licking through in hot, red, streams.

Cullen's grip on her tightened and he lumbered into an awkward run, burdened as he was with her weight. That was when she knew: they were going to lose the whole building. She turned her face against his chest, the first sob breaking loose as he reached for the last flight of stairs and fresh air.

Outside, Helena and Fleur ran to her. 'I think she's hurt her ankle. She took a fall.' Cullen set her down gingerly, but she clung to him, instinctively knowing he meant to leave, to turn back towards the danger.

'Stay with me,' she said fiercely, gripping his lapels. His face was sweaty and streaked with smoke and ash. She felt Fleur and Helena try to disengage her. No. She would not let go. There were two nightmares in her mind now: the sight of her beloved store in flames and the night of the flood—the night she'd let Keir go, how she'd unwittingly given him up without a fight. She would not make the same mistake twice.

'I have to join the men, Antonia. Every hand is needed if we are to save the building.' He peeled her dirty, gloved hands from his lapels with gentle force. 'Let me go fight for you.' She felt Fleur's arms about her and then he was off, running to join the newly arrived fire brigade. It would be all right. He would man a hose and it would be all right, she repeated, never letting him out of her sight as Fleur and Helena helped her to a place where she might sit. But then it wasn't. A cry went up and there was a commotion at the front of the hose line, men gathering around, Cullen among them, and then Cullen darted into the building.

She exchanged a horrified look with Fleur. Fleur was on her feet before Antonia even had to ask. 'I'll find out what's happened.' But Antonia knew what had happened. Cullen had run back into a burning building and for the second time she stood to lose the man she loved.

The minutes passed like hours as she waited for Fleur, as she waited for Cullen to reappear. The fire seemed to be getting worse, the dark flames lighting up the London night sky. Why was it getting worse? Why wasn't the water having any effect? Perhaps it was only her imagination. She had too much at stake. Damn her ankle. She was tired of waiting. She was grateful for Helena's grip on her hand.

Fleur returned breathless, her face pale. 'Someone reported a clerk was still inside, in the second-floor stairwell. Apparently, too panicked to move.' Too frightened to think rationally, Antonia thought. 'Cullen went in after her.' Her mind immediately went to the image of the second-floor ceiling slowly cracking apart with a river of flame.

'He'll be trapped in there; the ceiling was going to go,' she murmured, mostly to herself. Beams would fall, charred timbers would block off exit points. She squeezed her eyes shut, trying to shut away the images of Cullen overcome with smoke, or worse, burned alive by flame.

'Don't think about it,' Fleur whispered and hugged her close. Surely the fates would not be so cruel as to take both men from her. She would give up everything to see him safe—the store, the company, her reputation. She didn't care what the papers wrote, what scandals they unearthed or if he sailed for Tahiti without her. She only cared that Cullen walked out of the inferno alive, because knowing he was alive in some part of the world was better than knowing he was dead in hers.

A cry went up at the entrance and Antonia strained to see. She rose, leaning on Helena and Fleur. A man emerged, tall and broad, a black-clad woman in his arms. Profound relief swept her and she sagged against Fleur. 'It's him. He's all right. Help me get to him.'

It took a while to reach him. Cullen was the hero of the hour, having rescued the trapped shop clerk from the stairwell. She reached him with her eyes before she could make her way through the crowd. He saw her and began to move, cutting through the crush and taking her in his arms. 'I'm all right, I'm here,' he murmured into her hair, and she held on to him for dear life. How would she ever let him go in the morning?

Chapter Twenty-One

Morning was a subjective term. They didn't leave the fire until after three that morning. And they only left then because it was impossible to see anything of merit in the dark and because the town house was only a couple of streets away. They could rest, recover and return. Rest and recover were subjective as well. There was food and clean clothes waiting for them—someone on her staff had the foresight to go to Mivart's and fetch a change for Cullen—but even after washing up and food, sleep remained elusive.

'Come lay down with me,' Cullen encouraged from the bed where he lay stretched out an hour before dawn. 'At least close your eyes. You don't need to sleep. Just close your eyes, Antonia.'

'I can't stop seeing it, eyes open or shut.' But she did relent and lay down beside him.

'I know.' He combed his fingers through her hair with a sigh. 'What a night. My father was there. Cowden brought him.' He gave a hoarse chuckle, his voice still carrying the effects of the smoke. He'd said nothing of the ordeal once he'd gone back inside and she didn't ask. Saying nothing confirmed for her just how bad it must have been and how close. Maybe she didn't want to know, at least not yet.

'I was with him on the second floor when I heard the noise.' Cullen's fingers were gentle in her hair.

That was how he'd got there so fast, she thought. 'The noise sounded like fireworks the closer one was to it. Then there was fire everywhere and flames running up the draperies.' Antonia squeezed her eyes tight. She did not want to relive those moments of panic before she'd taken charge and tried to organise a retreat before it became a full-blown stampede. 'At the outset, I was scared to death.'

She paused. She'd never spoken these next words out loud, but perhaps a near-death experience brought them to the fore. 'A thousand things flashed through my head all at once. I had no idea I could think of so many things at one time. I thought I was going to die like Keir, in a freak accident. I wondered if Keir had felt like that—knowing without question that he was down to the last minutes of his life,' she whispered the words in the dark. 'But then I thought to myself, last minutes or no, how do I make them count? It's what Keir would have thought. How can I help others? Who can I save? And then I thought about you and suddenly you were there, and...'

'And you're safe, Antonia. You were brave tonight.' His grip about her waist tightened. 'I was scared tonight, too, when I saw that woman push you and you fell, and I lost sight of you. I know why you stayed and helped everyone, but in that moment I wished you had fled, that you'd been the first one down the staircase.'

'A good captain always goes down with the ship,'

she murmured. 'You scared me, too, going back into the building. You were a hero. Margery owes you her life. You went into a burning building to save someone you didn't even know.'

She felt him smile against her neck. 'It's what Keir would have done. He saved us both so that we might save others. I think that's his real legacy.'

Antonia turned in his arms, facing him, her arms wrapped about his neck. 'I think you're right.' She smiled into his tawny eyes. Sometimes the best way to defeat a ghost was to invite him in. For the second time Keir had been part of their conversation without haunting it. The first time had been at the cemetery. The realisation came to her that they could be themselves and they could still celebrate Keir, the man they had both loved and the man who'd brought them together. Why had she not seen it before? Why did she see it now when it was too late?

'I love you, Cullen,' she whispered, letting her eyes droop closed. There was always the chance things would look better by daylight.

Things did not look better in the morning. She and Cullen returned to Hanover Street when she woke. Smoke was still rising from the fire and its grey tendrils could be seen at a distance high in the sky. The smoke was only a prelude to the shock of seeing the building. The solid, square building looked like the jagged Gothic remains, the roof gone, the façade jutting into an empty sky. The structure remained, mostly, it having been heavily constructed out of brick, but the wood used to brace the internal structure had burned.

She leaned on Cullen's arm for support, her ankle still paining her. 'It's gone, all gone. Who would do such a thing? I cannot believe this was an accident.' Accidents were candles being left lit, or oil spilling on a stove and getting out of control, or a cigar left burning unattended. Accidents were not explosions that sounded like fireworks and draperies going up in flames.

The man in charge of the fire brigade and an inspector approached them. 'Do we have any insight into what caused this?' Antonia asked.

Both men looked tired. They'd been working all night. 'We do. We found the remnants of small explosives that were likely planted on the third floor near the draperies, probably behind the draperies, which is why they went up so fast and why they weren't detected.'

Antonia felt her stomach clench. 'This was deliberate?' It was one thing to assume it was deliberate in theory and another to have it be truth. It meant facing the fact that someone had wanted to destroy her store.

'Yes, Ma'am. This was arson,' the inspector replied solemnly. 'I am sorry. It is a great loss and while I understand that this is a difficult time, time is of the essence. Do you have any idea of who might have set the fire?' His gaze had drifted to Cullen, expecting a man to have the answers, but Cullen said nothing, his own gaze making it clear that she was in charge and the one of whom questions ought to be asked. Under other circumstances she would have revelled in the authority he conferred on her. After all, it was what she'd wanted in the beginning. But now she knew what it meant. He was leaving. This would be hers to handle.

'Possibly,' she said. 'We had a disgruntled site manager by the name of Mackleson. He was fired two months ago for skimming money, among other things. We caught him on the premises a couple days ago.' It wouldn't be 'we' much longer. Just 'I'. It was ironic to think that was something she'd once wanted.

When she finished, Cullen said, 'There was a disturbance last evening when the caterers arrived and our security were occupied with that long enough for someone to get into the building. That disturbance could even have been orchestrated on purpose.' He glanced at her, apologetic. 'I didn't have time to tell you and it seemed inconsequential when it happened.'

She nodded. 'Is there anything left worth saving?'

'The structure can be salvaged. If you're asking if you can rebuild, Ma'am, the answer is yes. It will take time and money, but you are insured,' the inspector offered. 'If you would like, I can walk you through it.' He extended his arm. 'We'll take it slow.'

She hesitated and shot a look at Cullen. 'Go on,' he said softly. 'I want to remember you like this, walking towards your new dream, hope springing quite literally from the ashes, because that's who you are,' he whispered for her ears alone.

He was saying goodbye. She'd step away with the inspector and he would be gone. His ship sailed in a few hours and she'd promised to let him go. Perhaps goodbye was better like this—simply stepping away, stepping into the work of the day so that she wouldn't feel the loss of him so keenly. She nodded, filling her eyes with the last sight of him.

'I'll write when I get there. Antonia, go build your store and whatever you do, don't look back.'

She swallowed against the thickness in her throat and took the inspector's arm. Her ear was only half tuned to the inspector's report. She felt Cullen's eyes on her as she limped towards the rubble, watching no doubt to make sure she kept her word. They'd had an incredible interlude. Now it was over. Eyes forward, eyes on the future.

By mid-morning, Antonia was up to her neck in work, in decisions and in people to help. The newly hired staff came to sort through the rubble. Robert Bowdrie came to handle insurance paperwork. Fleur came for mental and emotional support and to ensure the fire got a fair reporting in at least one newspaper. The architect came with the blueprints. The Duke of Cowden came to lend his gravitas to the process and seeing everything was done right. He came out of friendship, but also because his money was involved. In many ways it was as much his building that burned down last night as it was hers. Still, there was hope in the air after a night of disaster. But it did not inspire her as it once might have.

'Are you all right?' Fleur pressed a mug of coffee into her hands. 'You've been going non-stop.'

'Just overwhelmed.' Antonia found a smile for her friend. 'It was good of you to come.'

'Where's Cullen?' Fleur asked.

'Gone. He left this morning.' But it seemed longer than a handful of hours.

'Gone as in…?

'Gone to his ship, as in going back to Tahiti.' Gone,

as in not in her bed. As in his arms not waiting to hold her. 'It was what we agreed upon. It's what is best.'

'For whom?' Fleur interrogated fiercely. 'For him? For you?'

She didn't have an answer for that. 'He thinks it's best for the company, it will protect us from losing investors and having to contend with the old scandal.'

Fleur gave her a thoughtful look. 'So you're both willing to give each other up for the sake of the company? For an inanimate thing built by a man who is now dead?'

'Fleur, please, you're not making it better. It was very hard to let him go,' Antonia begged.

Fleur took her hands. 'I don't mean to make it better because you are making the wrong decision and what is worse is that you *know* it is the wrong decision.'

'Fleur, I have work to do,' Antonia said. She had to stay busy or she would lose what was left of her sanity.

'Yes, you always do, don't you? Why do you work, Antonia? To build a legacy or to bury the hurt?' Fleur challenged. 'How is that working for you?'

It wasn't working. She missed Cullen and she knew instinctively that she was repeating the pattern she'd used with Keir. The harder the work, the deeper she could bury what mattered without confronting it, without feeling anything. Only this time, she wanted to feel. She didn't want to forget the feel of Cullen's body, the sound of his low voice at her ear, the look of him, all broad-shouldered elegance in those jackets he claimed were too confining. 'It doesn't matter. It's too late now.'

Fleur looked at the little watch pinned to her bodice. 'No, it's not.'

'What are you suggesting?' But Antonia knew what her heart was suggesting—that she hail a cab and run to the ship, metaphorically, as her ankle hurt too much for any literal running. It was a half hour across town. An hour and a half until the ship left. 'I have a business to run, Fleur. It would take months to turn it all over. And there's the store.' She had responsibilities. She couldn't hare off to parts unknown at a moment's notice.

But thoughts of the store did not fill her with the old joy. She stood, hands on hips, and looked up at the blackened brick structure. When had this stopped being her dream? Before last night, she realised. It wasn't the work that daunted her, it was that she no longer had the heart for it and it no longer seemed important.

Keir's real legacy to us is that we have the power now to save others.

And perhaps they had the power to save themselves if they would simply take the risk. Keir's whole life had been about taking risks, taking chances on people as well as investments.

She spied the Duke of Cowden talking with the architect. 'Fleur, help me limp over there. I have an idea.' Her pulse began to thrum as new excitement took her. 'Then, be a dear and get me a cab, a fast one.' Fleur grinned and hugged her.

A half hour later, she climbed into a cab and urged the driver to make haste. She settled back against the cracked leather squabs with a smile of satisfaction. Apparently, she could drop everything on thirty minutes' notice. But she wasn't home free yet. She still had to convince Cullen.

* * *

He was going home. Cullen leaned against the rail of the ship, trying to interest himself in the busyness of the dock. He tried to convince himself that the feeling in his stomach was one of excitement. He'd promised himself he'd be back in Tahiti by September and he would easily make that. It was a good time of year to sail, fewer storms in the spring. He'd done what was needed, signed the papers, helped where he could. To stay now would undo that help. He had a life waiting, a place where he could do the work he was best at and work that made a difference.

Antonia would be fine without him. He'd seen her today with the inspector, taking charge. In fact, she would be better without him. If he stayed, she'd constantly be putting out fires of another sort and all set by him. He didn't want to stay and watch her respect for him turn into something else. And it would. One could only live with a troublemaker for so long before they got tired of the trouble and its consequences. But damn, he'd miss her. More than miss her because this wasn't about missing. It was about loving. He loved her too much to stay.

Down below on the wharf they were getting ready to pull up the gangplank, the last of the cargo loaded. Good. Soon it would be too late to do anything about. Soon, life would start again—life without Antonia Popplewell and he would navigate it. Someone gave a call that they were minutes away from getting underway to make the most of the afternoon tide.

Just then, there was a commotion on the wharf, a

carriage driving recklessly. Foolish driver. Horses near the water on the wharf was bad business if something startled them. As the carriage slammed to a halt and the door opened, a woman exited, her movements brisk— well, somewhat brisk; she was limping. It was the limp that made him look more closely.

'Antonia!' he called out and she looked up, shading her eyes against the light. He waved. He called again, but the ship's horn sounded, alerting the docks to its departure. No. Cullen raced down the stairway. He had to stop the ship.

'Wait! Wait!' Cullen sprinted towards the sailors at the gangplank. He could see Antonia gamely limping through the crowd as fast as she could. 'That woman is coming.' He gestured towards her. But what had she come for? To beg him to stay? Or— His heart gave a leap. Had she come to come? But that wasn't possible. She had work...

'Sir, we have orders, we have a schedule. Sir, the tide,' the sailors protested.

'Antonia!' He ran to the centre of the gangplank, knowing it made it much harder to move a gangplank when a man was on it. 'What are you doing?' he yelled into the crowd as she struggled to reach the ship.

'I am coming with you!' she shouted back and his pulse leaped with the confirmation.

'Sir!' It was the captain now, his tone strident and insistent. 'Perhaps you would prefer another ship at a better time? We must go!' He would not lose her now, but if he got off the ship, he'd miss the tide.

'Just a moment longer, she's almost here.' Then she

was there, breathing hard from her exertions. He grabbed her hand and pulled her aboard. Only when she was safe in his arms did he say, 'We can go now, Captain. I have everything I need.' Then he was with her, and they were laughing in each other's arms.

'You crazy girl, what are you doing?' He laughed down at her.

'Right now I'm just trying to stand up. Between my ankle and my corset, I'm done for.'

'That's what I'm here for.' He swung her into his arms. 'To prop you up when you need it.' He carefully navigated the steps, carrying her to the ship's rail.

'You're always carrying me.' She laughed as he set her down.

'That's what partners are for.' Cullen smiled. 'Seriously, though, do you know what you're doing? What you've done? You've jumped on board a ship bound for the South Seas with nothing but the clothes you're wearing.' The enormity of what she'd done was starting to sweep him now that the exhilaration of the dash was receding.

She flashed a wide smile. 'Isn't that how you did it? Only going the other direction? I have it on good authority there's clothes to be had in the Port of Cairo. Two sets ought to be enough.' She laughed. 'After all, I am told one does not need many clothes in Tahiti.'

'But one might need a husband.' He watched her eyes shine with tears.

'One might,' she said carefully.

'It can be arranged in Port Cairo.' He raised her hand to his lips. 'Will you be my wife, my partner?'

'On one condition,' she said solemnly. 'I want to marry you in Tahiti, on the beach you love, with the people you love. Can we do that?'

'Yes, we can do that.' He tugged at the ring on his finger. 'But perhaps I have a condition, too. For the sake of propriety, might you wear this until we get there?' It would solve the problem of a cabin and the inconvenience of enforced celibacy, something he was not looking forward to if she was nearby. Now that she was his, he had no intentions of wasting a moment. Life was short, happiness must be grabbed whenever it could be.

She smiled and slipped the ring on her finger and held her hand up to admire it. 'Compromise, hmm? I think that is a great start to this partnership.'

He bent his mouth to hers, stealing a kiss. 'Speaking of partnerships, do I dare ask about the business? Do we still have one?'

She wrapped her arms about his neck. 'Yes and no. I have sold my shares to the Duke of Cowden. The Prometheus Club will oversee everything. You maintain your shares until which time you'd like to part with them, if ever. Cowden expects you to continue with your South Seas operation and I will receive my own dividends quarterly as an investor. Satisfied?'

'The real question is—are you satisfied? You have given up everything.' Over her shoulder, London was fading as the ship began the long slip down the Thames towards the sea.

'I think you should rephrase that, Cullen Allardyce. I am satisfied because I have *gained* everything.' Of course she would think that, optimist that she was. She took his hand and led him to the prow of the ship.

'There's nothing to see here,' he murmured at her ear, drawing her close against him as they stared out over the water.

'There's the future,' she replied. 'We'll never look back, Cullen. We'll only move forward. Together.'

Epilogue

Tahiti—September 1853

The four long, clear notes of the *pu*, the conch shell, blew in the directions of the four winds, the sound calling the gods and the Mana to the beach. The significance of that sound sent a rill of excitement through Antonia. Today was her wedding day. She tightened her grip on the bouquet of island gardenias she held in her hands. The sweet fragrance of the flowers soothed her nerves as she stood on the beach, Rahiti's wife, Raina, on one side, the newly married Viahere, Rahiti's sister, on her other. About her was assembled the clan Cullen called family.

Her gaze was trained on the aquamarine waters, waiting to catch sight of her groom. The sun shone with pleasant warmth in the piercingly blue sky. Her bare feet luxuriated in the sand.

A light breeze feathered the fabric of her white *pareo* against her body. Cullen was right. There was less need for clothes here. Her crinolines and corsets were packed away in Papeete. Today, she wore the clothes of his clan, a simple single garment draped not around cages and hoops but just her own body. It felt both decadent and free, an outward expression of how she'd felt since the moment she'd jumped aboard the ship. She was free now, no longer weighed down by grief and limitations.

'They're coming!' Viahere whispered excitedly. 'Do you see them?'

She did see them and her pulse raced at the sight of Cullen at the front of the outrigger, the wind off the ocean in his hair, which had grown during the year he'd been away from the islands. It was still not down to his waist, but Antonia was sure it would get there. She positively adored making love with a long-haired man.

'He's a fine man,' Raina whispered appreciatively. 'Almost as fine as my Rahiti.' She laughed, squeezing Antonia's arm. They'd become good friends in the short time Antonia had been here. The clan had welcomed her warmly and rejoiced over Cullen's return. Rahiti and the men had immediately set to building a house for them in Tahitian fashion. The women had helped her set up that house yesterday with a housewarming ceremony and hand-made gifts that had made her cry at their generosity.

The outrigger reached the beach and Cullen jumped out to stride ashore. He was bare-chested, wearing a white *pareo* draped about his hips in a short skirt that showed off his exquisite legs. He was tan now, his hair sun-streaked the colour of honey. She liked this iteration of him very much. She liked this iteration of herself as well. She'd been busy learning the language, learning how to cook traditional foods and learning the customs. She especially liked the idea that meals were communal. Dinner was eaten together by the whole clan.

There were many hands to prepare the food, and there was always good company to eat with. No longer were meals lonely ordeals.

Cullen came to her and took one of her hands. 'Tahiti becomes you, my love. You look ravishing,' he whispered as Rahiti and Raina acted as their escorts and led them to the flower circle laid out on the sand. She passed her bouquet to Raina and Cullen took her other hand. The *tahua* raised his and the ceremony began.

It was unlike any wedding she'd imagined for herself and certainly nothing like her former wedding. Antonia's bare feet curled into the warm sand as the *tahua* began the handfasting blessing and bound their wrists with auti leaves. 'For spiritual protection, healing and purity,' Cullen whispered. 'I guess we need that last after all the time we spent in the cabin on the voyage.'

She smiled at him, letting her eyes say all that she could not: how much she loved him, how much she was looking forward to the life they would make together and every adventure they would have in this paradise. As optimistic as she was, she'd not imagined such a man or such a land existed or that they could be hers, that she would be allowed two grand, but different passions in her lifetime.

The priest bound their wrists together and poured out the water of purification over their hands. Purification, a beginning, a new start. There were many new starts ahead for them. Cullen gave her a sharp look and she knew her glass face nearly gave her away. She needed to be careful. She intended to keep that news for later tonight.

They exchanged flower crowns of island gardenias and leis of hibiscus as they exchanged their vows, pledging their commitment and devotion to one another in their own words. 'You brought me out of darkness, you showed me how to love again,' Antonia said, her eyes glistening with tears of joy. 'I pledge my heart to you for ever, in times of plenty and in times of paucity, I will stand beside you as your wife and your partner.'

She did not think the words adequate to express what he meant to her, but they shook him. She could see it in his eyes and then he reached for her, crushing her to him and holding her as if he would never let her go, never mind that the village looked on. She felt the slight tremble of his broad shoulders as he buried his face in her hair, letting emotion claim him for a moment before he found his voice.

'I may have brought you from darkness, but you brought me to life. You showed me what real love can make possible, what real love can forgive. I am yours for ever. I will spend my days worshipping your body and serving your happiness.' He barely waited for permission to kiss the bride before his lips found hers in a long kiss full of promise, full of passion.

The *tahua* offered the nature prayer to bless the marriage and then Rahiti's mother came forward to wrap them in a *tifaifai*. It was the blanket the women had given her yesterday at the housewarming and it would be the blanket they slept beneath every night. A perfect start to a loving marriage.

Rahiti's father came forward. 'You have married Kanoa. Now, we present you, our newest daughter, with a Tahitian name. You shall be known as Tereva, which means beginning.' She nodded, too overcome with emotion to speak. It was perfect.

Cullen took her hand and stepped with her out of the flower circle to lead the procession back to the village for the celebration. She had never known such happiness as that which followed—the feasting, the dancing. This was her new life, her new world. She and Cullen would live here as much as possible, with the understanding there would occasionally be business to look after in Papeete. She would stay here in the village while Cullen travelled the islands twice a year, but they would manage.

'Come with me, Wife,' Cullen whispered, leading her into the evening shadows. 'No one will mind if we slip away.'

Night in Tahiti was dark. There were no street lamps, only stars to light the way, but very shortly flames came into view from a bonfire on the beach of a lagoon. 'I thought you might like to swim before we go to our home.' He pressed a kiss to her mouth.

'I'd like that very much.' She'd taken to the warm turquoise waters with verve. There was nothing she liked as much as an evening swim with her husband. She reached for the tucked end of her *pareo* and unwound the cloth, letting fall to the sand, standing before her new husband naked in the new-risen moonlight, watching as he did the same. He was glorious nude, even more so in Tahitian moonlight. She moved into his arms, her arms about his neck, her body pressed to his. 'You're right. Clothes are overrated,' she whispered.

'Are you happy?' he asked, searching her eyes. 'It's so much all at once.'

'It is everything I could hope for. *You* are everything I could hope for, a dream I didn't even know I had.' She smiled up at him. The time had come. 'It is so much blessing all at once, but it's about to be even more, Cullen.' She took his hand and pressed it to her belly. 'This time next year, you'll have been a father for a couple of months, at least.' She smiled at the stunned look in his eyes. 'Now, I've overwhelmed you.' She laughed.

He laughed with her. 'You overwhelmed me from the start. One would think I was used to it by now, but I think you will never cease to amaze me.' She followed his gaze where it travelled to their hands at her stomach. 'A child, Antonia? Truly?' There was awe in his voice. 'I did not ever dare to let myself dream of being a father, or of happiness, or of love and now I have all three thanks to you.'

Antonia smiled softly at her husband. 'Don't you know by now that love always finds a way?' Overhead, the stars came out. It was hard to believe those same stars would be shining over London although no one would see them through the soot. Some people thought she was merely lucky, but Antonia knew better. She wasn't lucky. She was loved. 'Cullen, it's going to be a grand life,' she whispered. And they would live it to the fullest because life was too precious to waste a single moment.

* * * * *

If you enjoyed this story,
make sure to pick up the first book in
Bronwyn Scott's Enterprising Widows miniseries

Liaison with the Champagne Count

And while you're waiting for the next book,
why not check out her Daring Rogues miniseries?

Miss Claiborne's Illicit Attraction
His Inherited Duchess

Or one of her other recent stories?

The Captain Who Saved Christmas
The Art of Catching a Duke